THE RESTART AND THE REMEDY

ACES HIGH MC - DAKOTAS
BOOK 3

CHRISTINE MICHELLE

Cover Design ©2025 Christine Michelle
2025 Paperback Edition
ISBN: 979-8-89706-021-4

ABOUT THE BOOK

She drove into town with fresh betrayals nipping at her heels.

He was drowning in a similar misery.

MYRA

I was born lucky.

I was from a close-knit biker family. Another biker family had a boy two years older than me. He became my best friend, my lover, and what I thought was my soulmate.

Then I found out I wasn't as lucky as I thought.

My entire family had been in on his lies. They backed his play while they broke my heart.

Once I escaped that life, I found myself in the center of a different kind of motorcycle club. This one functioned as a family, but I knew all about how appearances could be deceiving. When a beautiful man with a slightly battered soul offered a hand out to me, I wasn't sure where accepting it would take me.

RABBIT

I stumbled into her life, half-naked on the outside and half-dead on the inside.

I made her regret being nice to me.

It didn't take long for me to realize she wasn't like the woman who had left me broken, and I vowed to make everything up to her.

TRIGGER WARNINGS

- Cheating (by exes of main characters)
- Sexual assault (of male characters)
- Other woman drama
- Strong language
- Use of drugs/alcohol
- Sexual situations described on page
- Violence
- Death
- Murder
- Family betrayals/estrangement
- Pregnancy during breakup
- A naked hitchhiker
- And more possible triggers not listed here.

AHMC
DAKOTAS
3

Myra & Rabbit

PROLOGUE - RABBIT

Her recently dyed pink bob blew in the blustery wind as she turned to face me before getting into the pickup truck parked outside of the house.

"It's not personal, Rabbit. We just want different things. You understand that, right?"

I understood jack shit.

Two days ago, I'd asked her how she felt about starting a family after we made love all night long. Now, I'd come home to find her pulling an overstuffed suitcase onto the front porch of the home she'd been sharing with me for the past four months. It was only a rental until the house I was building was finished. Once it was done, I planned on marrying Chastity and raising our children there.

It was something I had always wanted for myself, even before I saw how goddamn happy Rage and Tango were with their women. Then there was my brother and his ol' lady who managed to make me want a family of my own that much more.

Before my brother got his hooks into her, I thought I'd have that with Cherry, but she wasn't for me. She was made for Spinner. Her sister, on the other hand, had been wild and completely against even dating me at first. I'd had to work my ass off for a chance with her.

She knew I'd had a thing for Cherry, and she told me herself she was no substitute for her twin. She had not been wrong. Still, after finally pinning her down, I thought we had a chance to go the distance.

I thought that all the way up until the point where she turned around with that fresh new look of hers and waved at me. She didn't have a care in the world that she was breaking something inside of me as she slid into that old beat-up Chevy. The damn thing was lifted too high off the ground for its own good, considering it rested on those tiny little tires. The asshole who owned it couldn't even splurge on tires that fit his truck, and she was running off to be with him. I shook my head and tried to quell the sick feeling in my gut.

"Just like that?" I asked. Her lips pursed together in a move I knew spoke of her distaste for the question.

"Rabbit, I warned you," she finally called out. "I'm not Cherry. Never will be. Settling down just isn't in my blood. Be good, and..." I don't know what Chastity had been about to say, because the asshole in the truck pulled out, causing her to fall back inside the window. Her slender body didn't stand a chance against physics and she didn't care to finish her statement or poke her head back out, either. Instead, she tossed a hand outside the window, and her giggle was the last thing I heard before the roar of the truck's engine overtook it, and then they were gone.

I didn't know what to think. My life had just dropped my dreams right into the shitter and then promptly flushed.

I had been planning on asking her to marry me in three days. Christmas Eve had worked out well for my brother the year before, I figured it would do the same for me. I'd managed to get her to start dating me exclusively about six months back, after damn near a year of chasing her and trying to convince her it would be worth it. The joke had been on me the whole time. I hadn't been worth it. Not to Chastity Carson, anyway.

1. MYRA
SIX MONTHS LATER

I ONLY HAD A FEW MORE MILES TO MAKE IT TO SPEARFISH, SOUTH Dakota. The elation I felt at my trip almost being at an end was nothing compared to the confusion of seeing a mostly naked biker walking down the side of the road.

How did I know he was a biker?

Well, the kutte was a dead giveaway. Honestly, my curiosity got the better of me as I slowed to take in the fact that my initial assessment had been correct. The man had not one single stitch of clothing on, with exception of his leather kutte. According to his patches, he was a member of a local chapter of the Aces High MC.

I shrugged inwardly, having never heard of them before my friend Cherry informed me of who her old man was affiliated with. My GPS squawked at me, saying that my turn was coming up in two miles, and since I had been paying more attention to the nearly naked biker than the road, it startled me enough that I slammed on the breaks.

The next thing I knew, my passenger side door was flung open and the naked man deposited his ass – fine and bare as it was – into the seat of my car. Thank God for leather seats that could be wiped down. Not that he was dirty, but he was a biker in the middle of nowhere without clothes and that combination did not bode well.

"Thanks for the pickup. The rest of that walk was about to be brutal without my boots," he said as he beamed a smile my way that was probably responsible for melting the panties off the local women on a regular basis. I would know since it was doing the same thing to me. That was a shocking discover because I thought my lady parts had officially been toggled into 'off' mode considering my recent troubles. I guessed that I was still a woman, after all.

"Um, I didn't. Sorry, I-"

"Really, it's cool of you," he mentioned with a grin before turning to look forward at the road before us.

"Seems like you got yourself into a little pickle there," I mumbled as I took my foot off the break and gently eased back on the gas.

"Hey now, darlin'! There's nothing little about my pickle." His mock sincerity had me glancing over, and much to my shame, down as well. He chuckled and suddenly I wanted to put this biker boy in his place.

"If you say so," I mentioned as I rolled my eyes back to the road in front of me.

"It's chilly as fuck out there," he huffed indignantly. "Don't judge me," he added as he cupped his man parts in two hands. Yes, it was not lost on me that it took two rather large hands to be sure he had proper coverage. My GPS squawked once more about the impending turn I was supposed to take.

"Where exactly are you headed at this time of night?" he asked as he eyed the contraption that was suction cupped to my dash.

"I could ask you the same."

"You could, but it looks like we're going to the same spot," he informed me as he tapped the GPS.

"You're going to a bar with no clothes on?"

He shrugged his well-formed shoulders and grinned over at me. "It's a strip club. I figure why not let the ladies get a look for once."

'*Why not, indeed?*' I thought to myself. Though judging from his chuckle, I must have actually said it out loud. It figures, at the very start of my new life, I would be the one to accidentally pick up a hitchhiker. A naked, biker, hitchhiker. I rolled my eyes up to the sky, and silently asked what the universe had planned for me.

"Why are *you* headed to a strip club in the middle of the night?" He glanced around my heavily packed SUV before he brought his eyes back toward me. I didn't miss the way he glanced down at the way my hand nervously rubbed on my belly. Granted, there wasn't much of a bump showing yet, but since we were headed to a strip club, and I had all my possessions with me, it didn't take a stretch of the imagination for him to make the assumption that I was going to try to be a stripper. Instead of humoring him, I flipped the tables on his question.

"Why are you walking the roads naked?" I countered.

"Well, I was giving the goods to Wanda Sue since her man was out of town, but apparently the asshole wasn't as out of town as she thought. Only had time to grab my kutte and hightail it out of there before..." He stopped talking when he saw my lax jaw hanging nearly to the floorboards at his admission.

"You're a cheater?" I asked in such a vehement tone that he couldn't miss the disgust that dripped from my question.

"Hell no!" he all but yelled back. "Wanda's the cheater. I was just the poor, unfortunate soul she chose to use like I was a piece of meat or something." He said this completely deadpan with a slight twinge of victimized pain added in for effect. Then he burst out laughing.

"You should see your face right now. You don't know whether to be angry on Jerry's behalf or pity me. Don't feel bad for me, kitten. I've got fuck all to care about these days, and hurting Jerry's feelings isn't on my priority list of fucks to give either. Besides, he told Wanda he was out of town, but really he was over sleeping with Carrie Ann. She probably kicked him out, and that's the only reason he showed up to catch me with his other woman."

"What the hell kind of place have I landed myself in?"

"Only the best kind of place, sweetheart."

"Stop with the endearments. Can you even keep them straight? So far, I've been darlin', kitten, and sweetheart."

"Do you have a preference?"

"Yeah, none of the above."

"Well, snook'ems, it's hard to call you anything you

might approve of since you pick up strangers on the side of the road without introducing yourself properly."

"I did not pick you up. My GPS startled me after seeing a grown-ass, naked man walking down the street in temperatures threatening to drop below the 40s. You just took advantage and hopped on in."

"Hopped, that's cute," he muttered, and that's when I really knew I was in trouble. I had picked up some crazy asshole who was laughing in my passenger seat, while still without clothing, and it was all over the word 'hopped.'

He swiped at his face, leaving his junk inadvertently exposed, and damn my traitorous eyes. I looked. Again. Worse, he noticed that I looked again.

"I'm Rabbit," he proclaimed while grinning bigger than the cat who actually got the canary. "Get it now? It's funny, because I'm Rabbit, and you said I hopped..." His voice trailed off as he noticed that I wasn't really paying attention to his explanation since he still had his man parts uncovered. His shoulders bounced in a carefree shrug and he waved away the rest of his explanation then covered himself again.

"Look honey, maybe this would work better if you put your eyes forward. I'm all for showing you what I have to work with, but not if my dick is the last thing you see because you ran us off the road."

"Shit!" I managed to swerve us back onto the road, because yes, I had gone off on the shoulder just a bit.

"Damn, you left a whole rut back there," he murmured as he continued glaring at said rut through the side-view mirror. Eventually, he turned his attention back to me, though he still didn't bother to cover himself up. "I told you mine, now it's your turn."

"Huh?"

"Your name?"

"Oh, I'm-"

"You're going to want to turn here," he said, cutting me off before he could get my name.

2. MYRA
TWO WEEKS EARLIER

NOTHING GOOD EVER COMES FROM HEARING THE WORDS: "WE HAVE to talk," from your significant other.

Absolutely nothing.

You'd think I would have known going in that shit was about to get turned on its head for me, for my life, for everything. The problem was that my particular significant other had been my best friend since diapers, boyfriend since I was fifteen and he was sixteen, lover since I was seventeen, and the man I currently lived and shared my life with. So, when he asked me to meet him for breakfast so that we could talk, I honestly thought it would be about finally getting hitched like our families had been on us to do for ages now.

That was why when I met him for breakfast at the kitschy little bakery slash coffee shop in town, and I saw him looking completely out of sorts and unlike his usual confident self, I started to panic a little on the inside.

When I noticed he kept glancing at a woman, who I knew

to be the ex-girlfriend of one of his club brothers, that panic ramped up to adrenaline overload.

Still, I waited.

Still, he said nothing.

So, in an effort to move things along before I exploded, imploded, or got a severe case of the shakes from the extra adrenaline that would make me look like I was having a mild seizure, I spoke first. I was pretty certain, judging by the side-long glances toward the table with Phoenix's ex-girlfriend, that two and two was about to equal four. It was a little hard to fathom, though. Considering the news I had to share with the man I thought of as my soulmate.

"Spit it out and respect me enough to actually tell the truth and not the bullshit lies you're trying to spin," I told Michael "Blaze" Sanders as his shifty-eyes straightened and pinned themselves to my own. He knew that I knew his tells. He had been about to lie to me, had been thinking of the best way to spin whatever he had to say, and he had given himself away. We'd known each other far too long, and far too intimately for anything but honesty. His shoulders sagged as if a heavy weight had settled in on them.

"You know the party we had at the MC about two months ago when you couldn't come because you were sick?"

Of course I knew. My best friend, Lana, had come to take care of me because Michael had been unwilling to stay home from the multi-chapter shindig the Stoneridge Raiders Motorcycle Club hosted.

I had been extremely angry with him while also trying to support the club and his need to be there. I'd grown up in the life since my father was the VP of the Stoneridge Raiders. That didn't mean it wasn't a kick in the teeth to have my man basically tell me that going to a party was more important than seeing to me when I had a 104-degree temperature, the shakes, and couldn't hold anything down to save my life.

I simply nodded my answer to him. We'd fought about it after I had the strength to fight, but the damage was already done by then, and I had the feeling I was about to learn that the damage had been more than the way he disrespected me by going to a party while I was freaking dying.

"Well, I got smashed and Phoenix took me to his room to sleep it off. He said he'd just head back to his girl's place for the night."

That's when my stomach tightened because Jessica Finley, Phoenix's now ex-girlfriend, was the one sitting at the table that kept drawing Michael's attention. Michael sighed, obviously seeing that I was putting the pieces together.

"That's the night Jess and Phoenix broke up," I mentioned as I continued to glance back and forth between the two of them. "There was some big blow up, but no one would talk about it..." I shook my head then. "Around me," I clarified. "No one talked about it around me."

Sickness burned up my stomach as I shifted the little gift bag I had brought with me when I had hopes that this conversation was going to be something else entirely.

Stupid. I was so goddamn stupid.

"Babe," came from his lips on a tortured sigh as he attempted to reach for my hand. I snatched mine away and glared at the man I thought was my life, my soulmate, my everything.

"Finish your story, because if I'm not mistaken, you're keeping more than me waiting right now." The guilt on his face told me I wasn't wrong.

"I guess Phoenix was busy after he tucked me in his room. He got called away to handle something. Jess found her way to his room." He buried his head in his hands then. "I was dreaming. I fucking thought I was dreaming that you were there, blowing me."

I cringed because I had been down with a horrible case of strep throat mixed with an even nastier case of bronchitis at the time. No way was I blowing anything beyond my nose.

"Never even looked. Just laid there enjoying as my dick got hard from being sucked," he said without a care in the world to how it made me feel.

Meanwhile, my stomach's meager contents turned over at the fact that he wasn't even attempting to soften this blow with nice words. Nope, he was animatedly involved in telling this story like he was taking a pleasant trip down memory lane with the boys, not telling the woman he was supposed to love about another woman sucking his dick.

"Then you were riding me, but it felt weird. It was different because we always used condoms, and everything was so hot and wet, when I finally opened my eyes to ask you where you'd learned to do that..." he cut himself off there because he noticed I looked nearly ready to puke.

"It wasn't you. It was Jess, and she was riding me." He looked away guiltily again before his next admission punched me right in the heart. "I didn't stop her."

Despite the fact that he had so carelessly tra-la-laed through this story like my heart didn't matter, I could hear the remorse in his voice. I couldn't bring myself to care about his hurt feelings, though, especially when he started to speak again.

"I didn't stop her because I'd never felt sex like that before. I knew I should have stopped her. She was my brother's girl, and then there was you."

So happy to hear I was his second concern. He didn't notice my narrowed eyes narrow, though, and continued with his explanation.

"I was coming before I knew what happened and then Phoenix burst in the room."

"So, that girl basically started out your night by cheating on her man, your club brother, while RAPING you - an unconscious man. Instead of doing anything about that duplicity when you realized what was happening, you went with it because it felt better than anything you'd had before? That also means you were comparing her to me, since we were each other's firsts?" I asked and his wince told me that hadn't been true either. "So there were others at some point?" My heart hurt so much that my last question sounded more like a whimper than anything. My strength drained right out of me as I realized the implications of what he'd accidentally admitted. My man had been cheating on me for quite some time if his guilty face was to be believed.

"It was before we ever had sex, babe. I had to know what I was doing before we did it so I wouldn't hurt you, or make it bad for you," he explained.

"Yeah, because my soul's other half being with other

14

women wasn't going to hurt me more than a fumbled first time fuck?" I questioned angrily.

He snapped back like my words had struck him. Fuck him.

"I'm assuming the sex was so good with her bare that you're here to tell me we're done?" I finally managed to choke out behind the thick emotion clogging my throat, as I did everything in my power to hold back my tears.

"It's not like that, babe. I swear. I never touched her again after that."

"But you kept in touch for some reason, because her smug face keeps grinning over at me. Oh, and thank you so much, Michael," I sneered, using his given name instead of his road name. "Thank you for showing me the immense respect due an old lady by bringing your side piece here in order to ridicule me. You were my best friend on earth, my soulmate, the man I planned my entire future around, and you decided to destroy me in front of your side piece, as if the truth of what you've done wasn't enough? I needed to suffer a more public humiliation to go with it? I appreciate having her as an audience to that level of humiliation you've just heaped on me."

Again, he appeared as though I had struck him with my words. "Fuck. Fuck! Fuck! Fuck! You don't understand," he whined.

"Then fill me the fuck in so this horror show can be done, Michael."

"She's pregnant," he whispered and everything whooshed out of me in that breath. This man was supposed to be the father of my children. He was supposed to be my everything, our kids' everything, and he'd not only cheated, but he'd given some other woman the child I'd been dreaming of. He'd taken not only himself from me, but the future children we'd planned. Our future. It was all gone with those two words.

"I can't leave her to raise our kid alone, Myra. She said she'd terminate the pregnancy if I didn't break things off with you, and promise to be there for her."

"Have you verified her pregnancy?" I asked after glancing at the still smug bitch who sat at the table behind ours. She didn't appear to be having difficulty with morning sickness, and the drink she had did not look like a virgin one.

Interesting.

"What do you mean? She told me she was."

"You were with her ONE time, *supposedly*." I threw that last sentiment in because his word meant nothing. "She had a boyfriend and proved she had no qualms about cheating on him. If she's even pregnant, and doesn't miraculously have a miscarriage in the next couple weeks before you can get to a doctor's appointment with her..." I sighed. "If she's really pregnant and I'm wrong about that part of her bull-shit, then how the hell do you know it's even yours? It could be Phoenix's. Shit, you dumb fuck, it could belong to anyone." I informed him and didn't bother to hold back my vitriol.

At the rate the little color he had left in his face disap-peared, I knew he hadn't thought of any of that.

"She's drinking a Mimosa at breakfast, for fuck's sake, Michael. It has alcohol in it. Great choice of potential baby mama for you, because any truly pregnant woman would not be sucking back her third alcoholic beverage of the day before 10 a.m."

His eyes moved from me to glare in Jessica's direction. "What the fuck have I done?"

"You just admitted to cheating, multiple times, on the woman who thought you were her lifelong everything, Michael. You destroyed me and everything we were and you did it all based on that cunt's lies," I pointed to Jessica as I threw my accusations - that happened to be facts - at him. "The woman who started out what you had by raping you, and then destroyed what we had with a lie about a baby." I stood then, the gift bag I no longer wanted to use in my hand, as I slung my purse over my shoulder.

"No! Baby," He stood, too. All eyes in the café were on us by then, including Jessica's worried ones. I had to get out of there.

"Enjoy your life. Do not call, message, or come anywhere near me. Do not even let my name leave your lips on a whisper because you may have once been my everything and my future, but now you are nothing."

"Myra! Please, babe, don't do this."

"You did this!" I spat back angrily. "You get to live with the consequences of your actions, since you forced this whole heartless scene on me."

As if my words conjured hell to unleash it's demons, five of them stormed into the café at that moment. My father was in the lead. Phoenix wasn't far behind. He took note of Jessica, Michael, and myself and came directly to me, and whispered into my ear.

"I'm so sorry, baby girl. I wasn't allowed to tell you, and I begged for the right to do so." At least one person had wanted to do right by me. Too bad it wasn't any of the people who should have done it.

"All of you knew?" I asked. He nodded his head as my father raised unholy hell yelling at the "dumb son of a bitch," as he punched Michael.

"STOP!" I yelled at the top of my lungs. Everything stopped. My father pulled back mid-swing and glanced in my direction. "Just stop. Unless you're going to have someone beat the shit out of you, too," I told my father, my words laced with seething hatred. He paled when he realized it was all aimed at him.

"What does that mean?" he asked.

"You knew. That party was in the beginning of August, and every single one of you knew. Phoenix was allowed the opportunity to ditch the bitch who cheated on him. I realize I'm not, and never have been, as important as your fucking club brothers, but I'm your daughter!" I yelled. "And you let me continue to be with him. He was unprotected with that whore and who knows what she has besides a fake-as-fuck pregnancy."

Jess attempted to get up then to slink out, no doubt. Phoenix moved and held her in place.

"I get that it wasn't the place of the rest of the boys to tell me when my man was too much of a coward to admit what he'd done. But you..." I glared pure hate and hellfire at my father. "You're my daddy. You, above all, are the man who was supposed to protect me, to help ease my pain, and never to be part of causing me more. You knew. You probably knew about the others, too, huh? The ones he admitted to just now

– three years after the fact – the ones he used to practice on?" I could tell by his face that he did.

"You knew, and let him come home to me. You knew that I have never loved anyone else, that he was it for me, and you let me continue believing in a giant fucking lie! I've never been anything but loyal to ALL OF YOU!" My voice cracked as I shouted them all down.

"It wasn't a lie, Myra. I've always loved you," Michael spoke softly.

"Fuck you! When you love someone, you don't fuck another person. If you love someone, you don't lie to her face that they're your first, too. You don't keep fucking a bitch who is RAPING you because you discover how much better it feels without a condom. You love someone, you don't leave them home sicker than a dog, for their friend to look after, so that you could go to a party where this shit went down to begin with. You selfish piece of shit! You sure as fuck do not come home talking to the woman you love about starting a family so you can fuck her bare after you discover the joys of doing so with another woman."

Dead silence greeted my last jab. You could hear a pin drop in the café until Phoenix spoke.

"You also don't believe the lies of a whore who would cheat on one brother, take advantage of another, and has a fucking implant in her arm that prevents pregnancy." Michael's club brother pulled up Jess's shirt sleeve and showed where you could see the lines of the implanted birth control. Michael staggered back and barely managed to plant his ass into the chair he'd vacated only a moment ago. Tears streamed unchecked down his face.

"Baby girl," my father said as he approached me cautiously.

"Do not!" I yelled at him, and everything stopped again. "Do not call me your baby girl. Do not come near me. Do not touch me. Do not fucking address me unless it's absolutely necessary, and then you call me Myra only. Because you don't lie, hide shit, and condone his bullshit treatment of me behind my back and then think I have any respect or love left for you." My father jolted back with the last of my words. "You helped make this worse. If you knew he wanted, or hell, needed lessons, in order to please a woman when we were teenagers, YOU should have told him to put us on a break first. Instead, you condoned his cheating for stupid fucking reasons, and me being ignorant to it then doesn't make it hurt less now." My father flinched and took an uneasy step back from me.

"It just makes it all worse because everyone else knew, and I'm stuck looking like a fucking fool. You knew about her and did nothing. I know, because he hasn't had a mark on him in all this time. So he sure as fuck didn't get a beat down for it. I didn't get the truth." I moved my watchful gaze around the room. "I didn't get the truth from a single one of you. My own father. My friends. My uncle. The man I thought was my future husband. You all kept it from me. Every single one of you, every single bit of it."

My glare turned to Jessica then. "Thank you," I told her. "You're a filthy fucking cunt, but you're the only person here who bothered to make sure I knew what was going down. Maybe the rest of you, who supposedly loved me, should take note. The duplicitous whore who rapes club brothers, cheats on them, and lies to them about being pregnant is a better person to me than the rest of you lying, disloyal bastards. Enjoy your fucking brotherhood. You've all lost your daughter, your niece, your friend, and your lover." I pinned each of them in turn with my stare.

"Your brotherhood was more important than *my health.* Worse, it was more important than *my heart.* My heart broken into a million pieces because I'm not finding out about one betrayal. I'm dealing with a cheating ol' man who did this once. I'm dealing with an asshole ex who cheated on me multiple times throughout our relationship and my own fucking family condoned it! So, I get to deal with the betrayal I feel from each and every one of you mother fuckers." I heaved out a horrid sound that was half gasp, half sob before I turned to Michael again.

"Just so you know, I had something to talk to you about today, too." I huffed out a very unamused laugh as I held up the gift bag I'd been holding. "I thought, before I got here, that you were going to talk to me about finally getting hitched like everyone kept begging us to do, which would have been perfect, considering." I tossed the gift bag at his feet and watched as the contents of the bag spilled out when it tipped over.

A pair of tiny, black leather, biker boots fell out along with the note that said, "Congrats Daddy! A biker baby will arrive on May 23rd!"

Michael reached out his hand as shock, awe, and then devastation rolled across his features. My father's gasp made me glance up at him. He knew what this meant. I was having a baby. Only now, I'd be doing it alone instead of with my soulmate by my side and our families in the wings like I'd always planned.

"Congratulations," I stated coolly as I turned my focus back to Michael. "You got your wish. You knocked me up, but you chose a whore and her fake baby over the one you've been so enthusiastically trying to make with me." I scoffed out a heartbreaking laugh as I shook my head back and forth.

Glancing up at my father, I let the tears finally fall free. I couldn't hold them back any longer anyway. "Now, maybe you see why you should have cared more about your own daughter and her health, huh?" I pointed to Michael who was clutching the boots in his big hands and crying again.

"He was leaving me to take care of a whore's baby. He didn't even know for sure she was pregnant. No proof of her pregnancy existed, no proof that it was even his if she was able to convince him she was really knocked up. He loved me so much that it was that easy to walk away from me, and to make the break in public where she could be a spectator to my humiliation. Now, I have to raise my baby alone, one that wouldn't even be here if I had known he had cheated. I sure as hell wouldn't have gone bare or been with him ever again, had I known. None of you fuckers, aside from Phoenix, wanted to do the right thing, though. So, now I'm stuck with a cheater's baby in my belly and no one to help me raise it. That's how fucking much I'm loved."

"No, babe, you won't be alone," Michael adamantly declared.

I laughed. "You will have no part in my pregnancy, asshole. I suggest you snuggle up close at night with your whore's nonexistent baby belly. Plan what you're going to name your fake baby with her. That's what you were choosing to do when you called me here, knowing this could be a possibility since we'd been trying to have a baby together, right? You chose her."

"She said she'd terminate if I wasn't with her," he yelled.

"Yeah? And what did you think I'd do? Did you think I'd invite her in and we'd be one, big, happy family? Or were you hoping you hadn't knocked me up after all?"

I could see from his demeanor that was exactly his hope.

"I'll let you know when he or she is born. Do not contact me. In fact, stay far the fuck away!"

I turned to my dad who attempted to move closer to me. "You too. I'm done with you. I'm done with your club and the asshole men who don't give two fucks about the women in their lives. My child won't grow up around that bullshit and have to learn these fucked up lessons the hard way. My child will know I will always have THEIR back. Always!" I turned back to Michael. "Keep the boots, give 'em to your whore for her fake baby, or save them for the next one who is unlucky enough to believe your bullshit." I stomped my way over to the door.

"Do not come home. You can stay at the clubhouse and give me the week to process everything and then we'll decide what to do about the apartment," I told Michael as I began to push the door open. Then I looked back on last time at my father. "If you give two shits about redeeming yourself in my eyes, or even care about my heart or health at all, you'll see to it that he stays gone and gets tested for any diseases he might have transferred to me and my baby."

"You have my word," my dad's voice sounded broken when he spoke. I didn't relent, though.

"Your word means shit to me right now, so we'll call this a test to see if you can actually keep it. Keep everyone else away from me, too. I see so much as a prospect within spitting distance of my place over the next week and I will never see or speak to any of you again. I'll check in with my mom, so she knows I'm okay, but I'll be doing that by phone, too. No doubt she knew at least a little of this bullshit you've been hiding." She did. That much was obvious by the way my dad shifted his weight from foot to foot.

"Yeah, right. Like I said, stay away. Keep him away."

"If you promise you won't do anything stupid," my father stated.

"Like what? Hurt myself? My kid? Fuck you! You've all done enough to hurt me already. I'm not adding to your mess. I need a week to sort how I'm going to clean it all up and how to move on with my life." With that, I left. I left knowing I absolutely was going to do something stupid, but that it wasn't going to hurt any more than I already did.

3. MYRA

MY GOOD FRIEND CHERRY CARSON HAD GONE TO SOUTH DAKOTA two years ago for a Sturgis rally and she never came home. I knew she was a dancer in a club owned by bikers there, but she was also the only friend of mine who didn't live in my town on the Oregon coast or anywhere near it. When I called and explained the turn my life had taken, she was stunned silent at first. My whole life, there had never been Myra Adrian Chase without Michael Allen "Blaze" Sanders by her side. Until now. So, I got it. Even when I didn't want to deal with my own reality, other people had to get over their initial reactions before they could move on to understanding.

"You're coming here," she finally said to me as soon as she wrapped her head around the bomb I'd dropped. "There's a little apartment above Spinner's garage you could stay in, and I'll find you work, too. Did you finish your degree?" I smiled at that. I'd graduated high school early with almost two full years of college credits under my belt. Then, I'd gone into the nursing program to earn my degree.

"I have my degree and just need to take the exam for licensure," I explained.

"Good, in the meantime you can work for the club here. Study, do your testing, and then maybe Doc can get you in with one of the local doc shops or the hospital in Spearfish."

I had told her it sounded like a plan then, and that had been two weeks ago. Now, I was in South Dakota, right in the middle of shit that I swore I'd never be around again, another damn biker club.

I knew Cherry had become an old lady to one of the guys, and she swore to me that these men were not like the brotherhood I'd left behind. From what she said, her man, along with the rest of them, looked out for women. Supposedly, they treated them all like something precious. Sure, they had club girls here, too. They referred to the women as BRATs, though I didn't know what the acronym meant or even if it was one, but they were for the single guys to use.

According to Cherry, none of the brothers looked too kindly on those who struggled with infidelity. If you couldn't be loyal to one aspect of your life, it made that you might struggle with remaining loyal to the club as well. So far, it all appeared to be true, but I knew better than most that looks could be deceiving.

I'd have to wait and see because this was the only spot I had to run to and I was quickly running out of time to get adjusted to new places and faces before my baby was born. Running had been my only option out of my previous life. I'd left there in so much pain, but just a few hours later, I managed to put a plan together for my life. It took all of three days to pack up the only things I wanted to carry with me into my new life. If it was connected to Michael or the club in any way, it got left behind. So, everything else was shoved into my Suburban. My job received notice of my departure, and luckily my boss understood the lack of notice when I told her about my boyfriend's whore, her fake baby mama situation, and how the news was delivered to me. I did not tell her about my own baby, because I couldn't lose my shit again, and my emotions were pushing me over the edge too easily as of late.

I got a new prepaid cell phone and used it to contact my mother who cried and begged to come see me. I shot her down and told her I needed time to forgive her, too. She continued sobbing out an hysterical "I'm sorry," every few minutes before I finally just hung up on her.

I drained my savings accounts that no one but my mom knew I had. She'd helped me set them up when I was sixteen. She told me every woman, no matter how happy her life seemed, needed a rainy day fund that no one else knew about. I think she probably had been aware then that the love of my life was already cheating so he could "learn how to be a good lover" with the club whores. Making sure I was financially set was her way of preparing me for my real future, since she couldn't tell me about things that happened within the club. I thanked her, but also hated her for it. If she had just told me back before I'd given Michael my body, along with my heart and too many more years of my life, maybe I could have found someone who did deserve a woman like me.

Together, Michael and I had almost six thousand dollars in our checking account. I drove to the bank on my way out of town and asked to have my name and access removed from the account. Some of that money was mine fair and square, especially considering my last pay check had been deposited there. I took none of it, though. Had I taken any, it would have sent up a red flag letting the men know I was a flight risk. Instead, I simply emptied the accounts they didn't know about and signed the paperwork necessary to get my name off of anything connecting me to Michael financially. Then I hopped back in my vehicle – my Suburban was fondly nicknamed The Beast – and I drove north out of town. After I went roughly an hour out of my way in that direction, I finally headed east.

Six hours of driving straight through the first day wore me out. I'm sure taking the final steps to sign away my old life helped with that a great deal, too. I pulled into a hotel in some no-name town, paid cash, and slept like a log for twelve long hours before waking, grabbing food, and getting back on the road. The following day, I spent ten hours driving with a few bathroom and food stops along the way. I ignored the numerous times my cell rang. I ignored the beeps indicating I had texts, too. Judging from the amount of them, my mom had shared my number with someone. Probably my dad, possibly Michael, and either one was a betrayal to the confidence I had asked her for.

I continued to ignore the calls until the morning of the third day. After another night, in another no-name motel in the middle of nowhere, I picked up the phone and dialed my mom.

"Oh my God! Where have you gone? The boys have looked everywhere," my mom shouted in a panicked version of a greeting. "Your father is beside himself with worry and guilt. He knew you'd do something stupid." On that note, I hung up. I was beginning to wonder if anyone who I once loved had ever been more than a stranger to me. My phone rang. It was not my mother, so I answered calmly.

"Hello?" I had no numbers programmed in so this was phone roulette I was playing. No telling if I'd get the bullet or a telemarketer.

"Jesus!" I blew out a breath at the sound of his voice. "Don't hang up, Myra," my father stated quickly. "I need to know you're okay."

"Do you? Mom was only worried about how much guilt you harbored about not having me watched. So are you concerned for my wellbeing or because your ego was bruised?"

A heavy sigh blew through the speaker then. "I deserved that. I'm sorry your mom went off like that. She's scared and gets defensive when she can't control her fears. I really need to know you're okay, baby girl," he explained quickly.

"You lost the right to call me that," I huffed. Before he could say more, I continued. "I am fine. I went away for a while to think. That's all you need to know."

"You quit your job, took your name off the bank account, and cleaned out part of your apartment. No offense, but that doesn't sound like a quick trip, kid."

"Honestly, I haven't decided how long my trip will be."

"Michael says you didn't take any money from your account, baby."

I laughed. Of course he checked. "Nope."

My father surprised me then. "Do you need any? I can

wire it somewhere for you. Your mom says she set you up with a rainy day fund way back when, but she didn't know if you still had it."

"I'm thinking she did that back when she first found out Blaze was a cheating bastard. Pretty sure she was setting me up for the failure she already knew was coming, huh?"

"Yeah, baby." My father admitting that fact hurt my heart. They knew we were doomed and said not one damn word to me beyond helping me set up a fund in case I ever needed it to get away. It wounded me somewhere so deep I didn't think there would ever be a fix for the damage they caused. They could have just told me so I could have ended things then. I sighed.

"I fucked up," he admitted quietly. "Please, Myra, my only baby girl, please, let me help you fix this."

"I wish you had come and said those words to me months - hell, years ago. How could you let me stay tied to a man who didn't love me?"

"Because I knew he did love you, baby. And I could keep an eye on him."

"What good did that do, exactly? You knew and still did nothing to keep me from being hurt."

"I thought I had," he told me adamantly. "I thought I was protecting your heart."

"No, you helped destroy it, Dad. Protecting it would have been you telling me all those years ago. It would have been you asking what flavor ice cream would get me through the breakup when I was sixteen. It should have been you putting a stop to a man disrespecting your daughter by cheating on her, and doing it so openly in front of your brothers. Hell, I was friendly toward the club girls back then, and I bet they are who he was learning from, right? That way no bitches from school could run their mouths to me to try to break us up. Lyssa used to be nice to me, but then there came a time she wouldn't talk to me anymore or look me in the eye. I honestly thought it was because she was with you. You and mom were having problems then, so I thought it was about you."

My father sighed. "Yeah, it was Lyssa. Your mom and I…" He breathed deeply for a minute and then continued. "Our problems back then were about her not wanting to hide shit from you and me making a stupid choice. I thought if Blaze got it out of his system back then while he was young that he'd never cheat on you once you started to be intimate with him."

"How stupid was that?" I asked.

"He never did, baby. I know he was faithful to you once you…" He cut himself off, not able to talk about the fact that I'd had sex apparently. "Not until that cunt took advantage of him," he finally tacked on.

"He told me," I stated clearly. "He told me he woke up to her riding him, but that it felt so different, so good, being bare that he didn't stop her." My dad let out a string of profanities that could make a sailor blush.

"That dumb fuck said that to you?" His words were laced with anger that I didn't understand. Who cared what he said or how? What mattered was that he had cheated and lied and my whole family backed him on that play.

"Right before you all barged in on our happy little family breakfast. He sure as fuck did. So excuse me for pointing out the flaw in your logic. You made me an obligation to him because of my feelings. This is what it got us." I sighed, looking around at the big bunch of nothing that had become my new scenery and I wanted to throw the phone and cry. I wished there was a way to fix what everyone had screwed up in my life. There wasn't, though. They'd each had their hand in a very specific kind of damage they'd done to my heart.

"Here's what I know," I told my dad who had gone quiet on the other end. "Michael and I were best friends growing up because we were both club kids. Our moms wanted us together. They talked about it so much, I believed them. I believed he was my soulmate, my fate, my one and only." I almost laughed as I realized how they'd basically programed me to believe those things.

"Looking back, I remember how he used to watch other girls in school when he didn't think I saw. He longed to be with someone else, but out of an obligation he thought he had to me, because of our moms, you, and the club, he stuck with me. He came up with a bullshit excuse to get laid early on and that should have clued you all in that I wasn't what he wanted, but instead, you helped him hide it and continued pushing me as the main agenda. I blame him for not manning up and ending it. I blame you for perpetuating that problem for the both of us."

"I do love you. You're right, about high school. You're right that I felt stuck, but then I realized what I had, babe." Michael's voice came over the phone and my gut clenched. I'd apparently been spilling my heart and thoughts to an audience. Nothing was sacred for me anymore. No one from my old life gave enough of a shit about me that they could give me the same privacy, loyalty, and respect that they gave to that man who betrayed me repeatedly.

Fuck. My. Life.

"Un-fuckin-believable!" I shouted into the phone. "Do the betrayals against me never end? I'm F-I-N-E," I spelled out for them. "I am not coming home. You all just sealed that fucking deal by allowing that fuckwad to listen to my conversation with you. Do not look for me. Do not attempt to contact me. If I cool down and decide any of you are ever worth my time again, I will be the one to make that contact." I wasted no time after that as I turned the phone off, pulled the sim card and battery out, dumped them in the toilet of the gas station I ended up stopping at, and then I dumped the phone, too.

The call, along the emotional meltdown that ensued, kept me from leaving at the time I'd planned. Instead of getting to Spearfish by mid-afternoon, I didn't roll into that area of South Dakota until dark had already fallen and a man's naked ass walking down the road distracted me long enough that I ended up with a mostly naked hitchhiking biker in my passenger seat.

Welcome to South Dakota, and your new life, Myra Chase.

4. RABBIT
PRESENT AND STILL NAKED

THE TOO-BEAUTIFUL FOR HER OWN DAMN GOOD WOMAN WHO HAD accidentally picked me up on the side of the road was just about to tell me her name while simultaneously missing her turn into the bar.

"You're going to want to turn in here," I cut her off to say. She yanked the fuck out of the wheel sending the big ass SUV, and all its contents, careening wildly into the parking lot of Renegade Rosy's.

"Shit, darlin', you tryin' to pick up where Jerry wished he'd left off?" I waggled my eyebrows at her in a kind of crazy, offbeat manner. It was the same gesture I'd always used on my parents to get out of trouble. It always worked and my older brother hated when he saw me use it because he didn't have the same talent to be the class clown as I did. I wasn't too sure it worked on everyone the way it had my mom and dad back in the day. Instead of laughing, the woman in the driver's seat glared in my general direction before finally coasting her vehicle to a safe stop.

The huff she let out was my cue to get up and go. "Thanks for the ride, sweet cheeks," I called out to her as I opened the door. Just before I closed it, though, I caught sight of a man's sized sweatshirt on the floorboard, and I snatched it up and wrapped it around my waist."

"Um, wouldn't you rather turn that around the other way?" Little miss know-it-all called out to me.

I glanced down at the fact that I'd tied the sweatshirt with the front part open and the back covered up. "Honey, if I'm going to advertise one end of me, it's gonna be this one," I told her, as I pointed down to my cock. "The back door is strictly off limits, so it gets covered." I gave her a 'duh' look and then swaggered on out of hearing range as I made my way inside the bar and left her to contemplate my crazy-ass bullshit.

"Rabbit?" Flicker, one of our club's prospects, stood at the front door with a smirk cocked up across half his face. "Good night?" he asked as he looked past me to the woman I'd arrived with.

"Spectacular night, Prospect. You workin' or fuckin' off?"

He straightened as the smirk fell away from his face and his shoulders squared off. "Working," he told me.

I tipped my head back toward the Suburban I'd just arrived in. "Make sure you check her ID real well. I'm guessin' she ain't of age to be here."

Flicker's eyes dropped down to the cock I still had on display before he shifted them to the vehicle I indicated. Then they moved back to me and sheer fucking anger radiated from his pores. "You fuckin' around with underage chicks, now? I don't care if I lose my position in the club. If that's what the fuck y'all tolerate, I want no fuckin' part of it."

"Well, how about that?" I hummed. "I was worried you didn't have a set of balls until now." I clapped him on the shoulder reassuringly. He shrugged the gesture off. "First, I meant underage for a bar, not for sex. Second, I never had sex with or touched her at all. She gave me a ride here. That chick smells like desperation, though, and I'm pretty sure she has a bun in the oven, so politely turn her away from any attempt to try to snag a job." I winked at him, but didn't miss the outraged harrumph that came from over my shoulder. I didn't bother turning around.

"She's right behind me, isn't she?" Flicker nodded as he folded his lips between his teeth and bit down to keep from laughing at me.

"She can hear you, too," the woman called out with a whole truck load of sass added to those last few words for effect. I turned to face the irritated pregnant lady and then realized I had to look down and down some more. She was a short little shit. One glance back at the monster sport utility vehicle she'd been driving made me wonder how her tiny little feet even managed to hit the accelerator and brake.

"Damn you're small," I commented.

Her eyes swept up and down my body before landing back on mine. "And you're nothing to write home about there either, short stack. Unlike some people, I thought it might be rude to mention it." She threw in a little wink before dismissing me altogether as she turned to Flicker. The asshole was laughing at me.

"I'm not small. It's fucking cold out here!" Damn it, I was going to get a complex if I didn't get some clothes on soon. Shit, any more commentary about my dick's stature and I'd have to trade my Harley in for a fucking jacked up truck with wheels bigger than my body. I shuddered thinking about the last jacked up truck that had fucked off from my life.

"I'm supposed to meet Spinner here," the tiny little spitfire informed Flicker.

"I don't think so," I told her, cutting into her conversation once again. "He know you're in that condition?"

"As a matter of fact, I do," my brother said from somewhere just behind my shoulder. "What the fuck are you doing out here like that, Rabbit?" I turned to face him and grinned. Spinner rolled his eyes at me. "Jesus, man. Don't let that bitch ruin your life. You never used to get into trouble like this before. What the hell would Mom and Dad think?"

I shrugged my shoulders, pissed off that my brother would bring our dead parents into my issues. "Pretty sure they don't get an opinion anymore." I tipped my head toward the woman again. "You hiring pregnant dancers now?"

"What's it to you?" Spinner asked.

"Last I checked, this place belongs to all of us," I countered.

"And last I checked, you never bothered to have a say about who the hell works in this establishment." I narrowed my eyes at Spinner's response. It wasn't like him to be so hostile with me, even when I was fucking up.

"Myra, Cherry's waiting on you inside. Would you rather

go unpack and get settled into the apartment or check things out first?" My brother didn't bother waiting for her answer. Instead, he turned his glare back on me. "Actually, Rabbit can grab a set of clothes from the office and take over for me for a bit if you'd like me to escort you."

Myra, the short little bit of a woman who had picked me up on the side of the road smiled brightly at my brother, and for some insane fucking reason, I found myself envious that it was for him and not me. It reached all the way to her eyes and was something I hadn't seen in the time we'd driven here together.

"Thanks, but I think I'll just go in and say hello. Besides, I really need to pee. If you could show me to a bathroom, I'd appreciate it."

"Sure thing, come on, I'll show you the way." Spinner opened the door to Renegade Rosy's and held it while Myra walked right in underneath his outstretched arm.

"Who the hell is she?" I asked, but my brother ignored me.

"Get some fucking clothes on, Rabbit. Last thing we need is you running off customers." He glanced down at my junk and then smirked. "That sure as shit ain't gonna bring them in." The fucker took off, laughing as he went. I glared at Flicker when he couldn't hold back his laughter anymore.

"Sorry, I guess you've had a rough night," Flicker told me as he attempted to get himself under control.

"It's fucking cold out here!" I snapped at him before I snatched the door open and went inside. Before I got past the little entry hallway, I twisted the sweatshirt so that it was mostly on my side, but parts of it covered my junk and half of my ass. It didn't escape my notice that little miss Myra laughed as I walked by where she and Cherry were standing on the opposite side of the bar near the hallway that led to the office.

Thankfully, all the men of the club knew well enough to stash an extra change of clothes in the office. Depending on the night, Renegade Rosy's could be tame as ever or a wild fucking place to be. Sometimes, we ended up wearing more beer and liquor than we served, while other times it looked like we bathed in glitter and stripper sweat. A change of clothes was a necessary evil if any of us ever had plans for after we left work. Not that it was my night to work here, but I still maintained a change of clothes. It didn't take long to get myself together.

As I was about to walk back into the main room I heard Cherry ask Myra, "So you just left him there?"

"Yep," Myra answered back while popping the 'p' in the word very loudly.

"Huh! I always thought the two of you would go the distance," Cherry informed her.

"Yeah, well, everyone thought that. As it turned out, I was their pawn in some fucked up little matchmaking game. I can't believe how much of my time I wasted on him."

What a bitch!

It was like listening to a conversation that Cherry might have had with her twin before she left. It was all I could think and suddenly, I liked little Miss Myra even less than I had before I overheard her name. I had no respect for a woman who couldn't stick things out or at least let her damn feelings be known. No, these bitches had to just walk out on their men and run away. Must be something in the water where they're from. I definitely had no time for cold ass women like that. I'd dealt with my fair share of fallout from having put up with Chastity and her bullshit for far too long. I glared in the general direction of the table that the girls were sitting at before I left to head back to the clubhouse.

5. MYRA

"What did I ever do to that guy? You'd think I stabbed him with needles the whole time he was in my truck or something. He jumped in my truck buck-ass naked and I gave him a ride here. Now, he's acting like I'm the antichrist."

"Don't take it personally. Once he realized you were my friend from Oregon, he probably figured he was safer being a dick to you."

"What? Why?"

"Chastity."

"Oh no!" I knew what that meant. Cherry's twin was hell on men back before she was even legal. I could imagine the kind of destruction someone like her could be responsible for as an adult.

"Yeah," Cherry sighed. "Rabbit had a silly crush on me in the beginning, but all I could see was his brother." My beautiful friend shrugged her shoulders. "When he realized I didn't feel the same, he chased Chastity. She tried to do the right thing in the beginning and told him no."

"But?" I questioned because there was always a 'but' where Chastity was concerned.

"But, he finally wore her down. She did at least warn him that she wasn't like me. Not that he heeded that warning," she sighed again. "I feel horrible because Rabbit is usually a really great guy. It's sad to see the way he's unraveled since my sister took off."

"Well, I'll be honest, my first impression of the man did not lead me to believe he was a great guy in any sense of the word."

"He'll warm up to you and you'll see what I mean."

I ignored that and sipped on the Sprite that was giving me a second wind. I couldn't have caffeine, but the sugar sure did help after that last leg of that trip. I was worn out. I was so worn out, in fact, that I couldn't stifle the yawn that had my wide mouth gaping open as Spinner joined us at the table. He offered a sweet smile and then looked at my friend.

"Babe, I think maybe you should get your friend home so she can settle in and crash. That was a hell of a trip, especially for a pregnant woman to make on her own." I saw the wary concern in his eyes as he spoke and turned back to me. "Sorry my brother was an asshole tonight, too. That was a shit welcome for you."

I waved his apology off. "I'm not worried about him. I grew up in an MC remember?"

Spinner shook his head. "What I know is you also ran from one who mistreated you. We aren't like that here, contrary to my brother's behavior tonight, and he's not normally like that either. I don't know what got into him."

"Okay," I hummed out softly. "I'll take your word for it."

I wasn't going to argue with the man about whether or not his brother was the giant douchebag he presented himself to be. Spinner was the man giving me a job and a place to stay until I could get through my NCLEX-RN testing, get licensed, and then get a job working for a doctor's office or even at the hospital. I'd checked, and Monument Health in Spearfish wasn't too far to travel for work. There were a few other locations, but they might mean I'd have to move further away from Cherry and the club when the time came. I wasn't sure how I felt about that.

I didn't want to be a person who was stuck relying on others, especially another MC, but I'd never been a mom before either. I was pretty sure it would require me to have to lean on someone at some point in time. Wouldn't it? Frustration weighed heavily on my shoulders as I thought about that. When I first hoped that the pregnancy test would be positive, I believed I'd have the baby's father there by my side. I had a whole family, a club full of people who would have my child's back. Then everything went to shit and now, instead of being happy and planning all the wonderful things involved in pregnancy and bringing a child into the world, I had more worries than anything else.

The apartment Cherry and Spinner offered me was a little one-bedroom, one-bathroom place they had put in over the detached garage. The garage was Spinner's space for his multiple motorcycles. It was cute, although it wouldn't offer much room once I had the baby and had to fill the space with his or her stuff. My plan was to try to save enough to get a two-bedroom place on my own as soon as possible. Not that I wasn't thankful for the soft landing the garage apartment afforded me, because I was. It wasn't just me that I had to make plans for anymore, though.

"Is it going to be okay for you?" Cherry asked as I took in the older furniture that was already there.

"Are you kidding? It's perfect for me until I can find a place big enough for the both of us," I told her as I gently stroked my belly.

"That reminds me," my friend told me as I turned from the small kitchen back to her. "I'll pick you up at ten tomorrow morning, and we'll head over to the clubhouse. Spinner worked something out with Doc. He's going to do your initial exam for you and then he'll recommend an actual obstetrician who will keep everything off the books and do cash only visits."

"Is he having a hard time finding one that will do those things?"

Cherry shook her head. "No, there are plenty who will do that, he's making sure that they'll be the best care for you and the baby, though. You may want to live off the grid as much as possible, but that doesn't mean you should get shitty, shady care as a result."

"I appreciate that," I told my friend. "Did you have this place made up for Chastity?"

Cherry laughed. "Lord no! I would have killed her, or more likely, she would have killed me in my sleep, if we had to live in this close of quarters for too long. This is a place Spinner had before he met me. I talked him into updating the kitchen when I lived here for a while, though."

"Oh?"

"Yeah, like I said, Chastity and I may be identical twins,

but there was no way I could live with her constant string of men in and out of a shared space. We tried that before and it didn't end well for me when the drunk asshole thought I was my sister playing games with him."

I flinched, because I remembered why the girls had ended up running from Oregon. "So, you stayed here. Is that how you and Spinner ended up falling for one another?" I asked her, then winked, letting her know I was helping her avoid shittier memories. "Were you getting creative with your rent payments?" I mimed a blowjob and Cherry threw a pillow from the couch at my face.

"You bitch!" She tossed back at me, along with the pillow. She was laughing, though, so mission accomplished. I yawned again, unable to stifle it that time like I had the last four or five times since the exhaustion set in. "I'm so sorry. Here you are traveling halfway across the country while baking a baby, and I'm keeping you up even later. Maybe we should reschedule with Doc?"

"No," I waved off her concern. "I wasn't able to get to the doctor before I left, so it will be good to see someone as soon as possible so that I know everything is as it should be."

"Okay, well, I'm just over that way if you need anything. You have my cell, but Spinner's is there on the counter along with the bar and the clubhouse, just in case. Okay?"

"Cherry, I can't thank you enough for doing all this for me," I told her.

"Honey, you don't have to thank me. That's what friends are for. Besides, I'm happier seeing you taken care of than worried you might be out there somewhere hurt, being taken advantage of, or worse, only to have no one ever know what happened. I think you'll like it here too. It's a quiet life to bring your baby into."

I laughed. "Yeah, I just hope the bikers we're around here turn out to be a better breed than my family was."

"I'm so sorry they all hurt you the way they did," she offered as she moved toward the door.

"Me, too."

"Good night, My."

"Night, Cherry." I closed and locked the door behind her, and then I moved to the tiny bedroom I would be sleeping in every night. There were a couple of rolling garment racks in the corner for me to hang my clothes up on, a small dresser, a night table with two more drawers I could use, and a full-sized bed. As I looked around, I realized there definitely wouldn't be room for a crib in there, although I supposed I could always shuffle the garment rack to the living room and put a small pack-n-play type thing there. No, I would definitely need a new place before the baby was here. Luckily, I still had time to save.

It was my first time entering the clubhouse of an MC that didn't belong to the Stoneridge Raiders. I was blown away by the security doors, something they told me was not necessarily standard for the rest of the Aces High MC locations.

"Spinner said the building used to be some super-secret medical testing facility at one point. That's why you shouldn't be surprised by the offices Doc has downstairs."

"Ah, that was convenient for him."

"It was convenient for everyone, considering we are lucky enough to have a doctor in the club who comes in at a moment's notice most times."

"That has to be hard on his day job," I said. It wasn't that I was fishing for information, I just didn't understand how something like that would work.

"If he's with a patient, obviously, he can't leave right away to come help us out, but he doesn't work like a regular doc. He fills in and floats between the hospital and some offices around the area. If a staff member calls in sick, he's able to fill in for them. That way, if there's something coming up with the club, he can tell them he's not available. Most already know that he has other obligations."

"That seems like a weird lifestyle for a doctor."

"It is, but at the same time, the offices and hospital where he fills in for staff are grateful for the extra man onboard when they need him, and for not having to pay out a full check to another staff member."

"I bet," I agreed as we made our way through what must have been the main common area and bar for their clubhouse.

"This is a great space," I told Cherry. "Plenty of room to get rowdy without breaking shit, and the girls have a spot to dance, not to mention a great bar," I pointed out.

"Yeah, the guys seem to love it. Oh!" she cried out at the end, as her eyes turned to take in the bar I had just pointed out. "Come on," she glanced down at her phone. "We still have a little time, let me introduce you to my friend, Charlie." She grabbed my hand and dragged me, a little too quickly for my short legs, over to the bar area. There stood a woman who seemed sort of familiar at first glance, though I couldn't place her face. "Myra, this is Charlie. Her old man is our VP, Rage. Charlie, this is my friend from back home, Myra."

"The pregnant one?" The woman asked as she ducked to put some glasses away. She stood again to see me smiling and Cherry frowning at her. "What? Was it a secret that she's with child?" Charlie whispered as she leaned closer to us by resting her elbows on the bar and cupping her hands around her mouth so the whisper would carry to us only. I couldn't help it, I laughed.

"I like you already, and no, it's not a secret. At least one that won't be easily kept soon enough, so I don't see the point in trying to hide it."

"Well, that's good. Girl, you have a beautiful glow about you that pregnant women sometimes get."

That caused me to blush. It was nice to hear a kind word about yourself every once in a while, especially after my ego took that severe pummeling when my ex chose a lying whore over staying with me.

"Myra Chase?" A man called out from behind, causing me to startle and jump half way out of my damn skin – if such a thing were possible. I turned wide, fearful eyes to him just in time to see him swear under his breath. "Sorry, I wasn't thinking," he apologized. "I'm Doc."

My hand settled over my heart, trying to coax it to calm the hell down. "It's okay, you just caught me off guard."

"No," he told me sternly. "Don't make excuses for me. Spinner filled me in on your situation. I should have known better than to just go calling your name out like that." I started to protest again, but stopped as he held his hand up. "Let's just start fresh. Are you ready to head down to the on-site clinic?"

"Sure," I agreed before turning back to Cherry, just for verification that he was indeed the man I was supposed to go with. She reassured me with a quick smile and the nod of her head, so I followed along behind him as he led me down a set of stairs. I knew we were headed underground, but honestly, it didn't have that creepy basement vibe. The place was more reminiscent of a sterile hospital corridor, though it definitely had better lighting than most of the hospitals I'd been to. The walls, however, were a stereotypical white, which made the great lighting seem glaringly bright.

"Some color wouldn't go amiss down here," I mumbled, much to Doc's amusement.

"That's what I keep saying. This lighting on all that white is hard as hell on the eyes. I'm pretty sure Charlie already tried to convince Iceman to change things up down here, but it's never been a priority."

"As soon as I'm working steady again, I'm willing to chip in for some paint, you guys supply the labor, that's what prospects are for right?" I joked.

Doc laughed. "Ah, a breath of fresh air around here once in a while is nice, too."

"Do you usually only work with the men?"

"No. I take care of the club women, too, but they're usually trying to come on to me – the BRATs anyway – and that just makes for an awkward physical for everyone involved."

"Your definition here might help me to determine if that's a bad thing. What is a BRAT?"

He laughed. "They're what you probably call club girls. The female hang-arounds who have no problem servicing the men of the club in exchange for a roof over their heads."

"Ah, okay. So, then I guess my next question would be, what kind of a biker dude doesn't want to play dirty doctor with the club girls?"

Doc laughed so hard he bent over double trying to gain his composure before we both realized there was someone else in the room we had just entered.

"Oh, sorry Doc! Didn't realize you had to run another BRAT through her paces," Rabbit hissed out between clenched teeth. No doubt he had heard the last bit of what I said and I sounded like one of those women giving the man another unwanted come on line. Holy mother of miscommunications. The man already thought I was an opportunistic suckerfish here to do damage to the men of his club, apparently. Guilt by Chastity association was in full effect.

Doc, for his part, sobered from his laugh-fest pretty quickly when Rabbit said that. "I need you to leave unless you have an emergency, Rabbit. Miss Chase has an appointment with me."

"Yeah, you might want to make sure that one is clean, seems she might have some extra baggage along for the ride already. Don't want anyone here..."

"OUT!" Doc yelled at him as he pointed to the door. Rabbit didn't say another word, but he did toss a judgy little smirk over his shoulder before he left. "I'm sorry about that." Doc shook his head, exasperated. "I've never seen him be outright mean to a single soul on this planet, and that includes the BRATs we have here."

"Well, he seems to have decided that I'm all that is evil in this world from the moment he met me, so don't worry, I'm already used to his behavior."

"He's treated you badly before?" Doc asked, the shock on his face clear as day. I simply nodded and refused to talk about the man who seemed to hate me on sight for some unfathomable reason.

"Can we get this over with? I don't want to think about any of the asshole people in my life, past or present, more than I have to. I'm saving all my energy for this little guy in here." I patted my stomach and Doc's demeanor changed.

"You think it's a boy?"

I scrunched my shoulders up high and then dropped them. "I have a feeling, but I've been wrong before, so if you care to place bets, now would probably be a great time," I laughed.

Doc continued shaking his head at me as he chuckled. "You know, it's crazy that Rabbit took an instant dislike to you for whatever reason, because you remind me of him, always turning everything into a joke." With a raised eyebrow, and a stern look, I conveyed that we were not supposed to be discussing people who hated me. "Sorry," Doc amended. "Okay, last period?"

"Aug. 23rd and before you ask, I usually have a pretty regular period on about a 26 day cycle."

Doc grinned up from the little chart he held in his hand. "That's the kind of patient I like, the ones who know the answers to the questions before the questions are even asked."

"I aim to please," I teased, then realized what that sounded like. "But, uh, not like that. So, don't get your hopes up, Doc. There will be no dirty doctor being played down here while I'm present. I know I advocated for bikers to do that, but..."

Doc slapped his knee and burst out laughing again. "Oh, Myra, you don't even know how good you are for my soul right now." He patted my knee and offered up a genuine smile before turning his focus back to the chart that would tell him my due date. "Looks like you'll be expecting that bouncing baby boy to come out around May 23rd."

"Bouncing baby boy?"

"I sense the mother's intuition is strong with you, no way am I betting against a woman who not only knew right away when her last period was, but how long her cycle actually lasted. Honestly, that's a rarity among women around here."

"We can try using the Fetal Doppler to see if we can hear a heartbeat yet, but honestly, at just over 7 weeks, it could go either way. I don't want you to be disappointed if-"

I cut Doc off. "Once I take my NCLEX, I'll be a full grown, official nurse. I understand that it might be too early to easily find the heartbeat."

Doc's smile was positively infectious. "Sorry, I'm used to..." he waved his hand to indicate the building we were in. "I'm a bit jaded in my old age." Doc was not an old man. If he was 40, I would be surprised.

"How did you end up involved in a motorcycle club?" I

asked. Curiosity about how men found their way to the life always fascinated me.

"I came from a poor family, had mediocre grades because I couldn't get a decent meal, or a moment of peace to study. I went into the military, started as a corpsman and worked my way through school, then got tapped for a program, sent to medical school, did my time to pay off that training, and got out when I was wounded in a bombing on the ship I was stationed on."

My jaw dropped, but Doc continued on with his story. "I suppose I had a bit of a fatalist attitude after that, and probably a death wish, too. Did a lot of stupid shit. After physical therapy to get everything working right, I started riding. Ended up at a rally and picked a fight with the wrong motherfuckers on the anniversary of the bombing. Iceman was there, stepped in, and brought me home with him. The rest, as they say, is history. The brotherhood gave me something back that I didn't realize I'd been missing. These boys healed the broken pieces of my soul and I've been working on the survivor's guilt ever since."

"I'm glad you found what you needed here," I told him.

"Me too, Myra. Now, shirt up, so I can get to that belly."

Doc slipped the cool gel on my belly and started moving the doppler around to try to find a heartbeat. He picked up mine immediately, but we both waited to see if we'd be able to hear my little one's, too. Unfortunately, he wasn't able to find it. Not for lack of trying on his part. He patted my thigh as he removed the little wand from my belly. "Sorry, hon. If I had a transvaginal ultrasound working around here, I'd hook it up and we'd definitely be able to find that heartbeat, but it's not something readily available. I'll try to make sure we have a working machine for later on in your pregnancy, because paying cash, those exams are going to be super expensive for you."

"Thank you for trying," I said. I tried not to let my disappointment show, but that was tough. I was pregnant and the hormones were no joke to deal with, so the tears started. "I'm sorry, it's not like I didn't know the likelihood," I explained.

Doc smiled as he handed me tissues. "You'll be all right, Myra. So will that baby. I know you've been through some things with an MC before, but honey, the people here are all pretty great." He rolled his eyes after saying that. "Not that Rabbit gave you a shining example, but I promise his issues are solely his and if he doesn't get over them soon, I'll personally put a boot up his ass."

"Okay, Doc. Can you do me a favor?"

"What's that?"

"When you lodge that boot up there, can you give it a little sideways twist for me?" I asked in an innocent tone as Doc laughed.

"You bet. If he gives you any further trouble, you let me know and Uncle Doc will be there to handle him." He patted my belly as he wiped the gel remnants away.

"Uncle Doc?"

"Yeah, girl! That kid needs family at his back. I'm signing up for the top spot around here. I'll be the favorite, I just know it." I don't know what possessed me, but I leaned forward, reached out, and hugged Doc so hard, I thought one of us might break.

"I'll be your family too, Doc. Whenever you need a hug, come get one." I don't know what made me say it, but I just had a feeling that the man was going through something else, and whatever it was weighed heavily on him. Call it a hunch or some of the super-hormone, mommy intuition he spoke of, but I just knew he needed it.

"You are a gem, Myra. Never let anyone tell you otherwise," he said as he turned his back, presumably to put the doppler away, but I didn't miss the way he swiped at his eyes either. "You remember how to get back topside?" He asked me.

"Of course," I assured him.

"Go on up, I'll get you some appointments set up with a friend of mine who owes me a favor."

"Don't go using up your favors for me," I told him.

"Honey, if I can't use my favors up to help out a beautiful soul in need, then what's the point in collecting them?"

"You're quickly becoming my favorite person, Doc."

"Right back at you, girl."

ONCE I GOT BACK UP to the main floor, I noticed that Rabbit stood over by the bar watching Charlie work. When she went to move a few bottles on the higher shelf above her head, as she restocked the liquor, Rabbit hopped over the counter and took them from her.

"I've got this. Don't want you straining your back or nothing." His words were teasing, but it was sweet to see a man jump up to help a woman out without needing to be asked. Then again, this was Rabbit, so maybe he had another agenda. Everyone kept telling me he was a super nice guy, but I had yet to see it. I was really sorry for him that Chastity had apparently fucked him over, but boo-freaking-hoo. That didn't give him license to be a dick to other people. I'd been fucked over by my ex, too, and I certainly wasn't behaving that way. That would make me a hypocrite. And if we were being honest, I wasn't just fucked over by an ex, but by my entire family, so I had more reason to be an unbearable asshole.

I silently moved to the end of the bar to wait for Cherry, who I didn't see right away, but was supposed to be my ride back home once my exam with Doc was done. A man tapped me on my shoulder and I turned to him with a smile on my face. It was clear that he was a prospect because the front of his kutte held no identifiers and the back of it simply had the "PROSPECT" rocker below the Aces High MC logo of a skull in a top hat, sitting on top of four aces, while smoking a cigarette. Or was that a joint? Hmmm, something I could ask Spinner or Doc.

"Hi," I called out to the man who was grinned down at me.

"Haven't seen you around before. Anything I can get for you? A drink, appetizer, a little of me, or a whole lot if you have the time?" He winked as I laughed at his horribly cheesy pickup line. Granted, I knew that the men around the club didn't really have to try that hard since they were used to the easy-access club girls acting like they fell for those ridiculous lines. I was just about to tell him that I was waiting on my friend when Rabbit was suddenly there, just behind the bar, snarling at the prospect.

"BRATs are off limits to prospects, asshole," he hissed at the man.

"But she's not-"

Rabbit interrupted him before he could explain that he didn't think I was BRAT. "You forget your place, Prospect? I said BRATs are off limits."

I glanced down at myself. I was wearing yoga pants and an oversized t-shirt with some pink and white tennis shoes. My look didn't exactly scream 'girl of the hour'. Still, I stood from the stool, mouthed, "Sorry," to the prospect who looked quite pissed off, and then I made my way out of the clubhouse. I heard Charlie yell at Rabbit from behind me and then Cherry joined in. Either she'd find me in the parking lot or I'd talk someone else into giving me a ride away from this place. What I wasn't going to do was stand idle while Rabbit lobbed more insults my way. *The bastard!*

6. RABBIT

CHERRY CAME OUT OF NOWHERE AND SLAPPED ME WHILE CHARLIE
had me distracted with her shrieking. I didn't know what the
hell crawled up either of their asses because I was too busy
having an epic stare down with the prospect in front of me.
The bastard had been trying to hit on the new girl and she
hadn't even been certified safe yet. Not to mention, I didn't
know why everyone had a problem about me reminding him
that he couldn't go there until he earned a full patch.

"What the fuck is wrong with you?" Cherry's voice finally
permeated.

"What's wrong with me? What's wrong with you? You
just fucking hit me. You might be my brother's woman, but
you have to know that was completely out of line."

"No! You know what's out of fucking line, Rabbit? The
way you've been treating my friend. She's done nothing to
you. As I heard it, she did you a favor by allowing you to ride
to Rosy's with her that night you were walking the damn
streets naked as a jaybird. And you return the favor by insin-

58

uating – and not just once – that she's some sort of whore for the club?"

"Well, she is," I insisted. That time, Charlie hit me and the prospect stood there watching with his big Cro Magnon brow all furrowed and furious with me, arms crossed over his chest, and nostrils flared like he was going to come for me.

"She is my friend, and I am pretty much the only person she has to count on in this world right now. So help me God, if you just pushed her away and sent her running again, I will drag you to the town square, tack you up to a cross, naked, and let women from the whole state, and maybe a few more besides, take turns throwing rocks at your junk!"

Not gonna lie, I covered said junk and glanced around to see if anyone would help me. More importantly, I took note of all the people who might actually help Cherry instead as she stormed off to go after her friend.

"What the fuck?" I asked again, hands still covering the goods.

"Rabbit, I have never been disappointed in you since the day we met, but today, you actually jumped into the top spot on my shit list," Charlie informed me.

"Why?" I asked again.

"Because that woman is no whore, and you should be ashamed of yourself," the prospect beat Charlie to a response.

"She was just here to see Doc for her eval," I argued.

"No," Doc's angry voice came from just the other side of the bar. "She was here so I could check on her health because she has no insurance that she can use without it being tracked." He used a come-hither motion with his fingers, indicating I should move in closer. Like a complete dumbass, I did, thinking he was going to tell me something in confidence. He didn't. The motherfucker hit me. "That was for the prospect, because I imagine he was chomping at the bit to do it and knew he'd lose his chances at a patch if he did."

"Mother fuck me running," I spat out as I swiped at the blood pouring out of my nose. "You just hit me," I growled.

"I'm going to do it again, too," Doc slung the words back as he got ready to hop over the bar.

"Doc, out in the lot!" Rage's booming voice commanded. Doc's narrowed eyes landed on me as he tried to shake off his anger. Not that I understood where it was coming from. "You will apologize to that woman, and so help me, if you make her uncomfortable in this clubhouse again, we're going to have more than words next time."

"You fucking hit me," I reminded him. "That was more than just words."

"Nope. That was just me getting started on the lecture." Rage grabbed hold of Doc then and guided him toward the door. As they moved across the room, he looked back over his shoulder at Charlie. "Explain shit to him so he understands what he just did."

Charlie nodded and waited for the other men to leave. Then she turned back to me. I didn't think she was waiting on privacy, though. My best friend was trying to cool her own temper.

"I honestly can't believe you would treat any woman that way, even if she was here to be a BRAT." Charlie shook her head, disappointment brimming hot and angry in her eyes.

"The fact that she's here to become a nurse, and work with your brother until she can take her test, just makes it worse. She's probably someone who would be an asset to have around the club, especially since Doc has been worn thin lately."

"What? I need someone to actually explain what the hell she's doing here then, because I overheard her talking about how she left her man in the dust and wasn't going to look back."

"Did you now?" Charlie asked in that voice laden with sarcasm that told me I'd probably misunderstood what I'd overheard. "She did leave her man in the dust. Although, it didn't quite look like a bitch sporting a pink bob, waving at you from the cab of another man's truck, which is what I'm sure you were picturing." Well, she had me there, not that I was admitting to that out loud. "I'll tell you what I know, and even I don't know the whole story because Cherry thought Myra should be able to tell it, or not, as she saw fit.

"Myra has only had one boyfriend. They were club kids together and apparently their families made it impossible for them to not end up together. She thought he invited her to brunch to finally pop the question. He had her meet him at a café so his whore, who he was choosing over her, was there to watch him dump her. And this was after he had been actively trying to get Myra pregnant. They've been together for a long time, since she was 16. He had apparently been cheating on her that whole time and worse, her family knew about it and never said a word to her."

"What the fuck?"

"Suddenly that question takes on new meaning. So, you

have been treating a 24-year-old woman like absolute shit when she is trying to get over a million different betrayals. He was her only boyfriend, her first everything, she's pregnant with his kid, and he dumped her for another woman who he cheated on her with. Then she found out her family helped him keep it a secret, and other times he cheated as well. And you just added to the load of hurt she's carrying all because you overheard her say she left her man in the dust and was never looking back. Would you fucking look back on someone who did that to you, Rabbit?" Charlie huffed and puffed for a minute, gathering herself and trying to dissipate the anger she felt toward me. Anger, I realized, that I completely deserved.

"Fuck!"

"Yeah, fuck! You owe that woman a huge apology. And Rabbit?" she asked as I started to walk off.

"What?"

"Lose the chip on your shoulder. It's getting annoying and making me not like you very much anymore."

I hung my head and left the clubhouse. What could I say? I was ashamed of my own actions now that I knew what had been going on. Truth be told, I shouldn't have had to know any of that. The old me – the me before Chastity ripped me to shreds – would have never treated one of the club girls like that, even if she said she'd left her man somewhere. I took a ride out to the house I had built but refused to live in. It was where I planned to raise my family one day, where I planned to bring the woman I was in love with to settle down. I walked through the empty space, taking in all the extras I'd packed into the place, the detailed trim work of the cabinetry, the marble countertops, and the reclaimed barn wood door that slid away to reveal the walk-in pantry in the kitchen. The one that still remained untouched with empty shelves.

The thought of having Chastity move in and sully this place with her memories made me glad that she had never stepped foot inside the walls. I could continue to wallow in what I'd once thought of as a lost opportunity, or I could see things for what they really were. The bitch did me a favor by leaving before she could taint everything. Having a child with her would have been awful, and I might as well look into adoption and single parenting for all the help she would have been with a kid. I knew that. Somewhere deep down, I understood that she wasn't the right person, and still, I'd wanted something bad enough that I'd been willing to delude myself into thinking what I had would be enough.

I moved upstairs and walked through the hall, into what should be the master suite. It was just more empty space. Once I passed the giant sunken tub and free-standing shower that could easily fit five or more grown adults, I turned to the mirror and took a good, hard look at myself. There have been times where looking in the mirror meant there was room for improving on myself. This was one of those times, but it was so much more. The man staring back at me wasn't the person I wanted to be. He had been acting out, taking his anger out on the wrong people, and doing shit he normally wouldn't have done. It was then that I knew what needed to change.

"One big fuck you to the world party this weekend to get it all out of my system, and then I'm grabbing my life back by the nuts and getting my shit together," I told my reflection. It was rare that I let myself go completely wild. Some might say the crap I'd been pulling by sleeping with whatever women were available, whether they were single or not, had been me being wild. That wasn't wrong, in a way, but it was just a shot in the dark at all the things I normally kept in check. I didn't drink, do drugs, or indulge with the club girls. It wasn't because I thought they were beneath me, it had always been for the sole reason that I didn't want the future love of my life to ever have to walk into the clubhouse and look a woman in the eye who had me as a staple to her bedroom diet.

I'd seen how it crushed women's souls before. Some of my brothers should have been more grateful than they were that the women they chose had been able to look beyond those things. When I think about the trouble some of the club girls had caused Charlie early on, it made me cringe to think that I had been that same level of cunt to Cherry's friend, Myra. A simple apology would not be enough.

MY WEEKEND WAS ABOUT to kick off the right way. First, I was doing my research and getting some ideas for the night I had planned. There was something inside me, no matter how much better I wanted to be, that told me that the perfect woman and family weren't out there waiting on me to show up in their lives. I had never lived stupidly, and it was time to change that up a bit. Well, for the weekend, anyway. Charlie's latest romance novel had just been lying on one of the clubhouse tables, so I picked it up and skimmed to the good stuff.

A pool table, huh?

I glanced up at one of the pool tables we had in our clubhouse. It didn't exactly look comfortable, but this was about doing the unexpected and stepping out of my comfort zone. I'd missed the frivolous, fun, stupid times in my twenties. I was thirty-one now and time was ticking away from me. This weekend would be my one and done, free-for-all, booze and bitches binge, and then I'd go back to being boring old Rabbit. Sure, I was usually everyone's funny bunny, but I was also the safe guy in the room. Just once, I wanted to be the bad choice for someone else.

The slight hint of peaches and sunshine wafted to my nostrils. I knew that scent, it was one I had smelled all too recently. I glanced up in time to see her smirking at the book I had in my hands.

"It's Charlie's," I called out, halting her in her tracks. "I was just making sure Rage would approve of the crap she's reading."

She said nothing. The infernal woman just stood there, staring at me, the smirk never leaving her face.

"Fine!" I growled out. "You know what? I'm reading it for me. And I fuckin' like it. They blow shit up in this one. Legit — use bombs and whatnot, which is cool as fuck. And they aren't making love by candlelight either. Oh no. The hero of the story bangs her up against a wall, then on the pool table — which isn't really smart because bitches get rug burn from that."

When she just stared at me with a slack-jawed expression, I huffed out my frustration over getting caught by this woman as I read a romance novel. I don't know why it bothered me, as pretty much everyone here knew I picked them up periodically when Charlie left them lying around. All right, fine, I was a member of her goddamn book club, too.

"What? They do. Pool tables are not made for comfort when fucking, no matter how many of these books use them as a prop for just that."

"Rabbit?" Charlie asked cautiously after hearing my tirade toward Myra.

"What?"

"Maybe you should put the book down and step away from the scared pregnant woman before you scar her for life."

"She's not scared," I insisted while glancing between Charlie and Myra who was doing that slow-step, backing away thing you do when there's a feral animal in front of you. "You're not scared, right?"

Shit!

I to panic as she continued to creep away from me. This was the first time I'd seen her since I had been a complete jackass. I hadn't even managed to apologize yet, and now the woman was backing away from me like cooties were crawling from my crotch. I glanced down and took a peek.

Nope. Nothing crawling.

Fuck – I knew that. Maybe I was going crazy.

The woman gulped and halted her movement mid-step.

"FUCK!" I yelled. Then quieted my tone when her reaction was to damn near jump out of her skin. "Don't be afraid of me."

"Yeah, okay," she answered, then spun and ran to the kitchen. Literally, the girl ran away from me. Charlie laughed as she slapped me in the chest with her book.

"Idiot!" I tried to snatch the book back from her as she left, but the little minx was too fast. Once she made it to the kitchen, I took off and stood just outside the door, with my ear plastered to the wood, listening in, like a true fucking lunatic.

"Don't worry," I heard Charlie tell Myra. "He's a little touched in the head. Just ignore him and he usually goes away." They both laughed. At. Me.

"No," I hissed to myself. "Not my best friend." I quieted when Myra spoke and it became obvious she had been putting on a good show before. She wasn't scared in the least bit.

"Shame the good looking ones are always cheaters or crazy as hell, right?" Myra asked Charlie.

"You think he's hot?" Charlie countered.

"Well, I'm pregnant, not blind. Of course he's hot, but he's also fucking nuts. You know I met him when he was hitchhiking naked on my first night in town, right?"

"No way! Do tell," was Charlie's response.

I groaned and walked away, not needing to hear about that night. Getting the book back from Charlie wasn't worth reliving that particular embarrassment. I also knew I needed to get the new girl off my mind. Yeah, 'new girl,' because naming her in my head made her real. I couldn't afford to think of anyone else as real. I'd made that mistake with

Chastity. Sure, 'new girl' was experiencing much worse with her ex, but she was also having his baby and that made women a little crazy sometimes. No way was I going to get invested in her, only to have her flake and go back home to her baby's daddy.

Holy shit!

What was I even thinking? The woman hated me, thought I was crazy, and for good reason. I'd treated her like shit. How the hell was I even considering her as an option?

Instead of running further down that nut-job rabbit hole, I made some more absolutely shit decisions.

7. MYRA

CHERRY DROPPED ME OFF AT THE CLUBHOUSE. I HONESTLY DIDN'T want to be there, on the off chance that I'd run into the douchebag himself. Still, I had to learn how to run a bar from someone because there was no guarantee that I would even pass my nursing exam when the time came to take it. Charlie had apparently been running an airtight ship in the clubhouse bar, and Spinner wanted me to learn how she did inventory there because the girl he had in charge at Renegade Rosy's had screwed it up so bad, they were having to re-inventory everything. It was a headache I did not envy Spinner for having. Considering he and his woman were doing me a solid by not only giving me a place to live, but a job on short notice, knowing that I was pregnant...

Well, I couldn't exactly say no to the training session at the clubhouse. I was shocked to not only find Rabbit there, but to see him reading a romance novel. He seemed to be enjoying it, which I found odd. Not that there was anything at all wrong with men reading romance – more should do it. I had grown up a club princess, though, and there was no way in hell any of the bikers from my father's club would ever be caught dead with, let alone alive and enjoying, a romance novel.

"Earth to Myra!" Charlie called out.

"Sorry, what?"

Charlie laughed at me. "It was the book wasn't it? It always throws people off at first. You should have seen it when I finally got enough women together for a romance reader's book club around here only to have Rabbit come sauntering in one evening. I didn't know whether they were all going to duck and cover, or try to recruit him for their one-man harem. I mean, he does look like one of those guys," she finished as she tipped her head toward the book whose cover was facing us from where it was perched on the counter. Rabbit did sort of resemble the cover model.

Rabbit had what I liked to call a golden body. He was tall, probably around six feet, two inches and then he had beautifully defined muscles without being overdone. My ex had started out too scrawny, only to blow right past the perfect 'golden' zone into too much muscle. I swear, for every pound of muscle he put on as we got older, the idiot lost personality points. I wish he had stayed at the place where Rabbit was. It looked healthy, beautiful, and well, golden.

"It's not that," I started to argue even as I remembered what his body had looked like on that night he had hopped into my truck with nothing but a kutte on his back. Charlie gave me a look that called me out on being a liar without having to say a word. "Okay, not just that," I admitted. We both ended up chuckling. "It's a shame because the ones in that perfect body zone are always assholes."

Charlie frowned. "I know he's said some pretty crappy things to and about you, but I promise, Rabbit isn't normally like that."

I shrugged my shoulders, feigning indifference. She wasn't the only person to try to convince me of that. "Everyone keeps saying he has this great excuse for being an asshole, but to be honest, I don't see it." Charlie gasped, and I could tell she was about to argue with me. "Do you know my story, or at least the gist of it?" She nodded. "Have I been an asshole to anyone?" That time, she shook her head, and I watched as a frown deepened the creases on her forehead. "I don't normally like to compare people's pain, but if I could go through all of that with my ex while my family took his side, lied for him, and continued to have his back instead of mine, and still be nice to all the people I meet..." I didn't finish, I let the rest simmer in her own mind.

After a few moments she responded. "You're right. There's really no justification for the way he has been acting. I'm sorry," she tried to apologize.

"Don't. It's not necessary. I'm sure you know a completely different Rabbit than the man I've been introduced to. Your perspective makes a difference. For now though, I just want to learn your system so I can get gone before any weekend shenanigans kick off around here."

Charlie laughed. "Oh girl, that's probably for the best. I'll be honest, the guys aren't near as bad as they once were. I think that has to do with most of them growing older, though."

"Don't they get fresh blood in that often?"

"They do, but they're also hard on recruits. More of them either drop out of prospecting or end up being slightly older and more settled into themselves. The guys are picky. There are other chapters where they have some issues with a few of their men, and I think everyone here is trying to avoid that."

Thinking back to my own family and the MC they ran, I had to agree. "It sucks when a club starts to fester from the inside. At some point they forget that they're only as strong as their weakest link. In my family's club, they allowed the weak links to taint the rest and now they're all rusty pieces of shit where they were once indomitable steel," I told her.

"Exactly." Charlie grabbed a clipboard off of the wall and turned to me. "Okay, let's get started. I'm going to show you how to keep a paper tally, but then how I transfer it all to this program we have so that the electronic records are easily accessible. That way, if Spinner is ever gone, and one of the other men has to step in, they'll be able to figure everything out easily enough."

"Great! Let's do this."

"I'M SO sorry it took this long for me to get everything down," I said to Charlie after we finally closed out of the program. "This whole mom brain is a real thing, I think." She chuckled as I hung my head in shame.

"Seriously, My, don't sweat it. It takes however long it takes. If you want the honest truth, I'm great at making drinks, but it took forever for me to get this system in place for keeping up with what I was making. The first time one of the guys asked me what we needed to restock, I laughed and almost peed my pants."

"I hate to bother Cherry, but she brought me here this morning. I knew it was a bad idea. I hate being without my own ride and having to rely on others."

"Don't worry about bothering her, I'll get you home." She glanced at her phone and frowned. "Fair warning though, I'm sure the party has already started out there." Charlie shook her head and laughed as soon as the words left her. "What am I talking about? You were a club princess, I don't think it will be anything you've never seen before. Just remember, like I said earlier, most of the guys we have now are tame, so it shouldn't even be an issue."

I nodded my head in agreement, but boy was she ever wrong. While I had only ever seen the bad impression side of Rabbit, literally everyone who knew him sang his praises and talked about what an upstanding guy he was. So, imagine my surprise, and even disappointment in the man, when we moved out of the back storeroom into the clubhouse bar area, only to glance to my right and see the man himself, balls deep in a club whore he had bent over the pool table.

Of all the things.

It seemed like someone was putting what he learned from romance books to the test. Sweet, naive Charlies must not have realized her friend read them to get ideas for things to do with the women he fucked around the clubhouse. I couldn't knock the theory, because let's face it, most women wished men read more romance for that very reason. I didn't understand the gut-clenching reaction my body had to seeing him putting those ideas to action, though.

Charlie must have noticed what my attention shifted to, because as she turned her head, I heard an audible gasp. "Oh my God! That is so weird."

"Nothing I haven't seen before," I assured her. "No need to play like it's unusual when we both know better."

"For anyone else, I'd agree with you. Rabbit doesn't have sex with the BRATs, and he never, ever, does anything like that in public." Charlie seemed to grow unreasonably angry with her friend. It made me wonder if there was more between the two of them than simple friendship. She must have seen the curious look I tossed her way because she shook her head rather adamantly.

"You don't understand. I'm angry because Cherry's no-good, evil, twin bitch ruined my best friend when she left him high and dry."

I sighed, knowing how that kind of an abrupt end could leave you reeling. I still saw it as a cop out for bad behavior. Part of me began to wonder if all of the people in Rabbit's life really knew him at all. Maybe he had just been really good at hiding his wild side previously, and there came a point when it was too daunting to try to keep it all secret any longer.

"Honestly?" I asked Charlie who nodded in response. "If I weren't pregnant, I might go out and make some devilishly stupid mistakes, too. Instead, the only outlet I had was to uproot my life, drive halfway across the country, and hide from my family. Maybe, you guys should cut him a little slack and let him work his issues out of his system."

Charlie watched me for a long moment as I fiddled with

the zipper on my coat to keep from turning back to watch the action taking place on the pool table. I wasn't normally a voyeur, but curiosity – she was a bitch!

"I guess he's entitled to go a little nuts," she agreed after a few minutes. The knot of unease at seeing Rabbit go 'a little nuts', or maybe a better term would be 'nuts deep', still had me feeling a little rattled. Despite the way he'd treated me, and all of his assholish tendencies, I'd found Rabbit to be highly entertaining and worth a laugh now and then. That, coupled with everyone I knew trying to put the man back up on some sort of pedestal, were the only reasons I was feeling particularly queasy about what he was doing.

I shook that thought off as Charlie and I walked out of the security access door that always freaked me out when I visited the clubhouse. I had weird dreams where the door refused to let me out and I called my dad to come get me. Yeah, I know, that made me seem truly fucked up in the head, considering my father was the last person I would trust to save me. It made me wish I could drink and fuck it all away like Rabbit.

"He'll hate himself for that in the morning. He's a really private person and that BRAT will be preening and thinking she's his next old lady for weeks as a result."

"Really?" I asked, wrinkling my nose in distaste.

"Yeah, I told you, he never hooks up with them. They'll all assume it meant more."

"That's kind of scary. You'd think they'd get a better caliber of women in these places."

Charlie laughed. "Sadly, there seems to be a shortage of

women who aren't batshit crazy and still want to be a sex toy for a group of burly biker men."

"I don't know, I can see the appeal after what I just went though. At least when you're their whore you know exactly where you stand with them. No one tells them lies because they don't have to. There's a simplicity to their exchange that I envy."

The look of pity on Charlie's face made me shut down and stay silent for the rest of the short trip home.

8. RABBIT

"Wakey, wakey, baby brother!" I heard Spinner's voice about two seconds before stinging, hot pain shot through my ass cheek. I immediately yanked the jogging pants I had apparently fallen asleep in, down off my ass and craned my head around to take a look at the damage. Before I could catch a glimpse, Spinner's loud guffaw caught my attention.

What the hell did I do last night?

I thought about it a moment before I turned to look again. Bits and pieces came back to me. I got hammered, something I never really did that often. I tried to jog my own memory as I turned just enough to catch sight of the fiery red patch of skin on my ass and the ink.

"Is that a...?"

"I'm thinking it ain't the greatest idea for you to ever get drunk without supervision, bro." There was a tattoo on my ass of a rabbit pulling his own dick out of a hat, and it was on my left butt cheek. "Is he pulling out, or stroking it, I wonder?"

"Fuck!" I hissed just as I heard the click of someone taking a picture. I quickly pulled the joggers back up over the offending ink and glanced up in time to see Tango across the room laughing so hard tears rolled down his face.

That motherfucker!

"What the fuck did you get up to last night, Rabbit?" My brother asked as I continued to give a narrow-eyed stare to Tango that promised swift retribution. The evil bastard continued laughing until he was doubled over, holding onto his ribs like they hurt from the effort. It was a small comfort, but I'd take it.

Nah! Fuck that!

I was gonna go take that bastard out! I jumped up to do just that and immediately regretted the rash decision. The world spun, my stomach rolled, and the nearest trash can seemed too far away. I managed to make it only because a prospect standing nearby kicked the can toward me and the solid hunk of metal and I met in the middle.

Over the horrendous heaves my body manifested, I still managed to hear Tango's tormenting call, "Whatsa matta Wabbit?"

That motherfucker better be glad he was a safe distance away and my body was in full-on revolt. I heard a smack and then "That was mean," from Liza. His woman or not, that girl still had my back. I'd owe her some extra cookies at the next book club meeting. I thought so anyway, until I heard her laughter too when my brother snatched my joggers back down around my knees so he could get a better picture of the tattoo Tango had inked on my ass while I was drunk. Damn, I thought she had my back.

Some friend. She didn't even warn me that was about to happen.

I managed to yank my head out of the can long enough to call her out on being a traitor. "Thought we were friends, Liza?"

"Oh no! You did this to yourself. I wasn't here last night to talk you out of all the stupid decisions you made," she called to me and there seemed to be a little bit of censure in her words, too. What the fuck else had I managed to get up to last night? The minute I asked myself that question, a flash of one of the BRATs bent over the pool table came to mind.

No! Fuck no!

"Yeah?" I glanced around and noticed Charlie already working behind the bar, serving Iceman a beer far too early in the day. "Where were you, my bestie?" I asked as I continued to lean over the trash can, just to be sure the heaves wouldn't start again.

"I had to get Myra home, and honestly, after we witnessed you plowing one of the girls into the poor, defenseless pool table, neither of us were willing to stick around for any more of the show you were putting on."

"You witnessed?" I asked, horrified at the prospect of my best friend seeing me do that shit, but sickened for some reason as I thought about Myra being there, too. "Shit!" I grumbled as my stomach flipped and I heaved up bile but not much else. Being a naturally happy person normally, drinking had never been my thing. I didn't do drugs for the same reason. There was simply no need for me to alter my consciousness. The one fucking time I decided to just let loose and do all the things men in a biker club were supposed to experience, I ended up letting myself down along with some other people I cared a lot about. Some that I hadn't realized mattered to me at all. Namely, Myra.

"Sorry, Charlie," I finally mumbled as I was able to drag my sorry ass back out of the trash can and stumble my way to a barstool in front of where she was working. I wasn't stumbling because I was still drunk either. My asshole brother had left my pants around my knees as I had been puking. I'd have to kill him later, but by then, it would be too late. Everyone probably already had full color clips of my ass and balls, but more importantly of the rabbit on my ass who may or may not be fucking a goddamn top hat.

9. MYRA

CHERRY INVITED ME DOWN TO BREAKFAST, WHICH QUICKLY TURNED into brunch when Spinner got a call to leave and go handle something at the clubhouse. Part of me wondered if he had to go clean up his brother's mess, which led me to ask my friend stupid questions that shouldn't even be on my mind.

"So, Chastity must have done a real number on Rabbit, huh?" We both continued to work on putting together the frittatas we were making for brunch, but Cherry slid a little side-eye my way.

"Yeah," she finally lamented on a sigh. "Even I had hope that she would finally settle down and behave for a while." My friend gave me a hard look then. "Spinner told me Rabbit bought her a ring, was having a house built for them, and everything. I was so happy for her. You know? My sister was finally turning into an adult, and I thought that Rabbit was good for her, and that maybe we'd be able to have a normal sibling relationship as a result."

"So, what happened?"

"Who knows?" Cherry shook her head. "I don't think she could have found a better man than Rabbit. Something spooked her, though. The first clear sign of weather we'd had in a while, and she was in some asshole's pickup truck. That sister of mine drove off laughing and waving out the window while Rabbit stood there and watched."

"Ouch!" I knew all too well what that felt like.

"Yeah, he hasn't been right since. He's always been this genuinely happy, funny guy. Rabbit is the perpetual life of the party without ever drinking, doing drugs, or whoring around like a lot of the other guys in the MC life."

"Well, he's certainly not that way now."

"Why are you so curious about him and Chastity anyway?" she asked.

"Everyone keeps telling me what a great guy he 'normally' is, and I just haven't seen yet. Obviously, I've seen his wicked sense of humor put to good use, but mostly, he's been an asshole to me. Then there was last night, which totally contradicts everything you just said about him."

"Last night?"

I told her about the condition Rabbit had been in when we left the clubhouse and Cherry just stood there slack-jawed and gaping at me. "Seriously? He was having sex? With one of the BRATs? In the open?" Cherry asked, each portion of her question sounding more like it's own inquisition. "I want to say no way that was possible, but you have no reason to lie."

I shrugged. "Charlie was there, since she's the one that brought me home and we had to walk through the clubhouse to see it. Curiosity got the better of me, I suppose, because

82

the man I've met and known since moving here is nothing like the person everyone keeps trying to portray him as. Maybe he's just been damaged for a longer time than you guys thought, and he's just tired of hiding it?" I surmised.

Cherry quickly discounted that theory. "Spinner and Rabbit don't have a tragic history. They had a loving couple as parents who set the standards for a relationship at a pretty high bar for those boys."

"Had?"

"Caught that, huh?" Cherry offered a small smile. "Their dad died in a motorcycle accident. Mom survived long enough to be diagnosed with cancer while she was in the hospital getting patched up after the wreck. She refused treatment for the cancer and joined her man in the afterlife three months later."

"Oh no! That's horrible!"

"That's also the legacy of love their parents left them with. Spinner came home from the Army, hooked up with the MC, and Rabbit followed a year later when he graduated high school."

"You would think they would have been turned off of motorcycles after what happened."

"Nah! Their parents loved to ride and I guess the boys picked up the bug, too. They'd probably both cry like little girls if you told them they couldn't ride anymore." Cherry laughed, obviously imagining that exact reaction as she said it.

I groaned loudly, imagining something else entirely. "I miss riding," I admitted.

"How long has it been?"

"Too long." I had to really think about my answer though, which was disturbing in retrospect. "It was actually a couple of months before I got pregnant when I last rode." The weird noise in the back of my throat had Cherry paying closer attention.

"What?"

"I should have known then. He used to love having me on the back of his bike. At least he said he did." My mind drifted back all those months ago to how weird my boyfriend had been acting. "He wanted out then, I wish he had just manned up and told me instead of leaving me with a lifelong reminder of why people are not to be trusted."

"You can't tell me you regret being pregnant?"

"I regret that my son or daughter won't know their family. I always pictured raising my kids in the club with a huge extended family that would have their backs, you know?"

"It could still happen," she tried to tell me.

I laughed. "Oh yeah? You have a biker in mind for me?" I asked jokingly. I half-assed expected her to say Rabbit's name, but she shocked me further when she didn't.

"Well, if you don't mind sharing, there's always Whiskey and Fox. They're raising their kid together and I bet your little blended family would be cute as hell." I knew she was teasing me, but someone else obviously didn't.

"What the absolute fuck?" Rabbit asked as he and Spinner came into the house at the tail end of our conversation.

10. RABBIT

I couldn't believe what I'd walked into. What the hell did Cherry think she was doing offering Myra up to Whiskey and Fox like that?

"Calm down," Spinner whispered to me. "It's probably not what you think. I turned to frown at him because I knew my ears hadn't deceived me. Besides, Cherry was laughing at my reaction, while Myra blushed profusely.

"What?" My sister-in-law asked innocently. Myra was telling me how much she missed riding and how she had once hoped to raise her kid around a club who would always have their back. I was just giving her options for how to make that happen." Cherry's little miss innocent wasn't fooling me. She kind of reminded me of her sister in that moment. I could almost smell the manipulation in the air.

"Why the hell would Whiskey and Fox be your first thought?"

Cherry shrugged her shoulders and winked at Myra who silently pleaded with her friend to stop talking. "They're already daddies. So, it only made sense to pair her – what would the proper term be? – trio her with them."

"Cherry," Spinner called out to her, a slight hint of warning in his tone just as the oven dinged.

"Anyway, brunch is ready," the woman called out cheerily as she turned to pull something from the oven.

We sat through one of the most awkward brunches in the world when my brother decided to use me to break the tension. "You should see the tattoo Tango put on Rabbit's ass last night. It's classic," my brother chuckled before shoving another bite of frittata into his pie hole.

Both women turned their gazes on me at once. "You got a tattoo on your ass?" Myra asked as she winced, assuming appropriately that it must have hurt.

"What the hell did you do that for?" Cherry asked at the same time.

"In my defense, I didn't even know it was there until your asshole husband slapped me on the ass this morning," I admitted to Cherry, while not quite ignoring Myra.

"How could you not know that you got a tattoo?" Cherry's concern, at that point, was touching. I didn't get to answer her, though, because my brother slipped in with the truth instead.

"Numb-nuts decided to finally tie one on last night and got drunk off his gourd."

Cherry glanced at Myra who only subtly shrugged one shoulder before stuffing her face. I could see the disbelief in her eyes turn to full-blown shock. Myra must have already told her that I had been drinking and my lovely sister-in-law had most likely sung my praises and told her that was impossible. Normally, she wouldn't have been wrong. Unfortunately, that just made the rest of our meal even more awkward and stilted than before. Once we were done eating and the table was cleared, Cherry asked to speak to my brother alone for a minute and Myra took that opportunity to attempt to slip out of their house unnoticed.

I noticed.

I followed, all the way to her apartment, up the stairs, and through the door before she realized I had been hot on her heels.

"Can I help you?" Myra asked as she turned around to see why I was inviting myself into her space.

"I, um…" *Shit.* I didn't know why I'd followed her out here in the first place.

"You, um, what?" she asked as she tapped her foot impatiently.

"A couple things, actually. Mind if I come in?"

"I suppose not," she begrudgingly agreed. Once we were settled inside, I took in the changes she had made to the place since arriving in South Dakota. It looked homey and comfortable. Honestly, it was a smaller scale version of how I'd pictured furnishing my own home with Chastity. Only, I knew I'd have to settle for a very different look because it didn't match Chastity's personality at all. She was all wild and colorful, whereas Myra was more sedate and down to earth.

"You just going to sit there all day and stare at my place, or was there something you needed?"

I hadn't noticed that she had been scurrying around her

apartment, dropping things in a bag, like she was ready to head out on an adventure.

"Do you have somewhere to be?"

"Doctor's appointment in Spearfish," she informed me.

"Oh, well," I said as I stood back up, "I won't keep you then."

"I still have thirty minutes before I need to leave."

"Okay. Well, I have several apologies to make to you. When you first got here, I heard you'd left your old man and that you were hiding out. My last relationship didn't end on a great note, and I put my issues with Chastity on you while not knowing your story. I'm sorry I said the things I did, and treated you like the second coming of the cheating whore."

To my shock, Myra did not react at all the way I thought she would. Where I thought she would berate me for calling one of the twins a whore, since they had been her friends back in Oregon where they were apparently from, she threw her head back and laughed. "Second coming of the cheating whore..." she repeated as she continued to laugh. "I've heard Chastity called a lot of horrible things over the years, usually deserved, but that was the best! Did you mean the double entendre there or was that an accidental bonus?"

"Um?"

"You know because she's a whore... and second coming seems like it could mean she got hers twice..." When I just stared at her, she laughed again and waved her hand in the air. "Never mind. It was probably just my weird sense of humor."

"Well, technically, I called you the whore, not her but..."

She waved that thought away with her hand, too, as she continued to chuckle. "You know what I meant."

"And um, the second thing," I decided to go on and get all the apologies out while she was apparently in a good mood. "I'm sorry if you saw me behaving like an asshole last night." I noticed her questioning gaze. "Charlie told me you saw me before you left," I pushed.

"Yes, well, I did wonder briefly about your hypocrisy."

"Hypocrisy?"

"Mmhmm. You don't remember ranting about the overuse of pool tables in sex scenes in romance novels?" It was obviously a rhetorical question since she didn't allow me time to answer. "Then, there you were abusing that poor table like that." I could see the laughter she held back as her eyes twinkled with the effort.

I stood there, taking in her words, and the fact that she was laughing all of it off like some sort of sick joke. "You're..." I hesitated a moment before continuing, "kind of weird."

"Well, thanks, I guess." She leaned down and picked a coat up off the chair. "You're really bad at compliments."

"Out of practice, I guess." What the hell else was I supposed to say? I came in here with the intent to apologize, but I honestly expected a fight about it. Maybe I had been with Chastity too long and it had seriously colored the way I saw real relationships working, whether just friendships or the romantic kind. How else could I explain why I'd thought Cherry had an ulterior motive earlier and then I expected Myra to be a complete bitch about an apology?

"Listen, no offense, because I appreciate the gesture, and I accept your apologies, by the way. Not that the last one was even necessary because your night is your business, and I was just a guest in the clubhouse. That's *your* space. You don't apologize to people for what they see when they step foot in your home. Anyway, I appreciate it, but I really do have to get going."

I followed her out and was about to head back to my brother's place, since he had driven us here for breakfast, when I heard the familiar metal click, click sound and the failure of Myra's Suburban to start. I sauntered back over and tapped on the window, to find her head down on the steering wheel as her shoulders shook.

"Myra?" I called out when she didn't immediately look up.

She pulled the keys from the ignition, and motioned for me to back up. I stood there as she swung her short little legs around and hopped out of the truck. Yeah, she needed some retractable steps for that beast since the damn thing didn't even have regular running boards on it.

"How am I supposed to take care of another human being when I can't even get myself to a doctor's appointment?"

"Hey now!" I called out as I reached over, grabbed her shoulders, and pulled her to me. Myra was in my arms and wrapped up in a tight hug before she could even mutter a weak protest. "You're going to do just fine when the time comes, and who says you can't get to a doctor's appointment? That's what you have friends for, right?"

She leaned back, glanced over toward Cherry and Spinner's place, and then sighed. "I don't want to keep bothering them. They've done so much for me already."

Well, that hurt a little bit. "I wasn't talkin' about them, darlin'."

One of her eyebrows shot up in what could only be called questioning sarcasm. Okay, I definitely remembered her fussing at me before about calling her all sorts of endearments, and if I was being honest, I did it this time just to get her riled up so her mind was off the truck that wouldn't start.

"Wait here," I told her. "Give me just a minute." I ran to Spinner's house, grabbed a set of keys off the hook by the door and yelled out to him. "Borrowing the truck," before shutting the door behind me again.

"Let's go!" I told her as I headed toward Spinner's truck. She stood there, unmoving.

"You can't just steal your brother's truck to take me to my appointment."

"Borrow. I'm borrowing my brother's truck, something I would have needed to do in order to get my ass back to the clubhouse where my ride is anyway. Don't worry, I'll fill his tank for him when I bring it back."

"Okay, well, we have enough time to stop at the clubhouse if you want to leave it there for him while you get your truck and then I can see if Charlie can give me a ride."

I stopped what I was doing, threw the truck back in park and just stared at her for a minute.

"What?"

"I'm taking you," I explained.

"I just, I was trying to spare you the trip."

"I offered."

"You don't even like me," she muttered.

I felt like the complete dick that I was. She had every right to think that was true after the way I had treated her when she'd done absolutely nothing wrong. "Nah, see, that's where you got it wrong. The person I don't like very much right now is myself, and I'm making up for some of that, so how about you let me do it?"

Myra nodded her head, buckled her seatbelt, and didn't really say much else until I needed directions to the doctor's office. It took about thirty minutes to get there, but once we were parked, she turned to me and finally spoke again. "Did you want to come in and wait or just stay out here?" She glanced around at the snow that was still piled up on all the curbs and she visibly shivered.

"You not used to the snow?"

She shook her head. "I've seen snow before, obviously, but I lived on the coast in Oregon. We always got more rain than snow in the winter."

"I'll come in with you, if you don't mind."

"Sure," she responded as she unbuckled and opened the door. My brother's truck also sat up a bit higher, and I felt like an asshole for not remembering that when she had climbed into the damn thing.

"Wait," I told her as I jumped out and made my way around. "Let me help you down, so you don't slip on this slushy shit out here." When I reached my hand up to grab a hold of her, Myra just stared at me in awe. Then she shook off whatever she'd been thinking, and allowed me to help her out of Spinner's truck.

"Thank you," she whispered as her feet touched the

ground and my arm stayed around her waist until I was sure she was steady on her feet.

"You don't have to thank a man for having manners," I told her.

"Yeah I do, because there aren't enough around anymore who have any. If women don't reward the nice guys for doing the right thing, then they stop doing it."

"That's kind of a load of shit, if you ask me."

"Oh?" she answered back, sounding curious.

"Yeah, because if the only reason a man helps out a woman in need is to get something on the back end, even a compliment, then he doesn't have manners, he has an agenda. There shouldn't be a need to reward common decency."

Myra didn't have a response to that as we slowly made our way into the building that housed her doctor's office. I ended up sitting in the waiting room until she was done. Honestly, I kind of wanted to go back there with her and see what a baby doctor visit was like, but she didn't ask me to come back with her, and I wasn't about to invite myself. If it had been Charlie, I would have overstepped in a heartbeat. Myra hadn't exactly been given the best impression of me to start out with, though. That was a fact that I continued to beat myself up over. Fuck, I could be a stupid dick sometimes. I made myself a promise while waiting for her to finish up. She wasn't coming to another one of these appointments alone. It didn't matter if all she allowed me to do was sit in the waiting room like a chump, she'd have someone here for her.

11. MYRA

IT HAD BEEN A WEEK SINCE RABBIT TOOK ME TO MY DOCTOR'S
appointment and I couldn't stop thinking about the way
he'd helped me out Spinner's truck, or tucked me back inside
it when I was done. As if taking me hadn't been completely
out of his way or a waste of his time already. His words kept
rolling through my head and they probably stuck there
because it was the first time I saw Rabbit the way everyone
else obviously had. *"...if the only reason a man helps out a
woman in need is to get something on the back end, even a
compliment, then he doesn't have manners, he has an agenda."*

The text in the book I was studying from blurred before
my eyes as my mind wondered where it had no business
going. Rabbit's words rattled around in my brain as I thought
of all the times Blaze needed me to thank him or validate his
efforts in some way. Then there were the times he outright
requested, almost to the point of requiring, a reward for his
actions. He stopped and bought me roses one day, *'to be nice'*
but then demanded I show my appreciation for his effort. I

was allergic to those damn roses and ended up throwing them out the next day.

Maybe it had been a sign that I should have thrown the whole relationship out with those thoughtless flowers. It was crazy how one little sentence could completely mind-fuck a person. I wanted to be angry with Rabbit for ruining some of the memories I once thought of as good. I couldn't be mad at him for opening my eyes to reality, though. The times Blaze had gone out of his way or done something nice for me had always come with strings attached. At least I would know in the future that it wasn't okay. So in that respect, my anger dimmed and I found myself wanting to thank Rabbit for his insight.

I tipped my head back, rocked it from side-to-side, then in a rounded motion to the left, and back to the right, trying to knock the tension kinks out of the muscles there as I sat at the bar. You'd think Renegade Rosy's would be a shitty place to study but just before opening everyone was doing their own thing to get ready for their shift and the music was still turned off. The bar actually had an entirely different atmosphere to it. While I wouldn't call it a library-like space, it definitely helped me to focus more than my comfy, well-worn couch back at my apartment that kept putting me to sleep when I looked at the words on the pages for too long.

"What are you studying so hard over here?" Rabbit's voice startled me. I'd just been listening to the memory of it, playing his words from a week ago on repeat in my brain, but I realized that the memory paled in comparison to the real deal. I turned to see him smiling down at me from just over my right shoulder. "Looks complicated," he added.

"I have my NCLEX coming up, I'm just trying to get all the extra study time in that I can before I have to take it."

"Your N-what-now?"

I grinned at him, then patted the barstool next to the one I occupied. "My nursing exam, in order to be licensed."

"Oh, I didn't know that's what you were doing. You already went to college for that and everything, or is this the last step?"

"I have the degree, just need to be certified."

"Beauty and brains then?" he asked as warmth filled my cheeks. I hated that the compliment made me blush because I didn't want the man to think he affected me in any way. I may have forgiven him for being a dick to me, but that didn't mean I trusted his sudden personality change.

"So, that's what you want to do with your life? Be a nurse, help people, and stuff?"

"Yeah, something like that," I told him as I laughed at his assessment.

"Why?"

"Why what?"

"What made you want to do that?"

"I grew up around a motorcycle club. Some of the guys were always getting hurt, mostly from taking spills on bikes, and they were stubborn shits, too. So, my mom would end up being the one to patch them up and I watched her do it because they'd come to our house instead of the club-house. I think they didn't want to be seen as a bunch of pussies when they hissed and hollered as she poured peroxide over their wounds." Rabbit laughed at my assessment.

"I bet that was it. Then again, if your mom looks anything like you, they probably enjoyed her playing nurse."

"She was taken," I told him on a shocked gasp because I'd never thought about it like that. She was my mom, I'd never once thought of her as some hot commodity my dad got lucky enough to land, but thinking back... "You know what, you're probably right,' I told him. Thinking of her and those times made me miss my mom. I almost opened up to him about it, but he'd been a dick to me before so the trust still wasn't there. Instead, I decided to turn the tables on the conversation.

"What is it you want to do with your life, Rabbit?"

He laughed, glanced around the bar nervously, and then turned back to me and grinned. "Don't you already know?"

"Beyond the fact that you're a biker who doesn't mind nudity and showing off what you got, you're a dick to new women you meet, and everyone seems to have a high opinion of you in spite of that, I don't really know a whole lot."

He winced at my description. "I guess you're nothing, if not honest, huh?" If a person could shrug with their eyeballs alone, that's the response he got from me. I just waited for his answer. "Well, I guess, from your eyes, I'd say that was a fair assessment. Unfortunately, you've seen me at my absolute worst, so I can't deny any of that except to say, the behavior you've seen is almost all out of the norm for me."

"Okay, but that doesn't answer the question. What are you planning to do with your life?"

"You're sitting in it," he said. I glanced down, for some stupid reason I couldn't name. As if I was physically sitting in something he wanted to do with his life. Rabbit chuckled. "Well, I guess you can count it literally since your ass is parked on my barstool, but-"

"Wait!" I stopped him. "Your bar?" His grin widened.

"My bar," he confirmed. "After my parents death, pretty much all I had was my brother and the club. I wanted to make sure neither of them ever had to go anywhere again. Certainly didn't want my brother re-enlisting in the Army, so I used my portion of the money I got from their insurance policy and bought this bar. Unfortunately for me, the building and liquor license were where I ran out of money. It still needed some updates, all the logos and marketing, the actual liquor beyond the small stash that was here, and of course the up front money to pay salaries for employees until the cash started flowing." He laughed as he told me about his past.

"You needed investors," I summed up.

"Yeah, I had big dreams, but a too-small wallet as it turned out." He glanced around and the pride shone on his face as he took in what all his hard work and money had made. "When Spinner found out what I'd spent my inheritance on – the fact that I'd spent *all* of my inheritance on it – he flipped out, at first. Hell, I was just 21 at the time. Barely old enough to drink and this is where I sunk my money."

"Obviously, he had a change of heart about it at some point."

"Yeah, he realized I wasn't going to let it go, so he kicked in some of his own money to help me out. It still wasn't enough, though."

"That's where the club stepped in?" I guessed, accurately.

"You got it. So, now we're partners. Since I took the brunt of the financial burden, I pretty much get a sixty percent return on profits. Spinner and the club each take a 20 percent cut for their contributions."

"It's amazing, that you were able to put in so much and keep that much of the return."

"It is." He watched me for a minute before he asked, "What?" It was as if he could see a million different questions play out on my face all at once.

"That first night, you didn't want me in your bar and Spinner took me in anyway. I feel horrible now, because this is your place."

Rabbit shook his head. "Seriously? I was being a dick. Don't even worry about it. If I had known your situation before we met, I would have offered the same thing my brother did."

"Still, that wasn't exactly fair to you. I honestly thought the bar was fully club-owned and that Spinner managed it."

"He does manage it, which bumps him up from 20 percent to about 35 percent when we factor in the time commitment that he puts into the place. He gets paid a salary to manage it on top of his profit percentage for his investment."

"Oh, well, that's at least a little better. Why don't you manage it?"

"Do I really strike you as a numbers and business-sense kind of guy?"

I shrugged my shoulders. "I don't know. I try not to judge people based on looks alone."

"Fair enough. I'll just tell you that I'm not. At least, I'm not with the day-to-day stuff. I help out around the bar some nights when they're short staffed. I do the same at the clubhouse bar, too. If not for Charlie, I'd probably be the only full-time bartender in the clubhouse, truth be told. Those assholes can't mix a simple drink to save their lives."

"Everyone keeps telling me you normally don't drink. So why on earth did you choose to own a bar?"

He laughed and I loved the ways his eyes sparkled as he did. "I don't know if it's something that can be explained. It's where people come to be social, have fun, forget their worries, and I just wanted to give them the best damn place to do that. Plus, this was a strip club and the women weren't exactly treated well by the previous management. I wanted to make sure they had a safe place to go to work and make the money they need to get by.

I smiled at him. "So, you're a caretaker and a people pleaser, too?"

He chucked and ducked his head a bit to hide the heat that bloomed in his cheeks. "I suppose you could say that. Not quite as noble as patching people up, though."

"We all have our place in the world. There are many ways to make a person's life better. No one thing is better than another." I gave him a genuine smile as I spoke. "So, that's what you did with your life, where do you see it going? Do you continue on with the one bar? Add more? Start a family? How will the future Mrs. Rabbit feel about all the naked women you're around constantly?"

I was oddly curious about that last one because I don't honestly know how I would have handled knowing Blaze was headed to work with naked dancers. It was hard enough to think about the available pussy he had on tap whenever he wasn't with me at the clubhouse, or when they went on runs to other chapters. Granted, I was stupid enough to think he wouldn't cheat because my family would be around to stop him. Silly me, they didn't care enough about me to be bothered by the fact that my man cheated on me.

"I have plans to expand the bar out to some of the other chapters. We already have one set up near Charleston that's doing pretty well. I get a small percentage from that bar's profits since they're using all of Renegade Rosy's branding. As far as family goes, one day, I plan to have a big one. The future Mrs. Rabbit will be just fine with it because if she doesn't want me there when the dancers have their clothes off, then I won't be there unless there is a work emergency. That's the great thing about being the initial investor in your own business. You don't have to be there to run the day-to-day stuff. Everything I have to do can be done from the outside looking in, so long as I trust the person running the business." Wow, he really had thought about that. It also nearly knocked me off my feet to know he would put his woman's concerns above his business like that.

"The reality is that I would hope my woman would trust me enough to know it would never be an issue. Also, she can't be the type of person who would be embarrassed by the fact that I pay the bills with money that comes in from a strip club. I'm proud of what I've accomplished, and anyone standing by my side should be, too."

"You're not wrong about that." I noticed the time on the new burner phone I'd obtained for all of the local people in my life, my friend, work, my doctor; and reached over to close my book. "Well, I better start getting ready for my shift. Don't want the boss to think I'm slacking off," I told him and then winked as I took my things to the back.

"I saw you out there talking to Rabbit," one of the dancers, Mindy, mentioned as I stuffed my book into my locker.

"Yeah," I confirmed, not really wanting her to make a big deal about it.

"He's a mess," she said with zero elaboration.

"He'll be all right. He just needs some time and perspective."

"Is that what you needed after your breakup?" The woman was clearly fishing. Most of the girls knew I was pregnant, a few of them had seen me tossing my lunch here and there, but I hadn't really bothered to tell my story to any of them. "No. I needed a whole new life. Hopefully, I found it here."

"Well, Cherry seems to think the world of you." I said nothing, wondering where Mindy was going with her observations. Finally, when she realized I wouldn't respond, she huffed as if I was stressing her out by not answering. "It's not my business, or my place, but these guys gave me a shot when I didn't deserve one. They helped lift me up enough that I was able to start helping myself. We all saw the writing on the wall with Chastity. She was always going to leave him heartbroken. Those twins may look alike, but they are not the same person."

"That's for certain," I agreed.

"You have unfinished business out there somewhere. I'd

hate to see you break his heart when you go back to it," she continued on with her warning. That's what it was.

"My business was just as heart-wrenching, more so, and it is beyond done. That was another life for me. I won't ever go back to a place where everyone I knew betrayed me." I glared at her because I didn't like feeling threatened, especially in my place of work. "But make no mistake, you have it all wrong. My actions will never affect Rabbit because he doesn't give a damn about me anyway. The man barely tolerates me."

She shot me a knowing smirk. "We'll agree to disagree on that."

12. RABBIT

SPINNER MOVED IN CLOSER, AS IF I DIDN'T SEE HIM IN THE MIRRORS on the wall. He leaned in and whisper-yelled into my ear. "What are you doing here Bunny Boy?" I ignored him for a moment as I watched Myra pass a beer to another local who couldn't take his eyes off of her.

It wasn't even a little bit surprising that men were interested in her, even with the slightly protruding baby bump. Hell, most of them probably didn't even realize that was what she had going on. Not that it would matter to most of them anyway. Myra was gorgeous, always nice to everyone, and let's face it, the male to female ratio in these parts meant that there simply weren't enough women to go around. Many wouldn't care that she was already knocked up by someone else.

"Seriously, Rabbit, what's going on with you?" My brother asked again. Then he followed the direction of my gaze and said, "That's a bit of a surprise."

"Why?" I asked the question without taking my eyes off of her.

"I didn't think you two got along that well. Plus, she's pregnant."

"So?"

"So!" Spinner mocked my question. "So, it's not like you to take on someone like her with a past that could rear its head at any time."

I released a frustrated breath. "She ran from her past for a reason. Isn't that what Cherry did? You still chose her."

"That was a different kind of past and you know it, since you had Chastity for a bit and she was involved in all that mess, too. Hell, she was the cause of it being an issue for my woman."

"I know, but not everyone is Chastity."

"No, and thank fuck for that! I just want you to tread carefully, brother. She left a bad situation behind. Running won't be an option for her again before long. So don't screw things up."

"What the hell would I do to screw things up?"

"You have a past that could breeze back into town on a moment's notice. Are you going to drop everything for what you already lost or keep moving forward when that happens?"

"Is Chastity coming back?" I asked, my full attention now on my brother.

"See," he said as his accusing finger lifted in my direction. "That reaction right there is what I'm warning you about. If you start something with Myra, where does that leave her, should the woman you were going to propose marriage to, come back into your life?"

"We're only friends. It leaves her exactly in the same position."

"Yeah, okay. Do me a favor then, think with your big head on this one."

I grinned at my brother. "I always think with my biggest head," I reassured him as I grabbed my crotch before heading to the bar to get a fresh water with lemon. There would definitely be no more drinking in my future. If I happened to one day get my other ass cheek tattooed, I was going in knowing what was happening. I still had to get Tango back for that bit of fuckery.

On the way to the bar to refresh my water, I was stopped by one of the BRATs the guys had dubbed ABC. It wasn't because she was stupid or anything. Her name was literally, Audrey Boyd Carter, and that's how she always introduced herself, using all three names. She should have been at the clubhouse that night instead of Ruby's, but I decided to be polite as she tried to talk to me. I'd been so close to the bar, a fresh drink, and okay – another close-up peek at Momma Myra. I kept the disappointment at the interruption out of my eyes and smiled at the woman instead. I figured she was going to hit me up for a dancer position.

"Hey, Rabbit, I heard you're with Gabby now."

"Who?" I asked, honestly not recognizing the name.

"Gabby. You were just with her..."

"Oh, that! No. I was just blowing off some steam," I explained when I realized she must have been talking about my one drunken night when I banged a BRAT in the clubhouse. She was a new girl, so in my drunken stupor I didn't think she'd read too much into it being me that was banging her. I had become somewhat of a challenge for the girls over the years since I made it a point not to shit where I ate.

Yeah, they were there for the convenience of all the brothers, but the problem was, I eventually wanted to settle down with one woman and start a family. I didn't think it would be okay to start something with a woman and then drag her through the clubhouse where all of my previous conquests were collected and ready to give her shit. I knew how much flak my friend Charlie had endured over the years thanks to Rage's antics before she came along. I didn't want to ever put another woman through that.

I stopped and really took notice of ABC then. There was a devious little twinkle in her eye that should have been a warning to me. Unfortunately, I'd already turned and made eye contact, ready to brush ABC off, and I missed all the cues the BRAT had been sending me. "I could help you blow off a lot of steam," the woman cooed as she plastered herself to me and ran her hands over the crotch of my jeans.

Myra rolled her eyes before turning her back on me. Once our connection was severed, I returned my attention to the woman trying to attach herself to me like a leech.

"What the fuck do you think you're doing?" I asked the question in a low, menacing growl.

"Helping you to blow off steam?" Her voice wavered as she realized she had misread my lack of movement for wanting her attention.

"I didn't ask for, or want, your attention."

"But I thought-"

"What you claimed to think was that I belonged to one of your friends, another BRAT of the club. What you just showed was a complete lack of loyalty."

"That's not really fair to say to her," an all too familiar feminine voice chimed in. "Here's your drink," Myra took my empty glass and replaced it without acknowledging the fact that it was just water with lemon. "Club girls aren't supposed to be loyal to other women, especially where club brothers are concerned. You can't be mad at them for living by club rules that require them to be disloyal to other people and to keep their mouths shut about it when it happens."

I just stood there, not knowing what to say to that. When I didn't manage to get anything out, Myra walked back to the other side of the bar and started immediately serving another customer as if she hadn't just dropped a shitload of wisdom in my lap. Is that what the club had been doing? Were we inadvertently breeding disloyalty? The guys always thought that it showed loyalty to the proper people, since it was all about respecting the brotherhood above all, but now I had to wonder. Women tended to see things in a very different light than we did. Maybe this was why they had so many problems in the Charleston Chapter with the club girls? The Dakotas chapter frowned on married members doing the BRATs because we figured if you could be untrustworthy to your romantic partner, it was a slippery slope to fucking over your club brothers. I don't think any of our dumb asses thought about it the same way where the club girls were concerned.

"She's right, you know?" ABC broke into my thoughts, to inform me, even as she made it sound like a question. "It's the one thing I hate about my position with the club. I feel like in certain situations, I'm damned if I do, and damned if I don't. If a married man wants a piece of me, I have to be okay with it. Not that it happens a lot with the guys from your chapter, but you know what I mean. If his woman comes after me for it, you guys all think it's a fun sport to watch what happens." ABC had once belonged to the Tallahassee Chapter of the Aces High MC. When they came up for Sturgis a few months ago, she opted to stay. Chances are, those experiences she was referring to happened when she was with their chapter. Not that Tallahassee was a bad one, just that they were a bit on the wilder side and under their previous president, they had been prone to a few shit shows that ended up being a bit of an embarrassment.

"Would you still have sex with club brothers who had a claimed woman, if given a choice?" I asked her, suddenly disliking the whole system the club had in place.

"No, I would only be available for single men if given the choice. There's less drama that way. Most of the other women wouldn't care about it, though." She poked her bottom lip out in a pout then sighed. "I chose to leave Tallahassee and deal with the brutal winters here because your club was different. I don't have to fuck the married guys, at least not the ones who belong to the Dakotas Chapter. That means there aren't any angry wives coming for me when I least expect it." She rubbed the back of her head as if remembering an old wound, and I could imagine what that might have been. I'd seen a few old ladies throw down with club girls at other chapters over the years and there was almost always hair pulling involved.

"I'll take it to church and make sure you ladies have the choice," I told her.

She seemed frightened by that prospect. "I'm not trying to make waves here."

I swatted her worries away. "Don't worry. You won't lose your place for speaking your mind. I'll talk to Iceman about it in the morning, and we'll get some changes made. Sorry about before. I never thought about it from the perspective of one of the club's girls."

She shrugged her shoulders. "Why would you? Normally, our opinions don't matter, but we know that's our lot in life."

"I'll be asking for a few changes. It seems you ladies need a way to air your grievances where you don't feel like you'll be booted out the door for doing so." She nodded at me and then ducked away quickly, as if she was afraid she'd catch fire for standing too close to me.

When ABC left, I turned to see Myra grinning my way. "What?" I asked as I moved close enough to the bar to park my ass on a stool.

"If you're telling the truth, you just did a really good thing. Most club girls are there because they need to feel safe and the world has left them with too-few options. It sucks for them that they have to lie, hurt one another's feelings, and deal with pissed off old ladies and girlfriends all the time."

"You sound like you speak from experience," I told her, wondering and waiting to see if she'd fill in more information about her family, her ex, or whatever happened to force her to run. I knew he cheated on her, and the family took his back in that, but I didn't really know much else."

Myra shook her head in answer, and I thought that would be the end of it, but then she decided to elaborate.

"Not as a club bunny, which is what we called them instead of BRATs. What the hell does that even mean, by the way?"

"Bitches Relinquishing Ass and Tits," I told her with a straight face. It was a ridiculous name the men had come up with one night when we were all sitting around drinking years ago. It stuck because we all thought we were so fucking clever.

Myra laughed and shook her head in mock disapproval. "That's what I get for asking questions," she told me as she filled another order. When she came back to stand in front of me, she filled me in on a little glimpse of her previous life.

"I was a club princess, and more," she started out as a sad look replaced her amused smile. "I was friends with some of the club girls when I was younger. Our friendships were ruined when they had to betray me and keep quiet about it. They couldn't even look me in the eye anymore. At first, I thought it might have been because my dad was cheating on my mom. Then I wondered if my uncle was up to no good, too. I never thought the worst, though. The truth, as it turned out, was that they were sleeping with my boyfriend."

"Which club were you with and whose old lady are you?" I asked, feeling both anxious about her answer and oddly devastated that her answer might make her completely off limits.

"I am my own woman. My ex-boyfriend lost any rights to me when he chose a random hook-up after actively trying to get me pregnant."

"Wait," I held up a hand while fisting the other because there was no way I just heard her right. "What do you mean? He was purposely trying to knock you up, succeeded in getting you pregnant, and then left you?"

She was mid-nod when one of the waitresses inter-rupted. "My, I need three Coronas and one Tom Collins." Myra spun to make the drink while I turned my attention to the waitress.

"Who the hell orders a pussy-ass drink like a Tom Collins in a strip club? That for one of the girls?"

She laughed, shrugged, and then pointed to my drink. "Someone was having it made for you. They thought it was what you were drinking."

"They thought?" I glanced down at my water with lemon and dropped my head back. If I was a praying man, I'd take the moment to ask for better luck in life. "It's fucking water, with lemon." I told her as I slid the top half of her body across the bar to grab Myra's attention before she made that fucking weak-ass drink.

Myra was too busy to talk much after that, so I took off and headed home. There was a time when I loved living at the clubhouse, but my patience for it was running thin again. Hell, if I was a woman, I'd say my biological clock was ticking. There was just this drive inside of me to go have a normal family. Not that I would give up the club, but there was a difference between being a member and living there. It stopped being so much of an escape when it was both what you were escaping from and where you were headed to all in one.

The Next Day

"ICE, YOU GOT A MINUTE?" I called out when I noticed my club president slip out of his room at the same time I was leaving mine.

"Yeah, what's going on Rabbit?" I took my time, telling him about the discussion I'd had with ABC and how Myra put it all together in a different light for me the night before.

"So, you want to change our policies concerning who the club girls fuck, and whether or not they're able to complain about shit?"

"Yeah, I think it might keep us from having similar problems to what the Charleston Chapter is dealing with. There's also the shit that went down here with the BRATs when Charlie first came to stay here."

"I can see the soundness of a decision like that, but we're going to have to get the officers in on this and table the discussion."

"I figured as much. They should all be here within the hour," I told him.

"Well shit, you were going to try to bamboozle me, weren't you?"

I laughed at that. "Nah, just figured you might not be in the greatest shape to be up so early," I attempted to explain without calling him out on his recent behavior outright.

Iceman blew out a breath and ran his fingers through his short, cropped hair. It had once been a lot darker, but the silver that was peppered through the military style was becoming more and more evident since he'd kicked Carol to the curb. It most likely had to do more with the fact that he hadn't exactly been kind to his own body since she'd been gone, than it did with her no longer being around.

"It's okay, Rabbit. I haven't been much of a president lately, but that's going to change."

"Hope so, you know we have your back, no matter what, right?"

"Brotherhood," he answered back.

"Brotherhood," I parroted while meaning it in my soul.

There was a unanimous agreement once we were able to meet with all the officers. Unfortunately, they left it to me to tell the girls. That was not news I relished delivering, especially since ABC had insinuated that the newer girl, Gabby, thought more of our tryst than there was. Still, I got the ball rolling, so I went to deliver the news.

I had been right to worry about being the one to drop the bomb on the girls. Hell, as happy as some of them were, you'd think it was a straight up rainbow and glitter bomb. The worst reaction belonged to Gabby, as predicted.

"I knew you cared, but this just proves it. You made me so happy by looking out for my girls today, baby."

Charlie and Myra happened to be walking by as Gabby basically shrieked those words at me. Fuck my luck. How was it possible to have such horrible timing when Myra was around to witness shit? Hands grasped my face to turn my eyes from Myra's retreating form back to the woman currently acting like I did something specifically to please her.

"Why are you touching me without my permission?" I asked her, causing her face to wrinkle up as she frowned.

"Is this a new game you want to play? Are you going to be my daddy dom?"

"What the fuck?" I damn near shouted as I took a step back. "I don't know what you're on about." I admitted to her.

Gabby's bottom lip poked out in a pout. "After the other night-" she started to say, but I cut her off with a loud sigh.

"Are you the one I fucked on the pool table?" I asked as nicely as I could. For all the good that did me when tears started to spill from her eyes.

"Yes, of course it was me. You've never slept with any of the other girls." Yep, and that's why I phrased it like that. I knew it would hurt her a little bit, but better that than her deluding herself based on my lack of track record with anyone else.

"No offense meant, sweetheart, but I was plastered that night, pissed off, and honestly I don't remember much of it. You were there and available. It's not something I normally do, but I assure you, there was no hidden meaning behind it. We fucked. End of story." By the time I managed to set that record straight, Charlie and Myra were walking by again, close enough to have heard me.

Seriously, fuck my luck!

13. MYRA

AFTER OVERHEARING RABBIT HELP THE CLUB GIRLS AND SET THE ONE he had actually been with straight, he and I didn't cross paths again all week. It probably helped that I hadn't been back to the clubhouse since then. I sat there, at the bar, waiting for Charlie to get her butt in gear so that we could go do some shopping.

My boobs were already two sizes larger than my largest bra. There was no way I could continue to go without at least a couple of them to help hold up their newfound weight without squishing them into four separate entities on my chest. The rest of the clothing I could make do without. I needed to save money and men's sweatpants at Walmart were a whole lot cheaper than maternity pants. It didn't even matter that I had to roll them over a few times at the waist or roll them up at the bottom. Damn the store for being out of the cuffed versions that might have kept themselves up. Not that it mattered. What mattered were the giant jugs I couldn't figure out how to holster.

"What are you up to, little momma?" Rabbit asked just as I'd been checking out my swelling mammaries. Great, the man had perfect timing.

I smirked at the new nickname he bestowed me with. "Waiting on Charlie to get dressed."

"Were you naked together?" he asked as he wiggled his eyebrows in what I'm sure was supposed to be a lascivious way, but ended up looking goofier than all hell. "Just what are your intentions with my bestie?" he questioned before I could even answer the first one.

"I'm going shopping with the lovely Myra today," Charlie answered as she walked up and planted a kiss on my cheek. Then she turned her attention back to Rabbit and grinned. "Did you want to come?" Somehow, I think he only heard the double entendre that she didn't realize she'd made, and not the actual question.

"I always want to come," was his answer. I simply rolled my eyes as we all left the clubhouse and piled into my suburban.

Since there weren't many options in Spearfish, we had to go all the way to Rapid City to find a store with bras that might fit me. It wasn't until we were in Victoria's Secret that Charlie realized her mistake in inviting Rabbit. He took one look at me then the mannequin I was standing next to. His eyes bounced back and forth quite comically several times before a sales woman finally approached us. and back again several times. Right as the sales woman approached.

Before the woman could ask if we needed help with anything, Rabbit opened up his stupid, unfiltered mouth. "I don't know what Victoria's Secret was exactly, but it looks like you may have grown out of it."

"Oh my goodness!" The older woman looked absolutely scandalized and walked away from us before I could ask her to help. Honestly, what the hell was she doing working in a sexy lingerie store if she was such a prude?

"Rabbit!" Charlie hissed at him. I rolled my eyes and put the bra down because he wasn't wrong. I was short and curvy even before my pregnancy, now I was short and stupidly curvaceous.

"Nah!" I told Charlie. "He's right. I think I might need a specialty or maternity store for what I have going on now," I explained as I glanced down at my giant boobs.

"Do they need to be-" Rabbit started to ask a question, but Charlie punched him in the gut to shut him up.

"If you even think about asking what you were about to, I will make sure you never have the chance to find out with a woman in the future. You will no longer be able to spread your seed or use your grabby man hands." It was only then that I realized what he'd been about to ask. I rolled my eyes at him again for about the tenth time on our little fiasco of a trip.

"Seriously?" I questioned.

He blew a kiss at me and mouthed, "Mooo!" I couldn't stop the laugh from exploding free and Charlie turned narrowed, suspecting eyes on Rabbit.

"Don't encourage him, he'll only keep it going once you do."

"That's okay, it's just the stress relief I needed after studying so much lately."

"When do you take your exam?" Charlie asked.

"One week from today." I smiled at her then because it felt so good to have a new friend I could count on in my life. Charlie had become one of the best people I'd met in South Dakota so far. "I'll probably keep working part time at the bar, too, just so I can get ahead and hopefully move into a larger place before the baby gets here."

"Girl, you can't work yourself to death while you're pregnant," Charlie admonished.

"Don't worry, I'll be fine," I insisted.

"Why do you need a bigger place?" Rabbit asked.

"The apartment over your brother's shop is only a one-bedroom. It's fine for now, but once the baby is here, it'll get cramped pretty quickly."

The topic dropped after that in favor of peace and quiet for the rest of the trip home. My bra shopping had been fruitless, but one of the women who had overheard Rabbit make the crack about my boobs outgrowing VS, mentioned a website I could find the right sizes on. I hoped they weren't ridiculously expensive and that they had fast shipping.

Rabbit, who insisted on driving, dropped Charlie off at the clubhouse first, which was odd since he lived there, too. When he got me back to my place, he got out of the vehicle before I could and helped me down like he had the time he drove me to my appointment. It was sweet and once again showed me a flash of the person everyone else claimed him to be.

"Can I help you?" Rabbit asked.

I glanced down at the one bag I had with a couple of cute

baby things I'd seen. "What exactly do you think I need help with? This isn't even heavy."

"No, I mean with everything. Do you need help? I hate thinking about you being pregnant and having to work two jobs just to get by."

"Lots of women do it. I'm no different from the rest of them," I insisted.

"You are, though. You don't have to do this alone. They don't all have a Rabbit to pull out of their hat," he told me with a sexy little wink.

"I don't either. We barely know one another. I can't accept help from you." I turned and carefully headed up to my apartment, noting that I'd probably need to salt the steps again before evening fell and they iced over. Rabbit locked my truck and made his way over to his brother's truck. Figures, he planned to take his brother's truck again, and that's why he drove me home. I had to laugh as I watched him steal Spinner's truck without even a single thought. I hoped he at least texted him to let him know. Oh well, it wasn't my problem. That was between the crazy ass brothers who had somehow stepped in to make my life a tiny bit better. Warmth settled deep in my chest as I thought about him offering to help me out. It was sweet, even if it was an overstep coming from him.

14. RABBIT

Stoneridge Raiders MC.

That was the club Myra grew up in. Since I knew the town Cherry and Chastity had been from, it wasn't too hard to find out. I wasn't sure why it took me so fucking long to check in on things. Myra had said enough, the girls had filled in some blanks, and now I was beginning to get the whole damn picture of why the woman came here and wanted her location to remain secret.

"Yo, Rabbit, someone's here to see you."

I got up and went out to the front to find a man standing there who shouldn't have been. He was wearing a Stoneridge Raiders kutte, which was pretty ballsy of him, considering he was in our territory flying his own colors. "Can I help you with something?"

"Rabbit," he said, as if he knew exactly who I was.

"You got me!"

"You're the one who owns Renegade Rosy's?" I nodded my head, waiting to hear what came out of his mouth next.

"The place where Myra Chase works?" he asked, letting me know his real agenda. I crossed my arms over my chest, widened my stance, and stared the asshole down. Was this her baby's father? The asshole who cheated on her.

"Lots of people work for me, I don't tell anyone who they are for any reason. I also don't tell people when I've never heard of someone before, so don't get your hopes up."

He rolled his eyes and grinned. "I don't need you to tell me she's here. I already know that much. Listen up, I don't want Myra to know I was here, so you need to honor your claim in reverse, too. Don't want her to know that I am aware of where she is either. Her family won't find out."

"What's your game here then? Why are you coming to me? And for that matter, what the hell makes you think I'll be your secret keeper? I don't know you, and sure as fuck don't owe you a damn thing."

"I'm Phoenix, by the way," the asshole announced as if it would mean anything. When I didn't show any sign of knowing who the fuck he was, he continued, "I'm the unofficial tracker for the Stoneridge Raiders. Myra's whereabouts have never been a mystery to me. The thing is, I'm rooting for her to stay away from the bastards she left behind. They're no good for her or that kid of hers. Let's have a seat, and I'll tell you a little story."

He broke it all down for me, what Blaze – Myra's ex – had been up to, how Phoenix himself was involved and silenced by an MC order, and how Myra blew up when everything came out. I had to hand it to her, when he started telling me what she did in order to make a clean break from her hometown, family, and old life, I admired her even more than I had previously.

She hadn't even taken half the money from their joint account, the furniture, nothing. She just packed up her personal belongings, her personal savings, and took off. I was still finding things that were missing from the house I once shared with my ex. None of the missing shit belonged to Chastity, and that bitch no doubt pawned it all to fund her little adventure.

"Story time was really nice, but why are you your club's history with this woman?"

"I'm letting you know because she might need someone to have her back one day. Those people are toxic. She's going to need strong people in her corner. Besides, I actually wanted to tell you that if you betray her, if anyone from your club brings her family down on her, I will personally see to it that every single last one of you dies."

Well, shit!

Either the guy was crazy or he was seriously determined to keep Myra away from her family. It made me wonder what else they might be guilty of, because that seemed to be a pretty incredible and extreme measure to take for what happened.

"There's more to the story, isn't there?" I finally asked.

"The only thing more is my own story to tell, and that's not for you. Let's just say it's best for everyone if she stays here, unseen." He stood and moved to go to the door. "I meant what I said, you keep her safe or you will deal with me. She's the only family I care about."

The man hadn't been out the door for two minutes

before I had someone on him and checking into the club Myra had come from. This was a surprise visit, and we didn't need anymore popping up. It already felt as if I'd been gut checked, and now I had the worry of Myra's ex coming to collect her and their kid. For some reason, it made me feel a rage like I'd never felt before, not even when Chastity had left the way she did. Even then, the rage had been internalized because I wondered why I never listened to all the warnings about her. The thought of losing Myra was more crippling, and yet we were barely even friends.

'But you want to be more,' that annoying voice inside my head taunted me.

15. MYRA

WHILE DRIVING TO WORK A FEW DAYS BEFORE MY NCLEX, I thought I saw Phoenix pass by Renegade Rosy's as I pulled in, but that couldn't be the case because he would have stopped when he saw The Beast. Yeah, there were a million and one Suburbans out there, but mine happened to have some pretty easily identifiable stickers on it. Including the lovely one an old friend had slapped on it that says, "Nurses know where to stick it!"

I almost let that sighting get into my head and trip me up just before the test.

Hello, paranoia, my old friend. Good to see you again! Not really, go the fuck away!

I became anal about locking doors, checking again, and once more for good measure because nothing helps you feel more paranoid than adding obsessive compulsive traits to the mix. Still, I shook it off, took my test, and then allowed the worry kicked in again.

Instead of worrying about a Phoenix sighting, my brain

switched gears to wondering if I passed my test. During that time, I hadn't laid eyes on Rabbit. Our shopping trip was the last time I saw him. I wondered if he felt slighted when I refused to accept his help? Even knowing that was possible, it didn't change my stance on the fact that I wouldn't accept money from people to get by. I knew what it meant to rely on people and have them let you down completely. Not only did I have trust issues, but I needed to prove to myself that I could do it all. My baby was counting on me and I refused to let him down.

Rabbit wasn't at the clubhouse when I met the girls there. Charlie, Liza, and Cherry all sat around a table with books in hand when I showed up. "What exactly are we doing?" I asked while glancing around for any of the men to come tell them to get their own space. My father and the men in his club certainly would not have allowed the women to take over their space, especially for what appeared to be a book club meeting.

"We were just discussing the latest book we're all reading," Liza pointed out as she held her iPad up that was opened to the ebook version of what Charlie had in paperback. Cherry also had the paperback.

"I didn't know." Maybe I was still suffering from residual paranoia, but I took another look around the room and the girls finally caught on.

"Lord girl, the big, bad, bikers aren't going to pop out of the woodwork to kill us for having books in their space. We're waiting on them to get back. There's a lasagna in the oven, but it won't be done for another fifteen minutes." Liza smiled as she casually pushed her wavy bob of brown hair back behind her ears. I wasn't sure why she bothered because it wasn't long enough to catch there properly and ended up back in her face. Her eyes crossed as she tried to watch the hairs and blow them back out of her face. With a barely noticeable shrug, she finally gave up and offered me a shipping grin. "Since we have time, what's new with you and the little bun in your oven?"

I smiled down at my stomach. "The little one is fine, but I have other news to share!"

Cherry's phone rang, interrupting what I'd been about to tell them. "Hey honey, no just us girls still. I don't mind speakerphone, you know that." She leaned over and whispered to me, "Go ahead and share your news. Spinner's just checking in."

"Okay. Well," I paused to catch my breath because I couldn't believe I was about to announce this, or that I had people around me who would even care. "I did it!" Everyone started clapping and shouting their congratulations. Cherry tipped her head to the side, stared at me, and then started speaking into her phone.

"Hold on, Spin," she said into the phone before turning her attention to me. "What did you do, Myra?"

"I passed! I'm officially a registered nurse now!"

"Oh my God! I'm so happy for you!" Cherry yelled.

"Oh! It's too bad we can't get some male strippers out here at a minute's notice like the guys can get the female dancers. That's what we need for this celebration. Myra needs to know she's still a woman with working parts and that she can celebrate this start to her knew life!" Of course it would be Charlie to suggest strippers for my celebration. She saw everyone's slack-jawed expressions. "What? The poor thing can't drink to celebrate. The least we could offer is something nice to look at!"

Liza burst out laughing. "Only you, Charlie!"

"I thought it was a great idea!" I told Charlie. "It's too bad there aren't any male dancers at Ruby's."

"No kidding, I would throw down some serious money if there were."

"You better not let Rage hear you say that," Liza teasingly warned. "Although, if we were being honest, those poor male dancers wouldn't last long around these guys. I don't think they could handle their women ogling some nearly naked men on the stage."

"We might not have dancers, but you are coming out with us tonight to celebrate!" There wasn't a question in that. Charlie wasn't leaving any room for me to wiggle out of celebrating my latest milestone.

"I don't know, it's been a long day already. Truthfully, going out to celebrate doesn't sound like much fun."

"What if I promise it will be? Maybe we can get some of the girls there to give us some dance lessons?"

That had me intrigued. "Now, that might be worth the price of exhaustion. I've been wishing for a good way to get some exercise in, but with the constant snow, ice, melt, snow, thing going on outside; I haven't been able to come up with anything feasible that wouldn't involve me possibly falling on my ass."

"I feel that," Cherry said as she hung up with Spinner.

"Everything all right?" I asked.

"Yeah, he was just checking in to see if anyone was bothering us here."

"That's still weird," I told her.

"What? Why? Are you saying my man is weird for asking if I was okay?"

"No, just that it's not normal that you ladies are allowed to use the clubhouse this way." I swished my hand around to indicate them and their books. "My parents, well, my mom and her friends would never even think to ask because the answer would be a resounding no."

"That's kind of sad," Charlie said.

"Yeah, it is. I'm not sure why my mother put up with the shit she did, or for that matter, why I thought it was okay, too. It wasn't. There's such a world of difference between their MC and this one. It makes me wonder just how toxic our situations were there, because this is a much healthier place for women. Even the club girls here are treated with more dignity and respect."

"Come out with us tonight?" Liza asked, though it sounded more like insistence.

There was no way I could deny her request. Liza had never asked me for anything since I'd moved here. The least I could do was show up to lady's night and celebrate my own damn achievement with them. "How can I say no, when someone asks to celebrate with me?"

"I didn't need to ask," Charlie said. "I always knew your answer would be yes, eventually."

"Okay, well then, Miss I'm So Sure Of Myself, it's your job to keep me awake long enough to celebrate."

It was exceedingly difficult to keep my eyeballs from drooping, even with all the noise around me. I was used to the ambient sounds of the bar, if you could call them something so innocuous. It wasn't until the emcee came over the sound system, rather loudly, that I realized I'd gotten lost in the midst of a very long, slow blink. The girls were all laughing at me.

"Ladies in the house, you're going to want to come up a little closer to the stage, because Renegade Rosy's has a treat for you tonight!"

"You didn't?" I asked, turning to Charlie, because if anyone could pull off having a male stripper at the club on a few hours' notice, it would be her. She shook her head and seemed just as puzzled, though.

"I didn't do anything, I swear," she told all of us.

"Welcome to the stage, Electric Bunny," the emcee shouted.

"No!" Charlie screamed before she burst out laughing the moment the curtains parted and the spotlight hit none other than Rabbit.

"Oh. My. God!" Cherry stated as her jaw dropped.

"I've seen it all," was Liza's contribution.

I was speechless as I watched him glance around before his eyes landed on me and the music started in. It sounded a bit familiar, but wasn't something I could place right away. The music didn't matter in that moment because Rabbit taunted me with his eyes while wearing something resembling a tux. Instead of a top hat to go with it, he had on a bowler hat, and a cigar hung from his grinning lips. That sexy swagger of his as he moved his lithe body across the stage made it impossible to focus on just one part of him.

That was about the time my ears tuned back into the music blasting from the speakers. Rabbit grabbed hold of the pole, and started rolling his hips forward as he lip synced the chorus with every bit of big dick energy it was sung with. "All I wanna do is fuck! Fuck! Fuck myself tonight." It was one of those ridiculous songs by Steel Panther, but I couldn't lie, as hilarious as the lyrics were, Rabbit made it just the funny side of sexy, and if I hadn't know what tripped my sexy-brain trigger before, I did now. That man, gyrating his junk on stage to the most ridiculous song ever, the combination of humor and sex, that was it. That had my panties dampening at an unhealthy rate for a pregnant woman.

"Oh my God!" Charlie screeched again while clapping her hands. "I don't know if it's okay for me to look, he's like a brother to me."

"He's really up there doing this?" Liza asked, seeming shocked that Rabbit would stoop to this level.

"Oh, he is so doing this!" Cherry laughed out while clapping along with everyone else.

Meanwhile, I couldn't take my eyes off the spectacle before me. Unlike the other women, I had no problem believing Rabbit would get on stage and dance for us, considering how I'd met him. The man had zero shame when it came to his body. Then again, he had absolutely nothing to be ashamed of. The man took damn good care of himself. I had to laugh when he moved from the pole and started to hump the microphone stand that was set out as a prop for him. He continued to lip sync a song about being completely in lust with himself and that was all she wrote. I threw my head back and howled with laughter at Rabbit as he stood straight, did a little pelvic thrust, and then off came his tux jacket.

My laughter dried up a bit then. He had nothing on underneath of it. He was all tatted up, tanned, and ridiculously toned muscle. Another hip thrust, and his tux pants ripped away from his body leaving him in only...

"Holy shit!" I screamed. "Is that a banana hammock?" I had been so distracted by the muscles before that I totally missed the two strips of fabric going up his chest and over his shoulders. Yep, he was definitely wearing what should have been the least sexy thing on a man. Only, Rabbit rocked every little bit of fabric that kissed his skin like it was made for him.

Charlie finally answered me after she calmed down from a hysterical fit of laughter. "It's fucking yellow, too!" That started off new peals of laughter from her and the other women present.

There was absolute nothing left to question as the man moved, danced, shimmied, and shook every bit of his goods on that stage for our entertainment. Then, he turned around, and it got even better. The banana hammock was riding up the crack of his well-toned ass. That wasn't what caught my attention, though.

"Is that a tattoo on his ass?" I asked as I leaned further over our table trying to get a better look. Liza howled in laughter, so she must have already known something about the tattoo. I squinted, but the lighting and his quick movements kept me from seeing everything. It sort of looked like a rabbit using a top hat to cover his junk or something. I was definitely going to ask him about that the next time I saw him. By the time the song ended, Rabbit was directly in front of our table, on his knees, and singing into the fake microphone while staring me in the eye. His hips hadn't stopped moving, and while a huge part of me was screaming at my eyeballs to look down, the rest of me was hypnotized by his eyes on mine. When the last chord reverberated through the room, Rabbit stood and jumped right off the stage and made a bee-line straight for me.

"Oh shit!" I hissed out as I squirmed in the seat, ready to bolt. "He is so not..." I didn't get to finish what I was saying, because he so was going to do that. Afroman's Colt 45 started playing and Rabbit was swaying his ass in my lap to "...Colt 45 and two ZigZags, baby that's all we need..." I smacked the hell out of his ass and giggled so hard, trying to get him to stop embarrassing me. I wasn't so much worried about what people thought of me, or him doing this, though. I was more worried about the state of my hormones and the fact that I was about two seconds from taking things way too far and getting that back room happy ending people always talk about happening at strip clubs for men. We were both single, so it was okay? Right?

Before my nerves or my hormones could get the best of me, Rabbit leaned in and whisper-yelled into my ear, "Congratulations on passing your exam, baby!"

My body erupted in head-to-toe shivers and goosebumps. I reached out, not caring one bit what anyone might say, and grabbed his hips to still him as I looked up into his beautiful eyes. "You did all this for me?"

"Who else would I do something like this for?"

Who else, indeed.

I was dumbfounded though. "The girls said you needed a stripper to commemorate the occasion and here I am."

Thump! Thump! Thump!

My heart banged against my chest, letting me know I was still alive and it was okay to have feelings. Tears brewed, but I managed to keep them at bay somehow. "You're the best!" I told him as he turned to say something to me, too. Thanks to our proximity and both of us turning to hear one another at the same time, our lips collided, instead. When we finally managed to come up for air, the table was suspiciously empty and none of the girls were anywhere to be seen. Someone had been kind enough to leave a robe lying there at the table for Rabbit, though.

"Don't worry, I'll see you home safe and sound," he assured me in a voice that had both deepened and roughened thanks to the hormones riding us. For the first time since I left Blaze behind, I wanted that. I wanted another man to take me home, and hell if I didn't want him to still be wearing that stupid yellow banana hammock so I could peel it off his body.

With. My. Teeth.

16. RABBIT

I SLIPPED OFF MYRA'S LAP CAREFULLY, THEN LEANED IN ONE MORE time, knowing somewhere in the back of my mind that I was flashing my naked ass and that fucking ridiculous tattoo to everyone in the place who cared to look. "I need to go get dressed, but I'll be right back."

"Okay," she whispered so breathlessly that I only knew she said it because her lips moved to form the word, even if the sound didn't carry.

"Rabbit! Those moves!" One of our dancers yelled out to me the minute I stepped in the back.

"I wish my man would do something like that for me," one of the others called out.

I was just about to the office when a hand grabbing my shoulder stopped me in my tracks. Savannah Blue, otherwise known as Sapphire, was standing there with hard eyes trained on my own. "She's a good girl."

"I know that."

"Do you?"

"What the fuck is that supposed to mean, Sav?"

"I watched you pursue Chastity, even warned you about what would happen if she ever gave in. Myra is nothing like that bitch. She is all the sweet and good things in this world rolled into one person. That girl might be tough as nails, too, but you are the type of man who could break her."

"That's not a concern," I argued.

She arched a brow and cocked her hip, attitude ready to be unleashed. "You over Chastity, finally?"

Fuck. Not this again.

Why did everyone think I was just holding out until the bitch came back to me? Did I really come off as so weak that I would be waiting for her to return to me?

"Chastity made her choice when she drove off in some other man's truck," I confirmed.

"We've all watched you basically self-destruct since then, Rabbit."

And that was the point? I lost my fucking mind, standing in the hallway of Renegade Rosy's, wearing a fucking banana hammock, and with my brother down the hall watching as if I didn't see him there. "I didn't self-destruct because of her! I fucking went crazy because I couldn't trust myself. My own judgement bit me in the ass. My desire for things in life that I didn't have, but coveted, led me down that road. What I've been doing hasn't been to pine over a woman I'm waiting to return to me. It was because I was punishing myself for losing that much of myself to the pursuit of her - or what she represented - in the first place. So, don't come at me like I don't know what the fuck I'm doing."

Sav stream up at me with a huge grin on her face by the

time I was finished. Never mind that I was red-faced from rage-yelling at her. "Sorry," I huffed the quick apology as she continued to smile at me before patting my shoulder and walking away.

She turned back one more time. "Okay then," was all she said before she moved into the back room where the girl's had lockers and a private place to change.

"Fucking women!" I groaned as I turned to get my ass into the office and dressed again.

By the time I dressed and returned to the front room, the only people sitting at their table were Liza and Tango. I didn't even see him earlier. "Where's Myra?"

"She left," Liza answered.

"What do you mean? I told her I'd be right back."

Liza glanced down at her phone. "Rabbit, honey, that was like twenty minutes ago. The poor girl was already nodding off before you took the stage. She was exhausted. Spinner offered to take her home when he took Cherry."

Tango smirked into his drink as I cursed my brother for existing. There was no way Myra would turn down a ride from him since they were going to the same place. That mother fuckin' cock-block! Not that I thought we'd end up sleeping together tonight or anything, but my brother knew what the fuck he was doing.

I pointed to Tango. "You bastards are going down soon."

He held his hands up. "I can't help the woman took the first out to get away from you after you flaunted that you had a rabbit fucking a top hat tattooed on your ass."

I walked away without even attempting a comeback. It was that, or kill a club brother. The whole way back to the clubhouse, all I could think about was that kiss. Never, in my thirty-one years had I experienced another like it.

"HEARD YOU KISSED THE NEW, pregnant chick last night?" Whiskey asked, as if the gossiping men of our club hadn't been reliving all the details with one another.

"And?" I retorted as if I could care less.

"Be careful with her. Those pregnancy hormones are no joke, especially on top of whatever issues sent her running here to begin with." He would know all about the hormone issues. His and Fox's ex-girlfriend had a lot of mental problems when she carried their daughter. Unfortunately, they think it also led to her abandoning them and the baby once she was born too.

"You don't have to worry about anything," I explained to him. "Myra is just a friend."

"Friends don't kiss with tongues," Whiskey mocked me.

"Whatever!" I walked away before I had to admit the truth. I was falling for someone else's girl. Even knowing about their breakup, deep down inside, the truth was there. That ass-wipe, who put that baby in Myra's belly, would find her eventually. When that happened, I might just have a fight on my hands to keep her, to keep them.

"Treat her right, if you're going there." Whiskey added before he wrapped his knuckles on the bar and headed in the opposite direction.

It made me wonder if people thought I had treated

Chastity wrong and that's why she took off. I didn't think that was the case. The woman had been catered to like she was precious to me. I allowed that thought to trail off, knowing that was exactly where I had gone wrong. I treated Chastity the way I would have treated her sister, if she'd been mine. I held her in a regard that didn't match who she was. If only I'd realized that sooner. I might have saved myself some time.

"Rabbit, let's go. We have a run and you're driving today. No bikes. The weather may turn to shit later and there's still icy patches on the ground anyway." Spinner called out to me as he came through the doors like he was on a mission.

"Looks like Spinner woke up on the wrong side of Cherry's bed this morning," one of the prospects mumbled. I didn't bother giving him shit for it because he was probably right.

When Spinner was close enough, I asked, "Where to today?"

"Canada." The one word reply was enough. I knew what Canada meant. We were taking one of Tallahassee's hauls across the northern border. It also meant a nearly seven hour drive one-way.

"I'll go get something else on," I told him. The clubhouse had become my home again once Chastity left me. I gave up the rental we'd been in while waiting on my house to be built. The house was finished now, but I couldn't bring myself to live in it.

I built the damn thing with a family in mind. For whatever reason, Myra and that kiss popped into my head. I could picture her there, making my house our home. "Snap out of it!" I muttered to myself as I ripped the club shirt over my head and replaced it with a plain colored thermal. A hoodie on top of that would help stave off the chill, and jeans with sneakers instead of my normal riding boots rounded out my wardrobe. I grabbed a go-bag to take with me just in case we got stuck somewhere along the way. December in South Dakota already had harsh winters, but North Dakota and Canada didn't make it any better.

"Let's do this thing." I called out as I came back downstairs. Spinner nodded and started walking to the door without waiting for me to catch up. Something really must have been bothering him. My brother was prone to quiet, reflective spells, but he never outright shut me out like he had all morning either.

"What crawled up your ass?" I asked as I hauled my body up into the driver's seat of the box truck we were using to get the gear it contained into Canada.

Spinner turned and glared at me. "What crawled up my ass is you, little brother. You can go off the rails all you want after what that bitch sister-in-law of mine did to you, but you will not drag Myra down with you. She's been through enough." I sat, stunned that Spinner would even speak to me like that. "Stick to drilling BRATs on the pool tables if you must, but pregnant women shouldn't even be on your radar."

"Whoa! What is this all about?"

"Last night ringing any bells for you?" He huffed the question out, sounding both angry and annoyed. "Or maybe you were too blitzed to care about that?"

"I was stone cold sober last night. I danced to make Myra

laugh so she'd have a good celebration. You know, since she's pregnant and can't drink. That test she had to take isn't exactly easy, in case you didn't know. Besides, it was your damn phone call I overheard that gave me the idea for what the girls wanted." I started the truck and pulled away from the clubhouse. That didn't mean I failed to notice my brother's curious glances my way.

"I was talking about the kiss you shared while you straddled her lap."

"That started out as a part of my dance, and we accidentally bumped faces when we tried to talk to one another."

"And then?"

I shrugged my shoulders at Spinner's prompting words. "Then, I don't know. One minute we were both laughing and she was whispering something in my ear. The next, I turned to answer back but our lips met instead."

"Oh, yeah, I'm sure it was all a big grade school mistake, considering I watched you hold the poor girl's head to keep her plastered to your face."

His disbelieving tone only made me chuckle. "Well, it started innocently enough and then her hands gripped my hips hard, her lips parted, and-"

"Enough!," Spinner interrupted my recap. "She's come to be like a sister to me since she's been here. I can't listen to that shit."

"Like a sister to you?" I asked, frowning over at my brother.

"Cherry's her good friend." I shook my head and spat out a mocking laugh. "Have either of you offered to take her to a single one of her doctor appointments so she doesn't have to go alone?" I asked.

Spinner's mouth opened as if he would say something, then closed, and opened once more as he turned to me. "I honestly hadn't thought about it. I figured one of the girls was doing it."

"Well, I took her to the last one when her truck was broken down. If I hadn't been there, she just wouldn't have gone." I was sure she would have called Charlie for help, but I wanted to make Spinner feel bad. If he was going to play the big brother, protective card, he had better actually be fulfilling the role for Myra.

"I get it," he finally said. "Do better or don't come for you. Rabbit, do me a favor and don't go there unless you're completely serious. She had a rough time-"

"I already know."

"You know?"

"She told me the gist of it and I had a visit from Phoenix of the Stoneridge Raiders MC recently."

"What the fuck? Why wouldn't you tell anyone? Does she know they found her?"

"Calm down. Phoenix filled in all the details Myra left out before he went back home. He doesn't plan on telling his club where she is. It was his girl who slept with Myra's old man. He wanted Myra to know right away. Club forbade him from telling her. I think this is his way of repaying a debt he feels he owes her since it was his woman who ultimately tore apart her relationship and he had the opportunity to the ditch the bitch, but Myra was never given that same consideration."

"That's fucked, but I don't think the club will see it quite like that if they find out he's known where she is and kept it from them. That will be seen as an ultimate betrayal against their club."

"Not my problem. I have tabs on them, so we'll know if they attempt to head this way."

"You really do care about her," my brother said after a too-long moment of silence.

"She's growing on me."

"You hated her at first," he countered.

"I misunderstood something."

"You thought she pulled a Chastity and ran from her ex for no reason?" he surmised this, and the bastard wasn't wrong.

"Something like that," I answered reluctantly.

"Not everyone is going to be like her," my brother told me in a quiet, thoughtful tone.

"Let's not discuss my issues, and focus on the task at hand for now, yeah?"

"Fine," he agreed before he kicked back to take a nap. We would each only drive half way so the other could stay rested.

There was no way we'd show up and not be alert as fuck for one of these handoffs. We spent close to thirty minutes watching the offloading of the truck. Once their men moved out, Spinner released a low growl of frustration.

"I hate that we're wrapped up in this shit," he grumbled.

"Me too, but some things can't be helped."

He eyed me for a moment before tipping his head up in a

half-nod. "Others can. Let's grab a room in the next town and get a little rest before we head back."

I shook my head. "Nah. I'll drive. Let's just jump back across the border before we're here long enough to leave a footprint where we don't want one."

As it turned out, we ended up with a flat tire halfway home, in the middle of nowhere. We ended up having to stay until the next day to find someone who could get a fucking tire to us that worked on the truck we were in.

"That hotel seems like an amazing suggestion right about now, doesn't it?" Spinner had asked me before he cozied up in his seat with some of the blankets that had been in the back to offer a little extra cushion for the product we'd been moving.

"Fuck my life," I muttered before also trying to get a little shuteye.

WE MADE it all the way back to town, only a few miles left to pull back into the MC compound, when blue lights lit up behind us. I glanced down to check my speed.

"Two miles per hour over? Really?"

"Maybe your taillight is out," Spinner suggested as he rolled his eyes. "Pull it over, and don't be a dick. I don't feel like going to jail today, and you've been a cranky ass since the whole flat tire thing."

"What are you hauling here?" The first officer, Barker,

asked as he walked up to the driver's side of the truck, indicating the rear compartment with his hand.

"A whole lot of nothing," I explained as I offered a quick wink in his direction. "What? Were you expecting guns?" His hand immediately flexed to his weapon on his overburdened tactical belt. "Wait, a sec. I have you covered. Have you seen these guns?" I tormented him as I flexed my arm, causing my biceps to bulge for the man who did not look as though he was happy to have to deal with me.

"You fucking moron!" my brother hissed under his breath. "That is not something you say at a goddamn traffic stop."

"I'm going to need you to step out of the vehicle, slowly, and place your hands behind your head with your fingers interlocked."

"Well, I guess he wants a closer look," I quipped to my brother, though loudly enough for the cops to hear. Spinner shook his head and growled at me.

"You couldn't just keep your smart mouth shut, could you?"

"Aww, come on Sammy, when have you known me not to show off my smarts?" I laughed as he fumed, both over my behavior and the use of his childhood nickname. We couldn't exactly use our road names because then whatever we'd been up to would be associated with the club. I had no way of knowing if they had us on camera somewhere along the way, like say Canada - handing off guns. I still managed to get out of the truck and tuck my hands around my head in the manner the officer described. That didn't stop the prick from yanking me off balance and slamming my upper torso into the front of the truck as he kicked my legs apart.

"Hey now!" I called out. "I gave permission for you to look at the guns I was packing. I did not give you the okay to open up my backdoor."

"Fuck's sake, Rabbit, just stop!" my brother growled from where he was being frisked by dickwad's partner on the other side of the vehicle.

"What do you have in your pocket, here?" Officer Baker asked me. I couldn't help but laugh because the mother-fucker was holding my dick and he'd be pissed when he realized it. No doubt, if he had to ask what he was holding, the poor boy wasn't packing a whole lot himself.

"My dick, and if you could just," I squirmed as I spoke. "Yeah, a little tighter around the head," I told him.

The man stepped back as if his hand had been scalded by the heat of my junk. Served the fucker right.

"You're going down for that shit!" he seethed at me.

"You're the one who was molesting me at a traffic stop, dude. I don't think I'm the one in the wrong here. You're only making it worse by making threats involving having me 'go down.'"

Another vehicle pulled up before the asshole, who had a fist up, no doubt ready for a good kidney shot, could actually get that hit launched. I glanced to the side to see that the vehicle was a familiar one and it was my turn to groan. Please, don't let her get in trouble because of my antics.

Myra hopped down from her too-high vehicle and sashayed over toward the front of the police cruiser and the back of the truck I was currently hunched over. "Do I need to get bail money together?"

"Ma'am, you need to go back to your vehicle and move along."

"I'd love to, but that's my husband you had your fist raised to, and for no apparent reason from what I could see from the road," she told him innocently. "And that," she tipped her head toward Spinner, "Is my brother."

"Rabbit ain't married," the asshole said, proving he already knew who we were and that this had been a targeted stop. Too bad the assholes thought we'd be bringing something back from Canada and not dropping it off there. They might have actually been able to hem the Hastings brothers up for something had they got us on the trip to rather than coming back.

"Well, a quickie wedding in Vegas after he did this to me," Myra pointed at the baby bump that had been growing more prominent of late, "sure seems to tell a different story." She yawned, as if the whole scene was boring her. "Now, I need to know why the boys haven't managed to bring back my ice cream yet."

"Sorry, sugar-pop. They were all out at the first few stores we tried. If only you had wanted a normal flavor."

Myra threw her hands up on her hips and sputtered. "How hard can it be to find maple bacon ice cream and some dill pickles?" She looked dead fucking serious as she asked the question and I couldn't help the involuntary reaction I had. My dick went raging hard at the sight of her faux rage and quick thinking.

Both cops seemed stumped, especially after Myra added

a little foot-stomping to her tirade. "Now, I don't even want that flavor. I had to drive myself to the store to get Chunky Monkey instead, and it's currently melting in The Beast." She pointed back over her shoulder at the Suburban parked on the side of the road behind the cruiser. It was cold as fuck out, so her ice cream wasn't in any danger of melting, but the thought made it a nice touch. "So, if someone could tell me whether my man is free to go or if I need bail money, that would be wonderful!"

"I didn't see anything," the third cop, who I hadn't realized had been there, spoke up. The bastard had sneak attacked the back of the truck while we were occupied with dick one and dick two.

"He'll just be getting a ticket today, darlin'" the other one, who had been frisking Spinner, told her.

"A ticket!" Myra shrieked. "Like we don't have enough to worry about with a baby on the way? Now, we have to spend the crib money we saved on a ticket?" Real, fat tears sprang from her eyes as her lower lip wobbled. Even I wanted to console the beautiful little actress. She brought an Oscar worthy performance to a small-town sideshow.

"Ma'am, don't go getting upset. We'll send the boys on their way with a warning this time. Go ahead and pull yourself back together before you have to drive, okay?" If I could have rolled my eyes at his predictable response, I would have. Officer Asshole, I mean Baker, started to undo the cuffs he had put on me as I watched Myra strut her cute little ass, that had developed a bit of a waddle effect, back to her truck.

"Rabbit?" she called out, tears all gone by then.

"Yes, dear?"

"Bring some Cherry Garcia and Mint Chip home. I think I changed my mind again."

I was going to the store and buying every fucking flavor ice cream they had when I was released. "Yes, ma'am," I agreed as she got into her vehicle and pulled off with a fluttery wave of her fingers.

"Jesus!" The asshole cop hissed.

"Good luck with that," the other called to me from across the front of the truck while my brother stared at me in disbelief and shook his head. Yeah, I couldn't believe our luck either or her performance.

"We probably would have been doing him a favor by taking him to a cell," the asshole behind me said as he tucked his cuffs back in their holder on his tactical web belt that was just overkill for his job in this area. I ignored the fuckers as I hauled my ass back in the truck, unable to hide the mile-wide grin plastered on my face.

"You're sunk," Spinner informed me. Then he added, "I take it we're making a pit stop at the grocery store?"

I just my head, kept on grinning, and drove to the place that had all the ice cream that spunky little baby oven could ever want.

17. MYRA

My whole body shook as the adrenaline surge started to dissipate. I knew the guys had been gone on a run, but when I saw them pulled over, and Rabbit in cuffs, I had to do something. Even if all I was able to do was to get a message to Iceman, I'd be useful to the people who took me in when my own family forced me to leave.

When I pulled up outside of my apartment, Cherry was already there waiting. "What did you just do, Mrs. Rabbit?" she teased. I groaned in response. Of course Spinner would have told her already.

"They looked like they needed saving," I admitted.

"And now you're married?"

"I panicked. All I could think was that we're not allowed to give patient information outside of immediate family in an emergency. I blame the stupid test I spent all that time cramming for. Anyway, I just went with it."

Cherry laughed so loud and long that I grew concerned for her, then annoyed. Ignoring her hysterics, once again, I grabbed my bag that actually did have Chunky Monkey melting inside of it, thanks to The Beast's heater and my inability to get warm, and I headed toward my apartment.

"You know you're in trouble now, right?"

"For what? Because I helped club members out?"

"Oh, no, honey! You'll be thanked for that. You're going to be in trouble because Rabbit will never leave you alone now. I wouldn't be surprised if he swept you away to Vegas for real now."

"Okay!" I very sarcastically blurted back to my friend. "Whatever you say."

"Just wait and see," my pestering friend told me as she followed me into my apartment.

I pointed to my belly, which seemed to be my defense for everything these days. "You seem to forget all the baggage I'm packing."

Cherry swished her hand through the air in a dismissive gesture. "That won't matter to Rabbit. It's probably a plus for him. The one thing that man wants more than anything else in the world is a family to care for."

My heart stuttered a bit at that news. It made me both excited and trepidatious. "I don't even know what to say about that," I explained as Cherry followed me into my apartment.

"I know you've seen him at his worst since you've been here, but he's usually a really great guy. My sister ruined that man, but I don't think the damage is permanent."

"That might be true, but..." I hesitated, not wanting to overstep.

"But?"

"I don't see Chastity being a good fit with him. Maybe he saw things there that really weren't. I don't think it's really terribly fair that everyone keeps blaming your sister. He needs to acknowledge his part in their relationship disaster, too."

Cherry smiled brightly at me. "I think you're the only person who has seen it from that perspective."

"Well, I got a pretty rude awakening with my own situation." I'm sure she didn't mean it, but the look of pity on Cherry's face almost made me stop talking. I managed to keep going, though. "Everyone drilled it into my head, my whole life, that Blaze was meant to be mine. I believed it, especially when he made me his in just about every way, except the legally binding one. Come to find out, I wasn't all that to him. I was a club obligation, not a love interest."

"I'm sure he loved you, too. How could he not?"

"Any person who would cheat on another doesn't love or respect them. If they did, they would never hurt them that way. It's not just about the physical cheating. It's about the emotional stuff with another, the sharing of things that were meant to be for you only. It's about all the lies that keep piling up. It's the way you crumble inside, forget how to trust people - and worse, yourself. The way you'll over analyze the actions of the next person you're in a relationship with because you don't want to miss all those things that you should seen the cheater." Cherry's eyes brimmed with tears as I spoke.

"Sure, ending things first will still hurt, but then at least their future isn't clouded with mistrust and betrayal. That's where the respect comes in. You might not love them, but at least respect the fact that they gave a piece of themselves to you. Even if you don't want what they have to give any longer, let them move on without all the extra shit that will keep them from being whole." We both sat quietly after my little tangent and just let the sentiment simmer there.

"He was willing to give me up – knowing we'd been trying to make a baby – all because some whore lied to him and said he already made one with her." A shiver ran through me at the horrible memory of sitting in that café that day. "There's no way he loved me if he was willing to do that."

"Maybe you need to talk to him and hear him out?" she questioned. "He is your baby's father, even if you hate him right now."

"I gave them all time and they still betrayed me. I can't trust any of them. Not anymore. And I won't go back to live some obligatory half-life with a man who I know doesn't love me, and maybe never did." A knock on my door halted any further talk on the subject.

"I'll get it," Cherry said as she jumped up too quickly. I was sure she wanted to say more about everything, but ended up taking the out she was offered instead. "It's probably Spinner letting me know he's back and not in jail." She laughed as she said it before turning her head back over her shoulder to look at me again. "Thank you, again, for running interference for the boys."

I waved away her thanks, only to be stunned stupid when she opened the door and Rabbit breezed in carrying several plastic grocery bags.

"What is all that?"

Rabbit grinned as he made his way to my freezer. "All of

this," he said as he jiggled the bags. Rabbit was interrupted from further explaining, though, as his brother took over.

"That would be every flavor of ice cream we could find in pint size containers," Spinner answered, clearly exasperated with his brother.

Cherry giggled. "That was a sweet gesture," she announced. The twinkle in her eyes told me she was about to try to play matchmaker, damn it. I'd have to find a way to nip that in the bud.

"Why do I suddenly have more flavors of ice cream than can fit in my freezer?"

Rabbit popped his head back around the side of the open freezer door so he could see me. "What you did today was epic and deserved a reward."

"I didn't really do much," I insisted.

"Sure you did," Spinner supplied, unhelpfully, as he threw a wink at me while I glared at him.

"You cried on cue! You talked about your cravings and how we're married. How is all of that nothing?"

"You cried on cue?" Cherry chuckled.

"Only a little," I said as I threw her a quick shake of my head. I knew what she was hoping for.

"You lied to the police?" Her question was accompanied by over-exaggerated bug eyes.

"Yeah. So? It's not really a crime."

"I think it is, but don't worry, we'll make it official and then you can't get into trouble," Rabbit called out while his head was stuck in my freezer, moving things around to try to fit all the ice cream he purchased.

"What?" It was my turn to shriek.

Rabbit dropped the pint of Cherry Garcia in his hand as he doubled over with laughter at my reaction. "Now, you know how it felt trying to keep a straight face as you spun your web of lies to the Po-Po!"

"Noted! Next time, leave the dumb-ass bikers to their own devices. I'm sure you could have talked your way out of those handcuffs in no time."

"I would have-" he started to say when Spinner cut him off.

"You would have had both of our asses hauled off to jail if not for Myra's little interference. Thank you for that, but the way." Spinner told me as he turned his attention from his brother to me. Then he moved to Cherry. "Come on, let's leave them to it. I need a nap and it requires your presence."

Cherry giggled at her man. "Yes, sir!" came out of her mouth in sharp response to a smacking sound. I glanced back to Rabbit to see the horrified expression on his face just before we both started laughing.

"Does he tie you up and spank you?" The question came tumbling out of my mouth before I could pull it back. Rabbit then smacked my ass.

"Hey! That was my question! No stealing the good stuff."

"I'm not telling," Cherry called out just before Spinner popped her ass again, and all but dragged her down the steps before the door was even able to shut behind them.

"Well, that's a side of my brother I never really wanted to know about," Rabbit mumbled.

"I'm still kind of in shock," I muttered.

"Come here," Rabbit ordered gently as he grabbed hold of my hand and guided me toward the couch. "Take a load off.

Which flavor do you want to start with? I really did get them all."

"Mint chip?" I asked.

"As you wish," was his response.

"Okay Wesley," I joked, thinking of The Princess Bride, and wondering if he would even get it.

"Ah, she knows the classics!" Rabbit grabbed a spoon, the ice cream, and made his way back to me. "Maybe you are the perfect woman." His declaration made my heart leap, stutter, and then kick into overdrive. My brain was confused though because we used to hate him. He was mean to us – my brain and my heart. What the hell did it mean that I was starting to crush on the man, or that the little glimpses of the good man everyone else told me about were starting to have their effect on me?

It took me a minute, but I was finally able to get out a response. "Hardly," I scoffed, though there was no sincerity behind the effort.

"Definitely," he reassured me.

"If I was the perfect woman, I wouldn't be doing all this alone," I mentioned off-handedly while rubbing my belly.

"First, I already told you that you're not doing that alone. I'll be there with you for all of your appointments."

"Why?"

"Hush now! We're getting off topic. As to the rest, I never said you were perfect for everyone or that anyone else is right for you. Just that you're the perfect woman..." he winked at me and then added, "for me. That also makes me lucky."

Rabbit sat down beside me on the couch, plopped the

spoon into the ice cream, and then proceeded to feed me a spoonful at a time. Never mind my confusion over his surprising declaration, I was spellbound by the fact that the man was feeding me ice cream.

"Are you feeling all right?" I asked, thinking maybe something was wrong with him and he forgot that he didn't really like me all that much.

"I feel better than I have in a long time," he told me. "So, what's next?"

"What do you mean?"

"You passed your test, what's next? Do you have somewhere in mind where you want to work?"

"I do. Doc was sweet enough to give me references with a few doctor's offices in Spearfish. A couple are general, family practices and one pediatric. I'm hoping I'll be able to walk into a job with one of them." We were quiet after that until I signaled I didn't want any more ice cream, then Rabbit glanced down at his phone, stood, and told me he had to go. I felt like I'd been put in the dryer to tumble through a mess of emotions. Rabbit was a rollercoaster, and while I wouldn't mind riding him like one, I knew I had to guard my heart because there didn't appear to be a safety harness on that ride.

18. RABBIT

<small>MY THOUGHTS WERE ON ONE THING, OR RATHER ONE PERSON.</small> "I think the more I hang around Myra, the more addicted I am to her presence."

"Did you really just say that? Out loud?" Rage asked me. I nodded my head and gave him the dopiest, most lovesick grin I could conjure.

"Charlie, let's go! Rabbit grew a pussy and I'm not feeling safe in my manhood right now."

"Funny!" I deadpanned.

"Just fucking tell her that you're interested already,."

"It's not that easy," I told him quietly.

"Why not?"

"She's pregnant."

"Does that bother you?" Rage asked, eyebrows raised in question.

"Of course not."

"So, you'll happily raise some other man's child? What if

he comes back into her life and you're relegated to being the stepdad only?"

"Then I'd be the best fucking stepdad ever. Whatever is best for Myra and her baby."

"Then I'm not seeing the problem here, man."

"The problem is that she's been with exactly one man her whole life, she's having his baby, and he broke her heart. The asshole might not have felt the same, but for her – he was her one true love. The one she was supposed to get eternity with. I don't think she's ready to move on and have someone else in her life. Shit! What if she's never ready?" I asked after I realized that might be an issue.

"Yup, I was right. You grew a fuckin' pussy! Go get your woman, she'll be ready when you show her that you are, too."

"Rage, normally you're a horrible advice giver, but this time I agree." That was from my traitorous best friend who managed to sneak up on me as I sulked over my drink about the possibility of Myra never being ready.

"You're just saying that so he doesn't make you go without the dick," I told Charlie, deflecting.

She shrugged and laughed as Rage threw her over his shoulder and smacked her ass. "This is how you claim your woman!" Rage roared out a taunt.

"Except maybe gentler, since she's with child," Charlie added helpfully as Rage took the steps two at a time as she bounced with the movements while draped across his shoulder.

"Could I?" I wondered out loud.

"Could you what?" Spinner asked as he walked up. His sudden appearance startled me. I needed to get my head out of the clouds so I was more aware of my surroundings.

19. MYRA

There was a permanent smile plastered to my face. I got the job. Not only did I get it, but it was the one that I really wanted. Granted, I probably should have been gunning for the position at the pediatrician's office, because with a baby on the way, that might have been more helpful to me. However, I'd always wanted to just work with a general practitioner and soak up as much knowledge as I possibly could.

To say that I was shocked to have Rabbit show up and take me out for a celebratory lunch on my first day, would be an understatement. "What are you doing here?"

"You should be celebrating, and I wanted to take you guys out to lunch."

I glanced around, looking for the other person and wondering if Cherry or Charlie had come with him.

"What are you looking for?"

"You said, 'you guys,' I was just trying to see who else was here."

Rabbit chuckled as he pointed to my abdomen. "I meant you and your belly." I gasped, eyes going wide, at the audacity of a man to assume my belly had grown so large that it was its own entity. His laughter moved from a chuckle to a deep, full-on laugh that ignited something inside of me. He swept his hair back off his shoulders and tied it off into a low man bun at the nape of his neck while he got himself back together. "Come on, cranky pants, let's get you some food."

"You know, you're not supposed to tell a woman she's fat, even if she is pregnant."

"I never said you were fat, you assumed that's what I was implying. I was talking about the little bun you're baking in that oven. It needs to be fed, right?"

"Somehow, I feel like you just keep opening your mouth and inserting your own foot."

Rabbit glanced down with a sly grin on his face. "Nah, they're too big to fit, and besides, I think you secretly like it when I torment you." He reached over, bopped me on the nose with his fingertip, and then grabbed my hand and gently guided me around the icy patches to his truck. "You have an hour, right?"

"Yes," I managed to get out before he hefted me into the passenger seat, reached across to buckle me in, and then made sure all my parts were safely tucked away before shutting the door and rounding the front of the truck. I watched him with interest as he did so. His movements were so self-assured, and his smile blindingly bright as he caught me watching him.

"You having any special cravings right now?" Rabbit asked as he started his truck.

"No, I could go for pretty much anything."

"Good, then I know the perfect place. They're quick so that you won't be late getting back, but damn the food is sublime, even if it is fast."

Part of me wanted to know why he was being so nice to me, but then the other part – the one that remembered our kiss from that one night at the bar – told the nosy bitch-half of me to shut the hell up and enjoy it.

"Thank you for thinking of me," I told him instead of questioning it.

He glanced over at me, then immediately put his eyes back on the road. Granted, by the time he did that, we were pulling into the parking lot of a little restaurant anyway. As it turned out, the place was literally one mile from the office I worked in. He put the truck in park and then turned to me.

"You should never have to thank someone for thinking of you. The fact that you did just told me more about the people you had in your life before than anything else I've heard about them. I wanted to do something nice for you because I like you and the person you are is deserving of nice things. End of story. No ulterior motives and definitely no thanks needed."

I didn't know what to say to that. Where I came from, it hadn't been normal for someone to put me first, to think of me, and do something nice just because they thought I deserved it. Once again, I found myself split in two emotionally. There was the younger girl inside who wanted to cry for the life she'd settled for, and then there was the new me who was elated that someone was showing me the difference and I was starting to understand.

Our lunch was casual, fun, delicious, and over far too quickly. Rabbit got me back to work with five minutes to spare and earned a bunch of envious stares from my new coworkers. None of them actually said anything to me about him, though. I guess it was because they didn't know me well enough to be nosy yet. I'm sure the newness would wear off soon and those boundaries would disappear. Then again, maybe not.

Despite working at both the doctor's office and Renegade Rosy's, I didn't see Rabbit again all week. Christmas was steadily closing in on us, and I started thinking about what I wanted to do this year. Obviously, I couldn't go home, but there was also no way inviting myself to someone's party or home sounded good. It was mid-week when I was picking up a shift for the normal bartender at Rosy's that my idea formed.

"I don't really have anywhere to go either," I heard Sapphire telling another girl. "I guess that's what happens when you come from a shit show of a family.

"Do you guys maybe want to get together and have our own Christmas dinner? We can gather all the people between here and the MC, or any other friends you might have, who are the same as us with no family to go home to."

Sapphire's head tipped to the side as she took me in with a puzzled look on her face. "How is it that you have nowhere to go?"

I shrugged my shoulders. "Because I don't. You guys

know that my family are all far away and that I disowned them, right?"

"Sorry, I just thought..." I waited for her to finish that statement, but she didn't because Twilight, another dancer, jabbed her in the ribs with her elbow.

"It would be a fabulous idea for us to all get together and have a dinner of our own. Hopefully, some of us can cook. The rest of us," she pointed to herself, "can bring something store bought." I laughed with her as she said that.

"I can cook. Maybe Spinner will let us use Rosy's one afternoon next week?"

"As long as it's early enough that we can clean up and get the place up and running again before we open."

"They're not shutting the place down for Christmas?" I asked, having not looked at the schedule.

"Honey," Sapphire drawled out. "The holidays are some of our busiest days. Lots of lonely men out there don't have families and they come here so they don't have to feel so alone."

"They also tend to be way more generous than usual, so we don't mind working. Besides, what else are we going to do? Like you said, none of us have families to go home to."

"I guess. It just all seems so..." The words trailed off as I tried to think of a way to make sure everyone got a little Christmas cheer, even if some of us would be working the actual holiday.

My phone dinged with an incoming text, so I took that opportunity to go tuck my things into my locker.

Rabbit: Haven't heard from you. How's everything going?

Myra: All good. About to start work.

Rabbit: Thought you got off earlier?

Myra: At Rosy's now.

Rabbit: We need to talk about that. You just worked a whole shift. Who the hell scheduled you with a shift at Rosy's, too?

Myra: No one. I'm covering for someone tonight.

My phone stayed quiet after that. I guess that was all he needed to hear, that I was here because I wanted to be, not because of a scheduling issue. Spinner came by about two hours into my shift and headed right for me. He smiled, although it was a rather grim version of his usual, and then he spoke. "Get out of here, Myra. Go get off your feet and get some rest."

"What? Why? I'm fine," I countered.

"Nuh-uh. You worked eight hours at the office, you don't need to come in here now and work all night, too. I know you need the extra cash, but you also have to take care of yourself, for that baby."

Well, that made me feel bad. "There was no one else," I tried to tell him.

"Not true, there's me. I would have covered, and they

should have called me immediately, instead of offering the hours to you."

"Oh." The word slipped out as I turned around, and started the process of cashing out for the night.

"Myra, we're looking out for you, that's all. This isn't a reflection on you or your work ethic. Hell, I wish all of our employees were more like you."

"No, it's okay. I get it."

I didn't, though. Something told me that if there was another woman here who was pregnant, they wouldn't be as concerned with the hours she was working. Not that I thought they would take advantage and overwork her either, but if someone else needed the money and wanted to work, they'd be on the schedule. I didn't know whether to thank them or cry about my bad luck. As I moved to the back rooms and opened my locker, I decided that thanks was in order because my feet were beginning to ache right along with my back and legs.

When I got home, Cherry was coming out of my apartment. Not that I didn't mind Cherry being there, or that I had anything to hide, but that was a bit disconcerting when I didn't know it was happening. She immediately held her hands up to me and smiled.

"You'll see why I was there without letting you know. I hope you don't mind, once you do. It was supposed to be a surprise."

"A surprise?"

"Yeah, Rabbit said you were going to come home super tired and probably end up falling right out, so he asked me to stop over and take care of a few things for you."

"Rabbit?" I asked. Then, "A few things?"

She winked at me and then moved out of my way so I could go in. "You'll see." Cherry didn't follow me in, though. Instead she closed the door and yelled, "Lock it! Oh, and he'll be back by Christmas dinner."

I had planned on inviting Rabbit to the misfit Christmas that we planned to have at the bar, but I honestly forgot that he actually did have family here who he would be spending the holiday with. Cherry had just given me a great reminder, because I didn't want him to feel torn on where he needed to be, but more importantly, I didn't need to feel left out when he inevitably chose family over my invitation. Make no mistake, he should choose them over me, but that didn't mean it still wouldn't feel bad on my end.

Once I locked the door, the first thing that hit me was the dim lighting, then the second thing was the sticky notes. The first one, the biggest – as it was an actual sheet of paper – said:

> *Please, don't be mad at Cherry, but I thought it was better than me invading your space!*
> *Xo,*
> *Rabbit*

I moved to the next one that was on the counter.

> *You work too hard. Get your ass to the bath-room for some R&R.*

"You want me to go to the bathroom for rest and relaxation?" I questioned out loud as if Rabbit was there and could hear me. Still, I grabbed the sticky note and headed in that direction. That's when my eyes grew misty. The tub was full of bubbles and there was a glass with ice and juice in it sitting on the ledge. The radio was playing some alternative blues, which happened to be my favorite music to listen to when I had a moment just to kick back and let it all go. There was another sticky note, too.

> *Set a timer on your phone so you don't fall asleep in there. When you're done, grab some ice cream from the freezer, get in bed, and watch a movie until you fall asleep. Tomorrow is Saturday, and you have the whole day off.*
> *Enjoy it!*

He didn't sign that note. There were just a pair of bunny ears at the bottom of the paper. I ducked my head back out of the bathroom, though, because when I left that morning, there hadn't been a television in the bedroom area of the apartment. There was a small one out in the living room, but I almost never had time to watch it. When I glanced in the bedroom, there was a brand new television mounted to the wall across from my bed.

What in the world? Did Rabbit buy me a TV?

I quickly drew a different conclusion, that Cherry probably had one brought in for the apartment because there was no way Rabbit purchased a whole television for me. I quickly put it out of my mind and followed his notes to the letter. I didn't stay in the tub too long because I felt myself drifting a few times, and then once the ice cream was gone, and my relaxation coma was about to take me under, I reached for my phone and texted him.

Myra: Thank you. I needed that.

Rabbit: Sleep well, sweet momma!

That's just what I did.

20. RABBIT

My trip to Tallahassee ran a whole fuck of a lot longer than I had hoped. It meant barely making it back in time for Christmas. I hadn't asked Myra to join us because I honestly wasn't sure if things would work out with me getting there in time. Truth be told, though, I figured Cherry and Spinner would have her covered anyway. Then if I made it, that would end up being a bonus for both of us since we'd be at the same place together again, finally. I wished more than anything I could have been there the day that Cherry set up Myra's surprise night in at her apartment for me. If I could have been there to make sure she was catered to, I would have. Somehow, I didn't think Myra was ready for that yet, though. I knew that there was still work I needed to do, especially after my behavior when we'd first met.

"Glad you could join us," my brother said when I first walked through their door an hour before Christmas dinner was supposed to start. I hadn't seen The Beast outside when

I pulled up, so I wondered if they had sent Myra to go get something.

"Where's Myra?"

Cherry's head shot up from where she'd been peeking inside the oven. "What did you just say?"

"I asked where Myra is. I didn't see her truck out there," I hitched my thumb over my shoulder indicating the parking area beside Spinner's garage where she usually kept it.

Cherry turned a sorrowful face to Spinner who looked a little shocked himself. "I'm a horrible friend," she mumbled to him.

"No, you're not."

"What's going on?" I glanced back-and-forth between the two of them and then it dawned on me. "She has no family to go home to and neither of you thought to invite her to Christmas dinner?"

"Apparently, you didn't extend an invite either," my brother pointed out.

"I didn't think I would make it back in time and figured the two of you would have it covered since she basically lives in throwing distance of your house." Okay, so my voice was a little louder than it should have been. Still, worry had set in as I wondered where she could be and if she was all right.

I called Charlie. "Rabbit? Merry Christmas," was how she answered the phone.

"Yeah, to you too, Charlie. Hey, is Myra by any chance with you today?"

"Noooo," she drew out the word almost as if she was toying with it being a statement or a question. "We went to visit my aunt for Christmas this year. I would have told you goodbye, but you were already off on club business before we left."

"Shit, okay," I got ready to hang up when Charlie spoke again.

"Did you try calling her?"

"I'm doing that now," I told her and hung up before I could hear my best friend tell me how stupid I was to not attempt that from the beginning.

> Rabbit: Are you okay?

> Myra: Of course, I am. Are you?

> Rabbit: You're not here.

> Myra: Where is 'here'?

> Rabbit: Cherry and Spinner's place. Christmas dinner.

> Myra: Oh.

> Rabbit: "What does 'Oh' mean?

> Myra: It means I don't just show up uninvited, plus we're having Misfit's Christmas at the bar right now.

> Rabbit: Misfit's Christmas?

> Myra: Yeah, Christmas dinner for everyone who had nowhere else to go.

"FUCK!" I groaned as I tossed the phone to the counter in

front of me and reached up to push the hair back out of my face that had fallen free of the ponytail I'd had it in.

"What's going on?" Cherry asked as she swiped the tears from her eyes. "Rabbit, I'm so sorry. I thought one of you would have invited her, and honestly, I didn't think she needed an invite. We're her family now."

"Her last family let her down completely. You think she's showing up anywhere without an invite now?" I asked. Then I turned my attention to Spinner. "Did you know about the Christmas dinner they're having at the bar?"

"Oh, shit! I forgot that Myra asked if they could all use it for some sort of pot luck this week, before opening hours." He realized what that meant, in that moment, and swiped his hands down his face. "I didn't even..." he started to say and then turned to his woman. "Sorry, I let both of you down."

"I'm going over there." I glanced around at all the work Cherry had put into her own Christmas dinner. "I hope you won't miss me here, but she shouldn't have to think of herself as one of the misfits who got left out of Christmas."

"Oh God! Is that what she said?"

"Not in so many words. She literally called it Misfit Christmas, though, for all the people who didn't have anywhere else to go."

"Wait for us," she told me as she leaned over, turned the oven off, and started packing things up. "You can help me get everything over there."

"You don't have to," I told her.

"Are you kidding? I feel like such an asshole for not realizing she hadn't been invited and for not doing the damn inviting myself."

"I feel like a bigger asshole," my brother told me as he looked me right in the eye. "Not once have we ever thought about what all the dancers, club girls, and even our prospects and club brothers who don't have family have been doing at the holidays. We just went about our usual celebrations with one another."

"One thing at a time, Brother. I feel you on that, but right now, I'm only worried about one person."

21. MYRA

A<small>FTER</small> R<small>ABBIT</small> <small>EXPLAINED HOW UPSET HE HAD BEEN TO KNOW THAT</small> I had never been extended a formal invitation to Christmas Dinner at the Hastings' home, I felt kind of bad for not telling them about my Misfits Dinner plans sooner. The thought that I had caused any of them even the smallest bit of heartache over being worried for me, hit hard. After they all crashed the party the rest of the misfits and I had, I hadn't really seen any of them. It had been three days already, but that didn't mean Rabbit hadn't been in communication with me. I got texts from him several times a day. He had to travel down to Charleston the day after Christmas to go deal with some problem they were having getting Renegade Rosy's – Charleston established.

It was why I almost said no when my doctor's office called and asked if I would take an earlier appointment instead of the one I originally had on the 30th. I knew Rabbit said that he would be there for my appointments, but I was sure he only meant if he wasn't busy and definitely not if he was out of town. I figured a courtesy text was necessary though so that he wouldn't rush back from Charleston just to make that appointment only to find out that I'd already been.

> Myra: My appointment changed. It's today, 4:30pm.

> Rabbit: Be there to pick you up at 3:45. You at home or work?

> Myra: Home.

> Rabbit: Good, be ready early and we'll grab a late lunch on the way.

> Myra: Ok. Thought you were out of town?

> Rabbit: Nope.

Well, damn. The man honestly made my head spin sometimes. Granted, he had done a 180 with his personality in the past two months, but I still didn't know if I could trust the change. I wanted to. So, I hurriedly got dressed in some nicer sweatpants which were the only things I owned that felt comfortable anymore besides the scrubs I wore to work. I couldn't see spending a fortune on clothing I'd only wear for a couple of months during the pregnancy.

When Rabbit showed up, he was dressed in newish looking black jeans, a button-up, collared shirt, and he had his normally shoulder length dark blond hair pulled back toward the nape of his neck in a sexy as fuck, modified man bun. It rode so low on his head because the crazy bastard wore something akin to the a bowler-style hat. It was the same hat he'd worn during his little strip tease dance. That started me rambling to him right away, which was weird because I usually only rambled if I was really nervous.

"Did you know those hats were produced because they literally fought their way into existence?" I asked. Rabbit reached up and touched his hat.

"Um, I think the question is how do you know that?"

"I had to research it for a school thing. Well, I didn't. A friend of mine had to do a research project on hats and head-wear for a Trends and Concepts course." He looked puzzled so I continued to ramble. "She was going to school for fashion design. She bakes cupcakes and slings coffee now with that degree," I added needlessly.

What the hell was wrong with me?

"Okay, then," he hesitated. "I'm not sure I want to know how a hat fought, but it seems only logical to ask the question now. So, how did a hat fight?"

"Men used to wear top hats that bumped into low-hanging tree branches and poles which knocked the hats off their heads. So, the bowler hat was created to keep the hats from having to fight to stay on, but also to protect the men's heads from taking the beatings." I raised my fists and mimed throwing several jabs his way. "Get it now?"

Rabbit stood there stunned as he sucked his lips in and tucked them around his teeth to keep from laughing at me. Make no mistake, he definitely wasn't trying to keep from laughing with me. The bastard. I sighed as he gave me a once over.

"Did you still need time to get dressed?" he asked as he glanced at the watch held to his wrist by a thick leather band.

I glanced down at myself, realizing that I appeared underdressed in comparison. "I'm dressed," I puffed out, feeling a bit dejected.

"Right," he offered as he clapped his hands together. "And, might I add, you certainly look radiant in those sweats, Miss Myra." The grin on his face could have meant he was making fun of me or that I really didn't look that bad. I was going to go with the latter and hope for the best, even as I knew better. Maybe one or two maternity pants wouldn't kill me? I'd think on it.

I reached down and tugged lightly on the baggy pants. "I didn't want to waste money on pants that will only be worn for a few months at most," I shrugged out my explanation.

"Why not? If you're hurting for money-" he started to say, but I interrupted because there was no way he was going to offer me money again.

"No. I have plenty. I just don't see the need to buy pants specifically aimed at women who will only wear them for such a short amount of time." Yeah, it was redundant. He didn't need to know that I was always worried that I wouldn't have a job to come back to after maternity leave, or that no one would hire me knowing I had a new baby at home. He also didn't need to know that daycare was going to cost a lot and that I had to put aside part of all my paychecks now so that I would have enough later. Money might get tight, despite my rainy day fund I'd been shuffling savings into since I was 14-years-old.

"But the baby needs the extra room," he reasoned.

"Don't hit me with the baby guilt, mister. I still have a thousand and one things to buy for the baby, which is another reason to save money on the pants now. Babies are these teeny, tiny little creatures, but their stuff costs so much money. You'd think that I was birthing a giant who needed upgraded sizes and materials. Nope, just a wee babe and a blown budget." Okay, Rabbit had the crazy, wild-eyed stare going on, so that was me going off on another tangent again. Ugh!

Rabbit broke his crazy-man routine long enough to laugh.

"Sorry for my rambling," I muttered.

"Don't apologize. I happen to enjoy your little mommy tirades. Honestly, they give me more insight than a normal conversation," he admitted. I wasn't sure that was such a good thing. "Been meaning to ask, though, I thought you were seeing Doc for all your baby stuff? Why did that change?"

"He saw me when I first got here and then referred me to an OB/GYN he trusted. I didn't have insurance, so he also made sure it was someone who would give me a deal on cash transactions."

"You need insurance?"

"Once my 90-day probationary period at work is over, I'll have it."

"But how are you able to afford all the visits you've been to so far?"

"I had a little savings tucked aside," I shrugged my shoulders, a little uncomfortable talking about it since it was something I had never agreed with my mother about doing. I thought I'd surprise Blaze one day and have the down payment to a house instead of the condo we lived in. Little did I know, it came in very handy, and once I was able, there would be another rainy day savings plan started.

"A little savings," Rabbit murmured while I was planning just when I'd be able to actually start saving again. "We'll fix that later," he mentioned, bringing my attention back to the here and now. I wasn't sure what he meant by that and truthfully, it didn't matter.

"What happens at your appointment today?"

"What do you mean? It's a normal appointment."

"When do you get to do the fun stuff, like find out the gender?"

That question made me want to cry and set my cheeks aflame with embarrassment. "I don't know."

"What do you mean, 'I don't know'? Aren't all expectant moms chomping at the bit to see their little ones swimming around in their bellies?" I could tell by his teasing tone that he meant no harm. Unfortunately, our earlier conversation about my lack of insurance, dwindling savings, and expensive baby stuff tasted far more bitter on my tongue.

"I can't afford frivolities," I stated rather awkwardly. For most women, an ultrasound wasn't considered frivolous.

"Frivolities?" he parroted while also turning the one word into a question. "But they use those things to determine growth, if there are any potential problems, and-"

"And I still can only afford the basics."

"What about getting aid until your insurance kicks in?"

"Government aid can be tracked, so can the insurance

that I'm still on through my father, which would disqualify me from obtaining aid anyway," I informed him. I was in full-on, arms crossed over my chest, lip poked out, defensive pout mode. Rabbit seemed incapable of speaking after that, so I just continued to watch the scenery through the windows.

When we got to the doctor's office, I had to pee like crazy, so I ran off for the bathroom with a nurse since they always asked for a urine sample. I left Rabbit to wait in the lounge with all the other women and expectant parents.

When I returned to the waiting area, Rabbit was holding a toddler for what appeared to be a very frazzled new mom. She tried to find a pacifier that would stop the tiny little baby wailing noises coming from the car seat on the floor by her feet. Rabbit looked like a natural as he played with the little boy, keeping him busy while the mother took care of her youngest.

"Thank you so much," the woman finally said while looking up to Rabbit with relief and so much gratefulness shining from her tired smile. I sat on his other side without a word.

"Everything come out all right?" he teased.

"You try growing a baby inside you who uses your bladder as a trampoline, and see how badly you have to pee after 45-minutes in a car, lunch, and drinks during lunch."

"Baby bladder is the worst," the woman chimed in. Then she glanced between Rabbit and me before speaking again. "It looks like you have a good one helping you out, though. Don't ever let him go." I could see a cloud of sadness threatening to swamp the woman, so I looked away to give her a moment to collect herself.

"Where is your man?" Rabbit asked, rather insensitively.

"One was enough for him." She replied as she tipped her head toward the toddler in Rabbit's lap. "Two was too much. When he found out I was pregnant again, he took off."

"That's horrible!" I gaped at her and wanted to go maim the idiot on her behalf. "I'm so sorry you had to go through that." I reached in my purse and took out a piece of paper, wrote my number on it, and handed it to her. "If you ever need help, want to talk, or blow off some steam, give me a call. Us single moms have to stick together."

"Oh! I thought," the woman glanced at Rabbit again and then back at me. The question in her eyes was clear, but I already knew what she thought.

"He's a friend," I explained. Although, Rabbit did not seem happy with my explanation at all. He didn't refute my claim, but the tension in his muscles and stiffness with which he held himself after I made the clarification were all-too noticeable.

It wasn't long after that when my name was called. I felt Rabbit jolt, as if he were going to get up and follow me, but held himself back. It made me wonder if he was curious about what happened at these appointments. "Did you want to come back?" I asked him. His response was to jump up from his seat immediately as he nodded his head frantically at me. In that moment, the man seemed more excited puppy dog than his namesake animal.

Once my weight was done and we were taken into the room, I almost cried. The ultrasound machine was sitting there as if to taunt me with what I couldn't have. My heart hurt just thinking about it. It was cruel for them to put me in a room with the machine when they knew I couldn't afford to have the scan done. We sat there silently, waiting for the doctor to come in and see us until Rabbit finally broke the silence.

"Don't you have to get undressed and wear one of those paper gowns that your ass hangs out of?"

I laughed. It was actually a pretty apt description. "I don't think so. The nurse didn't tell me to do that when I came in."

"Wait, so you don't know on any given visit if he's going down to the promised land to check on the harvest or if you're just going to chat?"

I lost it. Never in my life had I heard someone describe a visit with a woman's doctor quite like that. A swift knock was followed immediately by the doctor and a nurse entering the room looking thoroughly amused by my laughter.

"Now, there's a sight!" he called out before turning to Rabbit. "I don't know what you're doing, but keep it up. This one needs more laughter in life."

Aww.

The nurse gave a sly grin to Rabbit, though. "Do we want to know what she was laughing about?"

Rabbit wasn't paying her any attention. "No clue," he mumbled quickly while watching the doctor set up the ultrasound machine.

What in the world?

"Dr. Murphy?" I questioned. He was too busy fiddling

with things to acknowledge me, though. "I think you might be confused about what we're doing today," I tacked on.

He glanced down at the chart in his hands then smiled up at me. "Nope. No confusion. We're going to get a look at your little one today and if the baby cooperates, we'll be able to determine the gender, too."

I wanted that so badly. This was a horrible tease. There wasn't an extra $250 for this, which is what they quoted me without insurance cost.

"If you could pull the waistband of your pants and underwear down and your shirt up, we'll get started." Dr. Murphy directed me as he turned my way with the transducer gel in his hand. The tears flowed, whether I wanted them to or not.

"Stop!" I blubbered as I started to hyperventilate, afraid I'd be charged for them going this far. "I can't do this."

"Myra," Rabbit tried quietly.

"No. I can't do this. It's not in my budget. I'm sorry. I know you think it's important," I said while switching my focus from Rabbit to the doctor. "I just can't."

"It's already paid for," Rabbit explained.

"What? How?"

"Don't overthink it. We'll call this your belated Christmas present," Rabbit said to me as he leaned over and placed a kiss on my forehead. What was it about those damnable forehead kisses that always melted my heart? Not that I'd ever experienced it before. It was something I'd started reading about in Charlie's books when she introduced me to audiobooks and the ability to "read" while driving.

I jumped when the gel hit my belly after I rolled my pants down, my shirt up, and exposed my growing belly to everyone in the room. "Sorry it's a little chilly since we didn't have it set up in the warmer ahead of time."

"I'm not complaining," I told the doctor as the image on the screen came to life and I could actually recognize little hands raised into fits in the air. We watched as one of them shot forward and punched me, but the amazing thing was I could have sworn I felt it, too.

"Did we just watch you get punched from the inside?" Rabbit asked, his voice sheer awe. I simply nodded, unable to look away from the screen or speak.

"Looks like we'll have a great view of what's going on down there, did you want to know the gender?"

"Yes," I whispered. Rabbit reached over and took hold of my hand, offering a squeeze.

"Do you have guesses before I drop this news in your laps?"

"Boy," I said at the same time Rabbit all but yelled, "Girl!"

Dr. Murphy chuckled at us, then he zoomed the little wand around my belly, pushed harder, and there it was. I knew immediately. "I was right." The doctor tipped his head and grinned at me.

"I forgot you were a nurse. Makes it easier and harder to do these things sometimes. No surprises when you mostly know what you're looking for."

I smiled at him. While Rabbit squeezed my hand a little harder. "Wait? Does that mean it's a boy?"

"That right there," Dr. Murphy showed him on the screen, "means he is definitely a boy."

"Definitely, huh?" Rabbit murmured before staring straight at my belly instead of the screen. "Way to go baby boy Chase. Already showing off your big man status."

"Oh my God!" I groaned but couldn't help when the sound bled into laughter. Dr. Murphy's shoulder shook as he tried not to laugh at Rabbit, too. My doctor was right. The man at my side was good for my soul. He was responsible for every time I'd been able to let go of my sadness and give in to joy.

"Did you really just say that?" The nurse asked with a bit of an attitude. I didn't like her and wondered if I could request she wasn't here the next time. Dr. Murphy may have been feeling the same way since he threw her a look over his shoulder that basically said, 'Shut the hell up!'"

"Where did we have your due date set?" Dr. Murphy asked as he glanced at my chart.

"May 23rd."

"Yep," he stated as he turned back to the ultrasound and what he was doing there. "Growth looks right on par, so we're going to stick with that." The doc did some more scrolling across my belly, stopping, and clicking, and then he said, "Okay, that's about it for today. Did you have any questions?"

"Can you go back?" Rabbit asked.

"Go back?"

"Yeah, move it back just a little," he made a gesture with his hand like he was in charge of operating the magic wand that produced the images. Dr. Murphy smiled and humored Rabbit.

"Here?" He asked.

"A little further," Rabbit told him.

"Ah, I see," Dr. Murphy said, and then he put the wand a little further to the left, and we watched my son's heart beating out a fast, but steady rhythm.

"That's incredible," Rabbit murmured. Dr. Murphy gave us a moment longer to watch and then he shut the machine down.

"Sorry, I know it's hard to walk away from that connection."

"No. You have other people to see. Thank you," I told him as I swiped at the tear running down my face.

"We'll have a CD and some pictures waiting for you when you check out." I nodded, but couldn't say anything because I was a little bit too choked up. Being able to see my baby was everything. Watching Rabbit's reaction to the heartbeat was something else, though. If I hadn't already been developing feelings for the man, seeing that would have been a game changer for sure.

As we were leaving the office, I took one of the images they had given me and I handed it to Rabbit. "What's this for?"

"Consider it a belated Christmas gift," I told him, and then I pointed to the image. It was one of my son's heart. I wasn't sure if he would understand the deeper meaning there, but I was done fighting. If he wanted to be in our lives, he wouldn't hear me complain about it.

22. RABBIT

Shameless knocked on my door and came strolling right in, reminding me of the visit Myra and I had with her doctor the other day. I smiled up at him without thinking about it and the asshole preened for me.

"Quit batting your eyelashes at me, old man. That shit is not okay!"

He laughed, but it was quickly replaced with concern again. "That MC you told me to keep watch on?" Shameless asked.

"Yeah?"

"They're neck-deep in shit right now."

"What kind of shit?"

"Seems to be internal, but at least one death so far and maybe more. My guy is trying to get accurate info." I just stared at him for a moment. Then I asked the only pertinent question I had because I needed to know if Myra should be made aware.

"Who died?"

"Young guy. Name's Blaze."

"You're shitting me?" I jumped off the edge of the bed, where I'd been sitting before he came strolling in. Not that it did me any good. There really wasn't anything to do with the nervous energy that just shocked my system.

"No. Why? He important?"

I moved around Shameless and shut my bedroom door so that we could keep this information just between the two of us until Myra could be notified. Though, I had reservations about telling her. "That was the road name of Myra's baby's father."

"Shit. What are you going to do? You planning to tell her?"

"I don't know. What do I do? If she finds out I had them all watched, will she be pissed or thankful?"

"Didn't you say you got a visit from one of them that prompted you keeping an eye out?"

"Yeah. Phoenix came here once."

"Phoenix?" Shameless stepped back as his brows furrowed a little deeper, concern clear in his expression.

I nodded. "Why?"

"Far as I know, he's the internal problem they're having. Kid went crazy. Started killing, or threatening to kill, certain members of the club."

"Fuck! Do you think we need to get Myra on lockdown?"

"That depends," Shameless drew out lazily.

"On what exactly?"

"You claiming her as yours?" When I didn't answer, he continued. "You know the rules. You don't claim her, she doesn't get club protection."

"I'll claim her." My hesitation to answer hadn't been about me. Myra had been claimed by another MC member before, and I honestly didn't know if she would be okay with it happening again. We didn't really have time to play nice and get permissions here, though. Her life might be in danger, and the worst part was, Phoenix had been within my reach, and I'd let him walk right back out of here.

"Then I think you might want to get her locked down. Phoenix was last seen headed out of town with a woman on the back of his bike. Might be headed this way if that woman of yours is any kind of unfinished business for him." He was quiet a moment before hesitantly added the rest. "Or that baby, considering who the father was."

"He didn't seem interested in hurting her or letting anyone from his club know where she was."

"Could be hiding her to hurt them, but Rabbit, we don't know what tripped his trigger either."

"I'll get on it. Not sure she's gonna be thrilled, though."

"I think she'll cooperate just fine if you tell her the news."

I agreed and hated it all at the same time. Telling her would mean breaking her heart a little more than it had already been broken. Whether the asshole had fucked up and lost her for good or not, Myra had loved him and she was having his baby. Hearing the news that her kid's dad was dead was not going to be easy to take.

> Rabbit: Need to talk to you. It's important, can I come by after work?

I waited a good twenty minutes for a response, and then what I got made me feel even worse.

> Myra: I'm not sure I like the sound of that. The last person who told me we needed to talk ended up breaking up with me publicly when I was trying to tell him we were having a baby.

> Rabbit: I'm not breaking up with you.

I figured that would at least get her to smile.

> Myra: Kind of hard to do when we're not together.

"Oh! That's what you think," I mumbled out loud before texting her the time I'd be at her place and then I stuffed the cell phone in my back pocket and went to have a talk with Spinner. He and Cherry needed to know what was going on, too, so they wouldn't be blindsided by what was about to happen.

MYRA'S SUBURBAN was already in the drive when I arrived. Spinner ducked his head out of the house and gave me a nod, letting me know he had been keeping watch on her until I could get there. I had called him before I ever left my room at the clubhouse to fill him in. It was nice to see he took things as seriously as I did. Not that I expected anything less from my brother. I was still watching as he shut his door when I heard Myra.

"You coming in or are you and Spinner going to continue with the long-distance, heartfelt glances all evening?"

I shouldn't have grinned. This wasn't the time to think things were funny. She made it impossible not to, though. I moved up the steps and followed her inside, locking the door behind me as I went through her whole apartment checking windows and making sure everything was secure.

"I wasn't actually nervous before, but now the feeling that shit is about to hit the fan just became real."

"Sorry," I leaned in and kissed her on the cheek, not wanting to get too personal until I told her about what had to happen. "Let's have a seat, okay?"

"Rabbit," she started as one hip cocked to the side, her opposite brow arched, and her arms crossed under her tits.

Might I also point out that those tits had grown much larger since the first time I ogled them. Then she sighed and her shoulders sagged heavy, breasts fell slightly, and the attitude changed to defeated really quick.

"I really can't deal with the lead up for important conversations anymore. If you could just spit it out, that'd be great, because honestly, I don't have the energy."

I got up, crossed the room, took her into my arms, and sat my ass right back down on her couch with her on my lap. "I claimed you with my club today," I told her. "I wanted you to know that I had a specific reason to do it, otherwise this conversation would have come first, but I don't regret it, wouldn't change it, and it would have happened eventually anyway. Understand?"

"Um," she hesitated a moment, then looked me straight

in the eye. "Yeah, I do." She leaned in and kissed me on the cheek that time. "Thank you."

"That's it? You're not going to ask me why? And you're going to thank me?"

"Club princess," Myra stated quickly as she pointed at herself. "I know if you're claiming a girl you aren't dating its somehow for her protection, right?"

I nodded my head, because what other response was there to her being so accommodating, thankful, and not angry with me like most women would have been?

"Rabbit, thank you for thinking of my safety and for caring enough to make sure I'm protected. Now, if you don't mind, I'd love to know why that was necessary."

"I have some bad news for you," I admitted and then watched as she took another deep breath, let it out slowly and whispered a quick, "Okay." I started rubbing comforting circles over her back, trying to relax her a little. "I know which club you're from because it wasn't exactly hard to track down since I knew your hometown." Myra said nothing to that so that I once again gave her a look like, 'Really? You're not mad about that?'

"Club princess," she stated again. "I didn't think the Aces High would allow me so close to everyone and their businesses without doing a background check."

"Right. So, we got word today that there's something happening inside the Stoneridge Raiders MC, Oregon Chapter." Her body tightened on my lap and she sat a bit straighter. "One of the members has flipped his switch and killed at least one Raider. There were threats, about others, but we don't have conclusive information yet if anyone else was targeted specifically, injured, or killed."

"Who was killed?" she asked.

"Blaze," I whispered, but I swear the name sounded as loud as a bomb going off in a monastery full of monks who took a vow of silence.

"Blaze?" she asked after a moment, her hand automatically sliding over her belly as if it needed protection. "You're sure?" I nodded and pulled her closer so that her head rested on my shoulder. I held her there as her shoulders shook. "I never had any intention of going back to him, or having anything to do with..." Emotions clogged her words and she had to take a moment to settle herself before she could continue. "He ruined any possibility of there ever being an 'us' again, but I had hoped that one day my child could meet his father and know him. You know? I never would have wished for that to be impossible. I thought, maybe he'd grow up some, and be a better dad than he was a man to me."

"I think that's what every good mother would hope for." It was the truth. I can't imagine my own mother would have ever wanted us to go a minute without knowing our dad, but then again, she was so in love with the man that she literally couldn't live without him. "I'm so sorry, Myra. No matter what happened in the end of relationship, he still had a place in your heart."

"We grew up together, literally from diapers," she told me. "Before we were a couple, we were always friends." She hiccuped the words out, but then cleared her throat and continued. "We would have been better off staying just friends. Then, we would still have been in one another's life. Maybe he would still be alive?"

"Don't put that on your shoulders. If you'd never been more than friends with him, you wouldn't be here now." I slid my hand around her waist and touched her smallish baby bump. "You wouldn't have this little guy on the way."

"That's true."

"If you want to look at things like that, then take this from it. You were meant to be friends, and then more, so that this little dude could be made. Maybe that was Blaze's purpose on this Earth, to create this life you carry."

"Let's not put that on his shoulders either," Myra told me. She wasn't talking about Blaze, though. She meant the baby, and that just proved what a good mother she would be one day.

"Is there anything I can do?"

"You can hold me for a little while," Myra whispered into my neck. Her hot breath and the wispy reminder that her lips were only like a millimeter away from my skin, made me feel things that were entirely too inappropriate for the circumstances.

We sat there, with her on my lap, as I held her. This woman's strength was unbelievable already, but even holding her as she cried for a lost friend, one she had already suffered a loss for, I could feel it in her still. "Myra, do you want to call home? I can get you a phone that can't be traced."

She shook her head into my shoulder. "No. It's strange, and I know I'm sitting here crying all over you, but I've already lost them. A part of me has already cried for everything I thought was mine in the past, the people, and the relationships. When I left, I knew I'd never be back and so it was as though they had died. If I call, I'll be tempted to go back, to see them, to try again, and that's not something that interests me right now. Maybe never. I'm sure this makes them worry more for me, but truthfully, they had a their second chance to show their love, concern, and loyalty for me and they failed." She shrugged her shoulders.

"They fucked it up, even then?" I asked, even though I already knew the answer.

"Even then. I don't want to call home. Thank you for helping me to say goodbye one last time, though."

"Anything you need, Myra. I meant that when I said it."

"I'm starting to see that," she whispered. "Do I need to pack a bag?"

"Yeah, I'm going to need you to get to your things together, but not until you're ready."

"I'm good. How long should I pack for?"

It was my turn to shrug. "Indefinitely, and we'll go from there," I told her. "Myra, you never asked-"

"Is it important?"

"Phoenix," I told her.

"Phoenix did this?"

"Yeah."

"Then it must have been justified," she said without hesitation.

"Really? That quickly, you think a man who started killing his own club brothers must have been right to do it?"

"Yeah, I do. Of everyone there, Phoenix was the only one with a true moral compass. If someone was guilty of something, he didn't usually let them slide on shit. If it was questionable, he'd find out the truth before passing judgement. I'm not just saying that because he told me he didn't want to keep what happened a secret. I'm saying that because Phoenix would never betray a brotherhood he truly belonged to. Something had to have happened – something major – if he attacked them."

"Well, considering we don't know what that something was, what he's up to, or where he's headed, you need to stay protected. He already threatened most of your father's club from what we're hearing."

"I'll go get ready. We can discuss this once we get to the clubhouse. Does your President need me to debrief them on the Stoneridge Raiders? I have to tell you now, I don't know much about club business, and what I do know, I wouldn't tell you. I might have disowned my family, and they proved they weren't loyal to me at all, but that doesn't mean I'll be disloyal to them by talking about their day-to-day shit."

"No one would ever ask that of you, and honestly that response says more about you than anything you could possibly contribute otherwise."

23. MYRA

Getting settled in at the clubhouse was easier said than done. Sure, I'd been there before. I knew some of the people who lived and hung out there. The thing was, my heart was kind of sad and battered, the whole being claimed by Rabbit thing was new, and I felt a bit like a fish out of water.

Once everything was tucked away in the room that I would apparently be sharing with Rabbit, I just sat there on the edge of the bed and rubbed my tummy. "I'm so sorry, little one. I know I ran away from that situation, but I'd like to think your dad would have wanted to know you and be a part of your life, even if I never wanted to be a part of his again."

The tears fell hot and wet down my face and crashed into the same little bit of a belly that I was rubbing. I didn't lie to Rabbit. I really did feel like I had already grieved Blaze, and I had, right along with my own family. The thing is I grieved for *me* and my loss before. Now, I was feeling the loss for my son – a son who would never have the chance to know his biological father.

I wondered if any harm had befallen my family, and why in the world Phoenix was that pissed off at the club I'd grown up in. There was a part of me that wanted to call and verify that all the people I loved were okay. Yeah, I wrote them all off because I couldn't trust them, but that didn't take away all the years I loved my old family. Still, the other part of me, the one that knew they'd drag me back home whether I wanted to go or not, told me to sit tight and just wait.

That, of course, led me to contemplate exactly where I was sitting tight. It was a new year, I was pregnant, claimed by another biker, and living in his clubhouse for my own protection for the time being. I laughed at myself. "I guess that vow of 'no more bikers ever' went out the window." I didn't even feel silly for talking out loud to myself.

"Hey," a voice called out to me as the door opened with an awkward bump. "I brought up some food." I turned to see Rabbit standing there with a tray in his hands.

"You want to talk about it?" He asked as he set the tray down on the table beside the bed. There was one on either side of the bed with a single drawer in each one. I hadn't yet felt nosy enough to go picking through Rabbit's stuff, even though he told me it was fine and he had nothing to hide.

I sat up and wiped my face on the sleeve of my shirt. "It's really nothing. It hit me that my son would never have the chance to get to meet his biological father. I planned to cut him out of my life, but honestly, I don't think that I could have cut him out of his son's life completely. You know? We grew up together. He was always a good friend to me, one of the best, really. Blaze was not cut out to be my boyfriend or anything more serious, but that doesn't mean he wouldn't be a good father. The more time I've had to think about it, the worse I feel about our whole relationship. Was he unhappy the whole time? Did he resent me and our families pushing him on me? It took what he did and moving here for me to realize that I was never his choice."

"Don't go feeling bad for the guy just because he died. He took the coward's way out by starting and maintaining a relationship with you when he didn't want one. It ended up hurting you and will end up hurting your son, too. He could have manned up from the start and told his family and yours that he didn't want to be with you that way. It would have saved you a whole lot of heartache, preserved your friendship, and made life easier on all of you."

"When did you become the wise one?" I asked, trying to deflect from the hard truth I was being made to swallow. Rabbit wasn't wrong. I knew my feelings for Blaze were partially because our families kept drilling in our heads that I was supposed to want that type of relationship with him. I'd had crushes on other people, but I knew it was 'wrong' in their eyes. Could I really blame Blaze for being the coward when the same burden sat in silent judgement at my feet? "Ugh. We are never doing this to our baby," I muttered without thinking.

"Our baby?" Rabbit asked in a hushed tone. I turned to him then, seeing his eyes on my stomach as his hands reached for me. "You know that's what I want, right?" he asked.

"Is it really what you want, or just what you think is best right now?" I had to ask. Questions never even occurred to be with Blaze. I wasn't traveling down that same path with someone else who thought they had a responsibility for me.

"You have your own life handled, Myra. If I didn't want you, both of you, we'd have put you up in another room and taken care of you without the need for us to be this close all the time. I both want and need you in my life because I've never met anyone who fit so perfectly into the vision I have of my future. Besides, you can obviously handle my ass at my worst."

"That's true," I admitted before winking at him and putting my hands overtop of where his rested on my protruding stomach.

"You know-" Rabbit didn't get to finish whatever he'd been saying because there was a very abrupt knock at the door.

24. RABBIT

THE KNOCK AT MY ROOM DOOR WAS THE MOST UNWELCOME SOUND I'd ever heard. Myra was opening up and it finally seemed as though we were going to move forward into becoming an actual couple. At least, I hoped that was what it meant when her hands were splayed overtop of my own that were holding her belly. Her son. Maybe our son.

"What?" I yelled at the door without moving, wanting to just live in that moment for as long as possible. Myra's eyes sparkled with the slight moisture there. I grinned to reassure her as a voice called out to me through the door.

"Rabbit, you have company downstairs."

"Be there in a sec," I called back before turning my head back in Myra's direction. "I'll be right back by your side shortly."

I stood and moved to the door and once it was thrown open, I glared at the prospect who had been the bearer of bad timing and news as I'd been having a moment with my woman. "Who the hell is it?" I asked.

He shrugged his shoulders. "Some broad," he managed to get out before I yanked his arm to stop him from moving further away from me.

"Some broad?"

"I didn't see her. I was on the stairs, heading up, when they told me to go get you."

Fucking useless prospect. Those motherfuckers were always nosy little shits until you needed them to be, then suddenly they knew nothing. By the time I reached the bottom of the stairs, it didn't take a genius to figure out who was there to see me. At first, I thought it was Cherry standing there wringing her hands and looking worried. That was right up until I turned to see Cherry and Charlie standing at the bar a little further away looking completely pissed off.

Fuck. My. Life.

"What the hell did I get called down here for?" I asked the room because it couldn't have been my ex – the one who ran out on me – who thought she had the power to summon me at will. Nah, that definitely couldn't be it.

"Rabbit," Chastity called my name in what would have been a reverent whisper, if only the sound would have projected to me. Instead, she had to increase her own volume so I would hear her, and it killed whatever affect she thought it might have on me.

I turned my glare on her and snapped. "What?"

"I stopped by our old place, but they said you didn't live there anymore and the house you were building for us was empty. It's so beautiful, Rabbit."

"Get to the point, and make it quick," I told her as coolly as possible.

"I need, I um, I'm back for you," she managed to fumble the words out, not quite knowing how to phrase whatever she was asking to get the best reaction out of me. It's funny, because thanks to hindsight, I was able to see her manipulations for what they were now. She'd played me before because I was a little bit desperate for a different life, and therefore easily fooled. That was no longer the case. Instead of falling all over her, like she apparently thought would happen, I laughed.

"No, you're not back for me. Let's get this over with and tell me what you really want," I demanded.

Before she could answer, Chastity's attention caught on something over my shoulder and her eyes narrowed to evil little slits in response. I turned to see Myra gliding down the steps with a grace and beauty that belonged on a movie set. Once my woman hit that last step, I threw my arm out in invitation.

"Come here, babe," I called to her and waited until she was tucked securely into my arm, by my side. I noticed that Chastity had taken a step closer to me before she realized I hadn't been talking to her.

"Myra?" My ex-girlfriend questioned. There was no shock at seeing the girl there, instead, she seemed resigned to the fact that she was in the clubhouse. Interesting. That meant she had to already know that Myra had been around. That was not necessarily good news considering the women came from the same town on the Oregon coast.

"Chastity," Myra called back by way of greeting as she wrapped her arm around my waist and held on. The only thing that gave away her discomfort with the situation was the fact that her fingers dug into my side with a bit more pressure than was necessary. Myra and I hadn't even mapped out our relationship with one another yet, let alone dabbled in public displays of affection with one another, outside of our one kiss at the club that night I danced for her. It felt effortless with her anyway, as though she needed the contact to ground her just as much as I did. Thank fuck, too. I'd never get back with Chastity after what she did to me, but it sure did help keep her at bay to be able to wrap my arms around someone else. More importantly, Myra just felt right standing there in my arms. She had been the one who belonged there all along.

Chastity sneered at me as her eyes shifted between Myra and me. "I see it didn't take you long to move on."

"You moved on before you even left me, so what does it matter to you?"

"I came back for you. Settling down scared me, and I fucked up because of it. I realize that now."

"Well, that's unfortunate for you then," I told her with little emotion in my voice. "What do you really want?" I thought my question might bear repeating because I wasn't fooled one bit that she was here for me out of anything other than some whacked out sort of convenience to her.

"I need protection," she finally answered. There it is. The real reason she was back. It had nothing to do with me. Chastity thought she'd get what she needed quicker if she tried to manipulate an emotional response from me first.

"You should ask your sister then," I informed her as I pointed to a very unamused Cherry over by the bar.

"I'm your old lady," she challenged, her eyes staring

daggers at Myra who never once flinched under the bitch's scrutiny.

"You were my girlfriend at one point. You might have been my old lady, if you'd stuck around. The minute you pulled out of here with another man, you gave up any claim to me or this club." I turned my back on her, ready to go upstairs and eat dinner with my woman.

"Wait!" She shouted. "Please! I beg you! He's coming! He's here in town and he'll kill me if he sees me here."

"Who is here, and why would he kill you?"

"Phoenix. He's here." She didn't say that in answer to my question. Chastity was staring at Myra as she spoke those words instead.

"Why would Phoenix want you dead?" I asked.

"That's not your business," Chastity spat out, obviously not knowing what was good for her.

"You're right. Nothing about you is my business anymore. Good luck with Phoenix."

"He'll be after your precious knocked-up little girlfriend, too. He's determined to wipe out the whole Stoneridge Raiders MC, that includes the missing princess," she snarled. "If you don't help me, I'll tell him where she is."

"I would have asked for help on your behalf, right up until you made that threat against Myra. What kind of awful person does that?" Cherry spoke up, asking her sister a question I didn't think was possible to answer. There was no way Chastity saw herself as a piece of shit human being. She was just looking out for number one, as usual.

"I'm sorry," Chastity wailed in response, changing tactics once again. "I'm desperate. You don't understand."

"Phoenix already knows where Myra is. That would have never been a valid threat against her. But thanks! Once again, you've shown your true colors. Those little reminders help whenever I start to forget and think you might actually be a little bit human."

"You knew he would come here and no one told me?" Chastity accused.

"First, it's not like you left a forwarding address or phone number. Second, how the hell would I know you have a beef with an MC in Oregon, or this person in specific?"

"I didn't even know that," Cherry added. "What have you been up to and how is it going to blow back on me this time?"

"Oh, that's rich! Blame the 'evil twin' again, Cherry."

"You wear the shoe so well," her sister fired back.

"Well, maybe I'll leave it behind, so Prince Phoenix has someone else to aim his sites on," the stupid bitch yelled at her sister without thinking."

"You're using again," Cherry accused. "It's the only time you willingly try to throw me under the bus like that."

Chastity stood there with a bland look on her face. "If you won't help me, I'll help myself."

"We're well aware of how you operate, you selfish bitch," I said. Chastity looked shocked when I spoke aloud what everyone in the room was thinking. Then she decided to try to punish me for it.

"Oh, look how perfect. Two goodie-two-shoes assholes who couldn't keep their significant others satisfied. How pathetic. Oh, and Myra? How was your ex in bed? Did he learn anything from all those lessons I gave him in high school?"

"Actually, he was a shit lay, so I guess like teacher, like student," Myra flung back, causing Chastity to charge her. Shameless and a prospect snatched her up before she could get far. "I already knew about his dalliances, you're not telling me anything new," my woman informed Chastity while inspecting her own nails, as if they were more concerning than anything the bitch had to say.

"Blaze is dead and Phoenix killed him," my ex shot out then, thinking that would be news to us. She stared at us, waiting for a reaction that she wasn't going to get. "You already knew," she whispered into the air.

"I think the question here is how did you know?" Shameless asked.

"I was with Blaze, bringing him out here to find her," she pointed an accusatory finger at Myra. "Phoenix killed Blaze and didn't realize I was there until it was too late. I ran, he tried to track me down, but then got a phone call and left."

"So, you witnessed a man being murdered and you came here for protection against his killer?"

"Yes!" Chastity huffed.

"That makes it too bad that you pissed off anyone who might have cared," Shameless told her just as there was a knock on the exterior security door. One look at the security monitor showed that it was Phoenix who stood there.

"Men with murder on their minds don't usually knock first," Shameless said as he continued to hold fast to Chastity. I went to answer the door, but Rage stopped me.

"Let me handle this. You hang tight with your woman, just in case."

For once, I saw no point in arguing. Rage took a while to unarm the man before he was allowed inside. Once Phoenix made his way inside, his eyes glanced right over everyone else until they found and settled on Myra. She shook visibly, obviously not knowing what to expect at that point.

"Are you okay?" Phoenix asked her and there was no mistaking the concern in his words. Myra nodded in answer and he smiled, the tension easing in his stance. "I had to check. We got word that she was headed here," he stated while swapping his attention to Chastity. The woman no longer appeared frightened. She seemed pissed.

"You were never going to be enough for her," Phoenix spoke while watching Chastity's expression. I knew he was talking to me, though. "You were too far down the totem pole of power for her taste." That had me interested. "Blaze was set to become President of the Stoneridge Raiders, Oregon Chapter. That was why the families wanted Myra and Blaze together so badly. They knew she would always have club protection even after her father was gone."

Phoenix glanced at Myra and gave her a sad look when he spoke. "This one," he continued, tipping his head in Chastity's direction, "was on her home turf while fishing for Blaze. You guys took care of her last problem in order to save her twin, so she would have ruled the town she was initially shunned from if she could get him on board."

"I don't know what you're talking about," Chastity spat at him.

"Her plan didn't work too well because Blaze was hell-bent on finding Myra and bringing her back." He turned from me back to Chastity. "You came with him so you could convince him what a horrible idea it was." Chastity said nothing so Phoenix continued. "A culling was about to happen and I couldn't let Myra be dragged back. She was the only truly innocent one there. She deserves a chance at a happy life."

"You killed Blaze to keep him from finding me?" Myra asked, her voice shaking as she did.

"I killed him because he was going to die either way. You don't need to know why. Doing it before he got to you was just an added bonus." The delighted twinkle in Phoenix's eyes made him seem a little more than just slightly unhinged. "Does this one have club protection?" He asked while pointing his thumb back toward Chastity.

"She does," Spinner spoke up. As his old lady's sister, it was his right of claim to make for Cherry.

"Pity," Phoenix stated. "I suggest you all watch your backs around her then. She'll stab you while you sleep, if she thinks she'll get something from it. I'm sure you're all soon to find out more about that, though," he tacked on cryptically, making me wonder what Chastity had been up to in the time she'd been gone.

"Did you harm them? The rest of them, I mean?" Myra asked when Phoenix turned to go.

"Your family, by blood, is intact. The rest, they suffered what they deserved."

Myra only nodded her head in response. It was clear she didn't understand why this was happening.

"Be happy, Myra." Phoenix told her and then he glanced

down to her belly. "Keep him happy, too. You two are the only family I have left." The man turned and walked out of the clubhouse then, just as quietly as he had entered, despite all the chaos he managed to stir up in his wake.

When my attention shifted back to the rest of the room, it was to find Chastity throwing herself – quite literally – into my brother's arms. "Thank you! I knew I could count on you to love me."

I smirked at my brother. Her crazy was his to deal with now. "I didn't do it for you. I did it because your sister would have a hard time dealing with your death."

"Still," she cooed as she attempted to wrap her body around Spinner.

"Get. The. Fuck. Off. My. Husband!" Cherry screamed each word as a separate entity before yanking her twin off of Spinner by her hair. "You have two hours to get yourself together and get gone."

"W-what?" Chastity shouted while staring with wild eyes at her sister.

"You heard me. I've had enough of your trouble to last a lifetime. I won't tolerate you being disruptive to my new family any longer. Phoenix will have a two hour head start getting out of town. It should give you ample time to pick a destination in the opposite direction."

"You're throwing me out? Abandoning me?"

"You bet your sneaky little ass that I am," Cherry ground out through clenched teeth.

When Chastity's eyes found mine again, begging for me to save her, I simply shook my head and turned to take Myra back up to our room.

"You can't possibly want her over me!"

"Every single day of the week and twice on Sunday. Make no mistake, I would take a used-up two dollar coke whore over you, though. Luckily, I don't have to do that because the perfect woman nearly ran me over one night, put up with my naked ass on the front seat of her truck, and made me realize that like her – I am worth far more than being shackled to someone like you for the rest of my life. I suggest you find a place far from here to settle, and don't come back."

"But my sister is here," she attempted to argue, as if we hadn't just heard how her sister felt about her.

"Your sister and her man can go to you, if they decide they want to visit."

Myra and I both silently slipped away after that, ignoring Chastity's ravings as we did so. "She will continue to be a problem, no matter what," Myra told me as soon as we got back inside our room.

"I'm sure she will. That's for Spinner and Cherry to sort through."

"I grew up with them. Trust me when I say, Chastity will do everything she can to draw you in and make you deal with her. She doesn't do rejection well."

"Will having her issues lingering around be a problem for us?"

"Us?" She asked, her eyes not meeting mine.

"You know there's an us by now."

"You claimed me to offer protection. I didn't expect-"

I cut her off by sealing my lips to hers. She opened for me to slide my tongue in and that's just what I did. I showed Myra how much I needed her to be mine.

"Wow!" Myra gushed out when our lips parted. "That was so different."

"You were told to love him," I managed to get out, knowing exactly what she meant. Blaze had been the only man she'd ever known. Myra didn't know what passion felt like, or chemistry, because she had been told to love the man and he had taken her out of obligation. "What we have is undeniable chemistry. Welcome to the next level." I winked as I added that last bit. I knew teasing her would help lighten the mood.

"Did you really just compare us kissing to leveling up in a video game?"

I shrugged my shoulders. "If the game controller fits," I responded. Myra laughed and playfully slapped my chest before getting serious again.

"I'm carrying another man's baby."

"No. You're carrying your baby. That kid is going to need a dad in his life. I'm applying for the job."

"Yeah? What are your qualifications?" She teasingly asked me.

"I look dead sexy carrying a baby around. Remember the doctor's office? Admit it, you wanted to jump my bone," I pointed down to my cock, "and get pregnant all over again when you watched me showing off my potential dad skills."

"You are unbelievable!"

"Unbelievably sexy, baby. We just went over this. Do try to keep up, pretty momma."

25. MYRA

PRETTY MOMMA WAS A NEW ENDEARMENT, AND I FELT MYSELF blush as Rabbit used it. My knees quaked with nervousness as butterflies tumbled around my stomach. Wait. No. That wasn't butterflies. It was my baby. "He's moving," I informed Rabbit.

"Do you think I can feel him yet?" he asked. Instead of answering, I placed his hand on my belly and we both waited. "Maybe he's shy?" Rabbit questioned just as I felt another jolt. The way his eyes lit up, I knew he felt it, too. "Our boy just tried to beat me up for touching his mom."

I laughed and the baby kicked again. "Maybe, he just likes to hear your voice and he's rewarding you by making his presence known."

"It has to be that one, definitely. I'm too awesome to be kicked away."

"You really are," came out of my mouth in a dreamy tone, completely without my permission.

"Now you've done it!" Rabbit announced.

"Done what?"

"You just admitted that I'm awesome. There's no giving me back now."

What was I supposed to say to that? If I was being honest with myself, I didn't want to give him back. "I don't want to," I whispered in his ear before nibbling there on his earlobe.

It was completely out of character for me to initiate things with a man. I had rarely done it when I'd been with Blaze, and if I was honest with myself, that was probably a tiny part of a problem as a couple. Thinking back on things like that also made me realize that I hadn't done it because I never felt the need to. He didn't inspire that reaction from me. Rabbit did, though. I was tired of fighting myself and holding back with him.

"Do you know what you're doing?" Rabbit asked me, his voice a gruff whisper against my neck as I leaned back slightly so that I could see his eyes. The black of his pupils had already begun to swallow up any color that would have been visible. Instead of answering with words, I leaned in and gently nipped his bottom lip with my teeth before licking over it lightly, and that's about the time Rabbit lost control. "I'm going to take that as a *'yes'*, but I'm going to need you to spell it out for me in words. Is this what you want, Myra? Are you ready for this? For me?"

"I'm more than ready," I hummed against his mouth as his lips met mine in an almost brutal claim. Rabbit pulled me down so that I straddled his lap, facing him as his hands palmed my ass.

"You don't know how long I've waited for this," Rabbit said as he started to tug my shirt up over my stomach. I reached down and grabbed hold of the hem, afraid for him to lift it. "I've seen your belly before, Myra."

"That was different," I muttered while refusing to look him in the eye. Rabbit reached up and dragged my chin upward so that I was forced to meet his gaze.

"No. You are a beautiful woman," he said as he stared into my eyes, so I could see the truth there. "I won't allow you to do this, because it's completely unnecessary with me. The fact that you're growing a human in here," he started as he gently ran a hand across my belly, under my shirt. "This means that you are doing something so amazing, that it's difficult to even conceptualize. You are gorgeous. You fucking glow like this, and this belly you have, that is you bringing life into the world. It only makes you more attractive, not less."

He didn't wait for a response. Instead, he swiftly lifted the shirt free of my body and dropped his hand back to unclasp the bra as well. Once that was gone, he stared for a moment. "This body," he said before he leaned in and stole a quick kiss. "This should be in a museum, because it is pure perfection."

Wow!

If I hadn't already started to fall in love with the man, I would have fallen hard and fast right there in his lap as his eyes roved over me with hunger in them and his words sewed the broken pieces of my heart back together.

"Rabbit," I whimpered against his lips.

CHRISTINE MICHELLE

"Yeah, baby?"

"I get that you're enjoying the view, but I need you," I told him as I helped him off with his shirt, too. He pulled me close, our bodies squished together, chest to chest, as he kissed me deeply while his hands went to work on my body. One was gently massaging my breast, while the other was being less than gentle with my ass cheek. I groaned in appreciation for all the attention he was showing me, while also making myself busy getting his belt undone, then the buttons and zipper of his jeans.

"Babe, I'm not even kidding when I say if you touch my dick, I might detonate early," his husky request made me remove my eyes from his gorgeous body and instead meet his eyes. "I really don't want to embarrass myself here," he added.

"It's okay, you already embarrassed yourself the night we met," I chuckled as I told him that.

He quickly picked me up and flipped me so that I was on my back on the bed as he towered over me, his pants undone and the gorgeous golden brown treasure trail that led into his unfastened pants taunted me. "You're going to pay for that, I told you, it was cold outside." That response only made me giggle louder.

"Aww poor Rabbit," I laughed and leaned up to playfully nip at his collarbone. The quick, hissed intake of air on his part told me he enjoyed the little nibbles on his skin. My Rabbit was super sensitive. I pulled him closer so that I could get to his nipples and offered up the same treatment there.

"Totally forgiven," he said.

I laughed again. "Already? You're way too easy!"

Rabbit lifted my legs so that my feet touched the edge of the bed, and then he quickly did away with the sweatpants I'd been lounging in. My panties went with them, all in one fell swoop. Rabbit's grin widened as he glanced down, dropped my clothes to the floor and then winked at me.

"Oh, baby, I will never have to worry about being cold again!"

"Huh?" I mumbled out in a complete lusty haze. Then the infuriating man ran his hands up my legs. "Oh God!" I groaned, and not in a pleasantly sexed-up way either.

"Yeah, these babies should keep me nice and warm for the winter. Why have you been holding out on me Myra?" My giggle was less humorous then and more the nervous kind of 'oh shit' laughter.

"Seriously? I didn't think I'd need to shave my damn legs, and the bump is starting to make it a chore, so..." I started to explain, but stopped the minute his hands reached the apex of my thighs and then without any hesitation, he dove in and licked me right up my middle. And let's be honest, if I hadn't gotten around to shaving my legs, there were other areas I'd forgotten to take a razor to as well. I was slightly mortified that he wasn't seeing me polished and primed for our very first time, but what else could I do?

"Why are you worried about it?" Rabbit asked, completely serious before he leaned in and took another swipe at me. I hope he didn't expect me to answer, because my lady bits hadn't seen any action in far too long, and they hadn't seen any mouth action in a ridiculously long time. "I prefer my women to look like women instead of little girls."

Another swipe of his tongue. "Then again, this is my first time with a woman going full Sasquatch."

"Oh for fuck's sake, Rabbit!" I managed to get out before grabbing his head and shoving him where I needed attention the most. Forget my embarrassment, I wasn't going to let him come up for air ever again, then he'd never be able to talk about my mortifying level of body hair. Yeah. That sounded like the perfect plan until the bastard started laughing against my pussy.

"Holy shit!" The words hissed out of my mouth. I'd never had someone laugh while down there before and the vibrations certainly kicked things up a notch. Rabbit mumbled something, but it was incoherent since his face was smooshed into my pussy.

"Yes!" I hummed as he started doing something amazing. It was almost like he was writing his name, right there, on my pussy, with his tongue.

"Rabbit," I moaned his name as I loosened my hold on his head, fisting his hair in my fingers instead. I'd been secretly dying to run my hands through his gorgeous, wavy, golden brown tresses since I met him, but definitely since that night he did a strip tease for me at the club. His tongue slid down from my clit to penetrate me as his thumb took over making sure my clit stayed stimulated. "Fuck! Rabbit!" I panted as he managed to coax an orgasm from me, surprising both of us with the intensity of the thing. "Raaaabbit!" his name was a long moan on my lips before he slowed his efforts and crawled his way up my body, moving my boneless form further up the bed as he did.

"You taste like the best dessert," he complimented before

leaning in to suck my bottom lip between his own. We kissed so slowly and languidly that I damn near had another orgasm just for the sheer joy of the moment. I'd never been tended to that way before, so reverently, as if he cherished every single touch and taste.

"I don't even know your name," I whispered when he finally pulled away from my lips. "How have I not even thought of that before now?"

He grinned at me again before swiping away all the left-over moisture from his mouth. "I have news for you little momma, you were just moaning my name loud enough for the whole clubhouse to hear you."

I smacked his chest playfully. "I was not, and that's your road name. You've never actually told me your given name."

"Nathaniel Hastings," he was quick to tell me before leaning in and giving me another kiss. "Great to meet ya!" I laughed at that.

"Are you ready for more?" He asked as he leaned down and placed sweet little open mouthed kisses along my jaw, my neck, shoulder, collar bone, and then across the top of each breast.

"Yes, I need you," It was more demand than answer to his question. There was no way we were calling this done. He'd already had his face down there, so there was nothing left to hide.

"Good, now tell me, what's going to be the most comfortable for you right now?" His hand was caressing my thigh while the other slowly teased my nipple. He remained propped up on an elbow while hovering over my body with his own and I had to admit I liked the feel of him there, but I wasn't sure how comfortable it would be for long. Lying on my back felt weird if I stayed in that position too long.

"How about this?" He asked as he lifted up and gently turned me over. Rabbit reached past me and grabbed some pillows to stuff underneath of me to take some of the weight from my belly. I actually let out a low moan as it also took some pressure off of my hips. "I take it that was a yes?"

"Yeah, definitely," I agreed as I glanced back over my shoulder and watched him roll a condom down his length. "Nathaniel," I tested his name on my lips. "Or Nate?" I asked.

"Rabbit," he growled. "No one has called me Nate or Nathaniel in a very long time," he told me before he ran his fingers down the length of my back only to smack my ass before plunging himself inside of me.

"Rabbit," I grunted as the force of his movement pushed me forward, face down into the sheets. He didn't leave me there like that. Instead, Rabbit leaned over my back, grabbed a fistful of my hair and yanked just hard enough for the tiny bite of pain to register before his other hand moved under me and pinched my still-sensitive clit.

"Oh God!" I hissed out as my body seemed to move of it's own volition. Up and up and up until my back was plastered to Rabbit's front and we were both sitting upright on our knees with him still inside of me. He used the grip on my hair to turn my head slightly, then leaned in and kissed me. His tongue fucked my mouth at the same pace his cock moved inside of me. Slow, languid strokes mixed with primal, rutting thrusts until he let go of my hair and ran his hands down my arms. Rabbit grabbed hold of my wrists and placed them on the bed frame in front of me.

"Hold steady baby," he called out to me as he then grabbed hold of my hips and started hammering into me with a force I had never known before. The slapping of our bodies became a symphony of noise in the room. I didn't listen to Rabbit, though. Instead, as his pace increased, so did my desire to come again. I thought that I might actually come just from him fucking me, which would have been a first, but I took things into my own hands and slid one of my palms down the sheets until I made my way between my legs and started stimulating my clit while he fucked the absolute hell out of me.

"Mmm," he moaned as he leaned in further. "You playing with yourself, baby? One of these days, you're going to let me watch you do that, but for now, let's get you there, because I'm not going to last this time." Rabbit then reached up and pinched one of my nipples, rolling it between his thumb and forefinger at the same rate I strummed my own clit. As he stroked in and out of me with desperate movements, I tipped over the edge, almost over-stimulated to the point where the world blacked out and faded for just a second before the contractions brought on by my orgasm had me panting.

"Myra, God, so fucking good!" Rabbit grunted to me as he found his own release thanks in part to my orgasm milking his cock. "Jesus, woman," he huffed as he slowly maneuvered us to where we were lying on our sides with the pillows in front of my belly and Rabbit playing the part of big spoon to my little one.

"You're perfect," he whispered in my ear before kissing my temple. "Fuck! I don't want to move, but I need to go deal with this condom," he finally groaned as he slowly released his hold on me and moved to get up. Rabbit was kind enough through the fleece blanket he had at the end of his bed over me when he saw that I shivered in the wake of his absence. Losing his body heat as the sweat on my own body cooled, left me slightly chilled, so I was grateful for his thoughtfulness.

When Rabbit came back, I watched as he rounded the bed, and slid in behind me. His warmth up next to my body caused me to make a noise of absolute delight as his fingers trailed through my semi-damp hair. "I like that noise you keep making," he murmured in my ear as he placed a sweet kiss there. "You keep doing it and we're going to be down for round two."

"I'm okay with that," I told him as I rolled over so that we could face one another.

"I didn't hurt you, did I?"

I shook my head in response and then smiled at him. "It was perfect."

"That's good," he said as he pulled me tighter to his body. "Don't worry, you didn't hurt me either. There was a minute there when I thought maybe, I might die being smothered in the sweetest fucking pussy on the planet, but there was just enough air getting through..."

I laughed so loudly that I actually snorted for a minute. "Oh God! Just shut up now!" I hissed at him as I buried my heated face into his chest.

"No, it was all good, because I think the hair on your legs worked to pull me back out just enough so that I could get some much needed oxygen before we took you over the top."

The giggles and mortification levels were both off the

charts as a banging at the door startled me. "If she's laughing at it, you're doing it wrong! We can always send you to another chapter so you don't embarrass us further." The disembodied voice from the other side of the door laughed at his own crass joke. I didn't recognize who it was, but apparently Rabbit did.

"Fuck off, T. You're not even an important word in your trio."

I laughed again because he was referring to the three guys named Whiskey, Tango, and Foxtrot, being collectively referred to as WTF or What the Fuck whenever they were together as a unit. Tango being the "the" in the equation did actually seem to be the least important when you looked at it like that. Though, I'd bet money Liza would disagree.

"That's just rude, Rabbit. When you're done embarrassing yourself, Spinner requested your presence downstairs. Seems pretty important, so might want to hustle." He tapped the door and I thought he was gone but then he called out, "Sorry, Myra, we're not all like that."

"Fuck, A guy can't catch a break around here," Rabbit muttered as he shook his head. I ran my fingers over his back in a comforting gesture.

I laughed at the man. "That's what you get for the leg hair comments," I told him before I slid out of bed and grabbed his hands in mine. "Come on, I'm pretty sure your brother can wait long enough for me to help clean you up in the shower."

"You have the best ideas, little momma."

"I think you like that about me."

"Your best idea ever was when you picked up a naked bunny on the side of the road."

Once again, I found myself laughing. "I didn't exactly pick you up."

"Keep telling yourself that. We both know the truth." He motioned to my very naked, sexed up, pregnant body. "Obviously, you liked what you saw.

Lord help me! I did.

26. RABBIT

AFTER GETTING CLEANED UP AND DRESSED AGAIN, I TOOK MYRA downstairs with me. Everyone's eyes immediately locked onto my hand intertwined with hers. As I glanced around at everyone, only some of them were smiling about the fact that Myra and I had obviously sealed the damn deal.

Children. Gossiping ass bitches.

As I turned closer to where my brother stood, I finally noticed why the rest of the crowd seemed to be a bit on edge. Chastity was still in the clubhouse for some odd reason.

"What's going on now?" I asked.

"My sister failed to mention the extra someone who needed the club's protection," Cherry stated sadly as she glanced over to an infant carrier.

"You stole a fucking baby?" I shouted. "That's a new low, even for you."

"It's *our* baby, you idiot!" Chastity yelled back.

"That's funny, because I don't remember ever getting you pregnant or even trying to." I shot back.

Myra tried to let go of my hand, but I held on that much tighter. No matter whose baby that was, it wouldn't change my mind. Myra was the woman who I should have been building my dream life toward all along. And not to sound like a complete pussy, but I needed her to have my back right now. If there was any truth to the bullshit Chastity was spewing, I was about to be tied to that cunt for at least a solid 18 years.

"She's yours, she's the reason I took off."

"That doesn't even make sense. I told you how much I wanted a family. Obviously, an unplanned pregnancy wouldn't have been anything to cause me to turn you away. What I would get angry about, though, is a woman knowing she was having my kid and running off and never saying a word about it. I think you knew me well enough to under-stand both of those things. So, again, I'm asking whose kid you have there, because I am 99.999 percent positive it ain't mine?"

"You don't understand," she whined, just like I knew she would. When Chastity didn't get her way immediately, she knew how to turn on the drama fast. I still wasn't sure what happened to make her the evil twin to Cherry's beautiful soul, but they were night and day in personality. "I didn't think I was cut out to be in a functioning family or to be a mom."

"So, instead of running to terminate your pregnancy, like a normal psychopath who didn't think she could be a mommy, you went and had the baby and kept it, despite your admission that you didn't think you could be a mom? How the fuck does that make any sense, Chas?"

I moved to walk away when she didn't answer the question. Of course, it was Chastity, so she wasn't done yet. The bitch had to stab a little harder with that knife she was wielding.

"Don't you want to meet your daughter?"

"Sure, one day, when I have a daughter with my woman. Until then, if you want to continue with this charade, we'll have a paternity test done. If it says I'm the father, we'll go from there."

"Where are we supposed to stay until then?" The calculating bitch had the nerve to ask.

"Most definitely not with me," I answered.

"We could stay in our house you haven't moved into yet." The hopeful tone in her voice made me want to be sick. As if I would ever allow that to happen. "This is what you had it built for after all, our family."

"It's not now, nor ever will be *'our'* anything. And you will never sully the inside of *my* home with your presence."

"But-"

"Do something with your sister," I told Cherry as I cut her sister off. "If she keeps asking more of me, I'm liable to kill her myself."

"I have enough saved for a place closer to work now. Why don't you have her stay with you for a few days to give me time to move the rest of my stuff out of the apartment over Spinner's garage, and then she can stay there?" Myra asked Cherry.

"That's perfect," Chastity cooed. I'd honestly never contemplated violence against a woman before, at least not in the very serious way that my brain was running through scenarios to get this woman out of all of our lives for good. Truthfully, if that was my child, I would do whatever it took to make sure Chastity had little to nothing to do with her. There was zero doubt in my mind that the woman would ruin that child otherwise. I had other things to worry about for the moment, though, like Myra thinking she was going to be getting an apartment of her own.

Not happening.

I didn't bother disagreeing with Myra in front of everyone, but we were going to have a serious talk in private. "Come on," I demanded in a whisper, and that time she followed along behind me, our hands still locked together. I stopped at the bottom of the stairs. "Someone give Doc a call and get him on the DNA test immediately before the bitch can skip town with the kid again," I called out.

"No need. I know you're the father," Chastity called back.

"There is most definitely a need," I answered through gritted teeth. "She doesn't leave here until Doc has had the chance to swab both of them." I ordered, pointing down at the baby.

"I know of a place where we can get it done quickly. No need to call Doc." Chastity's bright smile made me cringe. Either she was positive it was my kid or she had something up her sleeve. My bets were on her having something to hide and needing a way to control the situation.

"And why would a woman who was sure of her child's paternity just happen to *'know of a place'*?"

"Girls talk," she suggested.

"Doc will do it," I growled.

"I don't trust Doc," she muttered.

"Funny, he's the only person I trust with this. I suggest you watch bad mouthing a brother in his clubhouse before you find yourself locked up downstairs while your sister cares for your baby."

I didn't stick around for any more of Chastity's drama. Myra and I both let out a heavy breath when we were back behind closed doors in our room.

"You are not looking for a place closer to work when I already have one," I informed Myra.

"If that's your baby-" she started.

"If that's my baby, and I seriously doubt that, then I will take care of it. Would it be a problem for you if we both bring a child into our relationship?"

"Of course it wouldn't. My issue is more along the lines of whether you would end up wanting to keep your family together since you have the opportunity."

"Would you do that?" I asked. "I can't trust Chastity with anything. There's no way I could be with her again. And that would be my answer only if you weren't in the equation. With you here, the answer becomes, FUCK NO! I'd never give you up, my beautiful little momma bear. Not for anyone, but certainly not for a cheap imitation and a shitty mother figure."

I pulled Myra down on my lap after I sat on the edge of the bed. "You are mine to protect, mine to love, mine to take care of. My house is half-way between the clubhouse and where you work. That makes it perfect for both of us. No one has ever lived there before, so we can move in and make it our home together."

"You don't think we're moving too fast?"

"No. I think we're moving at just the right speed, especially since this baby will be here before we know it. He's going to need a place to come home to. I want that to be with me. With us." Myra seemed to contemplate my words as she leaned more heavily on my body. "What do you say? Move in with me?"

She leaned in and kissed my lips. "I would love to live in sin with you and maybe coparent a couple of babies together."

"You giving me more babies?"

She shrugged. "You know, just in case that little girl does turn out to be yours."

"Myra, I always used condoms with Chastity. I know that's not something easy to hear or talk about, but it's the truth. I was never comfortable even considering going without protection with her. So, the chances of that baby being mine are pretty damn slim."

"Things happen, they're not foolproof."

"I get that, but even if that turned out to be the case, I want us to be able to deal with it together, and I'm really going to need you because there is no way I'd ever leave my kid with that woman to raise."

"You think she'll let custody go that easily?"

"There are two things in this life that Chastity cares about. Money and power. I have money, if I need to buy her off, I will."

"Let's hope it doesn't come to that," Myra managed to say before hugging me tighter.

"I liked what you did with your little apartment. Can we

do something similar with the new house?" I asked her, trying to get Chastity out of our heads for a few minutes.

"You really liked it?"

"Yeah, baby. I want that, but obviously, on a bigger scale."

"That can be arranged."

27. MYRA

My LIFE BECAME A SERIES OF EVENTS THAT REQUIRED MORE patience than I had. We were waiting on furniture to show up at the house Rabbit was moving us into. We were waiting on the DNA test to come back to see if Chastity's daughter really was Rabbit's. Then there was me, waiting on this baby to grow big enough to be able to come out and meet me properly. Not that I was complaining about all of it. Rabbit managed to turn every day into an adventure for us. Our relationship was completely different to the one I'd had for so long with Blaze. We had fun. We laughed. Even when there were heavy topics being discussed, Rabbit and I made sure that we always ended them on a light note because there was no need to stay stuck in the negatives all the time. Despite all the waiting, I couldn't remember a time in my life when I had been happier.

"You didn't have to come get me, Deanna was going to bring me home," I told Rabbit when he picked me up from work unexpectedly. The Beast was in the shop again, this time for routine maintenance to make sure it wouldn't crap out on me somewhere between work and home.

"I wanted to come get you," was all he said for a little while. I noticed the tension in his shoulders and his hands as they tightened around the steering wheel though.

"Are you okay?"

He pulled in a huge breath, held it a moment, and then let everything go. "Doc called. He has the results waiting for us at the clubhouse. Spinner went to get Chastity and the baby. They're meeting us there."

"That's a good thing. Now, you'll know for sure if she's yours or not." He didn't acknowledge me at first.

"What if it is my baby? I'll have to deal with Chastity's bullshit for the rest of my life. I don't want you to have to do that, too."

"Whoa! What are you saying?"

"If it's my child, I'll give you an out. You can take the house and keep clear of me as much as possible."

I gasped audibly. "Is that what you really want?"

"Fuck no! I want to build a family with you."

"And I want that with you. We'll deal with whatever the test results are, but we're doing it together." My words were a demand. There was no way I would let Rabbit self-destruct over this. I could handle Chastity and to be honest, something Rabbit said to me the night she showed up kept playing in my mind. 'Money and Power' were the two things that woman wanted. Granted, playing games with my head and the relationship I had with Rabbit would give her a huge power trip, but I honestly thought the money would be the bigger motivator. Either she would sell that kid or end up trying to fleece Rabbit slowly with outrageous child support asks.

"She'll never stop her cunning plays. She'll try to tear us apart at every opportunity." It was as if he were speaking the worries spinning in the back of my mind.

"The only way she'll succeed is if we let her," I reminded him. "You forget, I grew up with the twins. I know exactly what she's capable of."

We both sat quietly contemplating that on the way back to the clubhouse. When we got there, none of Spinner or Cherry's vehicles were in the lot, which made me uneasy right off the bat. We got inside and sat at the bar waiting for word from them, or for Spinner to walk through the doors with Chastity and the baby in tow. We were sitting in the clubhouse for about fifteen minutes when Rabbit's cell finally rang.

"Yeah?" He called into the receiver.

"She's not here. The apartment was cleaned out, man," I heard Spinner voice rather loudly on the other end of the call.

"What the fuck? Why would she haul ass now?"

"My guess?" Spinner questioned. "She knew it wasn't your kid."

"All right, well, Doc's here. I'm going to go get the results. I'll call you back in just a minute." Rabbit looked to Doc who had moved to stand beside him. "You have them?" Rabbit asked him.

"Right here, but Rabbit, I think maybe you might want to open them in private." Doc glanced my way briefly, and my stomach felt like I was on a roller coaster and the bottom just dropped out from under me. Did that mean that Chastity hadn't been lying and now she was in the wind with Rabbit's kid? Was that my fault? Did she take off because of me? Crap. Panic was creeping in as Rabbit shook his head.

"It'll be fine, let me see," he told Doc who then handed him the envelope.

I watched as Rabbit's shaking hands peeled the envelope apart, reached in, and grabbed the papers to pull them out. He glanced over them quickly, but then his eyes went back to the top and he just sat there stunned for a moment.

"No! She wouldn't." The disbelief in his voice was startling.

The anticipation was too much so I leaned over and took a quick peek at what was there. An audible gasp flew from my lips when I realized why my man had asked that question. "Oh no!" I managed to get out. "Cherry will be devastated."

Rabbit pulled his phone out and called his brother back. "You need to get to the clubhouse now!" Once he hung up again Rabbit glanced up at Rage and Shameless, who were standing near us, too, waiting with Doc as we read the results. "Find her. Don't come back without that baby."

"Shit, is it yours?" Rage asked.

"No, but she's still a club princess."

"Fuck!" Shameless hissed, immediately understanding since there was only one way I would know that for sure based off Rabbit's DNA test.

28. RABBIT

Spinner came running into the clubhouse with Cherry hot on his heels. "Is she here? Is the baby yours?"

"We need the two of you to come with us," I told my brother as I headed downstairs to where the club had sound-proofed rooms set up.

"You have her in a cell?" Spinner asked incredulously.

"Not yet," I answered. "Our brothers are out there searching for her as we speak."

"Shit!" Came out of Spinner's mouth. "It was your kid," he surmised.

I waited to answer him until we were all inside the room and seated. How the fuck was I supposed to ask my brother this shit with his wife sitting right next to him? My heart hammered against my ribs so fucking hard, I just knew everyone in the room had to hear it. I couldn't even meet Cherry's eyes, though I knew they were on me because I felt the burn of her stare. "I need to know if there was ever a time you remember being with Cherry that she didn't seem to recall," I started.

I watched as Cherry blanched and looked stricken. "No," she whined so low and pitifully that I almost missed the word. There was no way to miss her complete devastation, though.

Spinner glared at me then turned to his wife. He immediately must have remembered whatever Cherry had already thought of. "You told me it must have been a dream because you hadn't come into work that night," he mentioned.

My brother turned back to me, all the color having drained from his face. "Nate, what in the hell did your results say?" Spinner already knew. That was the only reason he'd call me by my childhood nickname. My big brother looked to me to make the reality of the situation untrue, and I didn't know how to do that for him.

Instead of answering, I passed the paper across the table to him and waited until he opened it. "It says I'm not the father, but I am a close relation."

"This was why she left," Cherry tells us in a wooden, detached voice. "She knew we would find out what she had done." While she sounded as emotionless as a robot, the tears that were on a steady drip down her face belied her true feelings on the matter. My sister-in-law was devastated. There were still questions that needed to be answered, though, because according to the timeline of the baby's conception, Chastity and I were very much together still.

"How did you not realize?" I asked my brother. Part of me was angry with him for having slept with the woman when she had been mine, and after he had already claimed her sister. Logically, I knew he must have been tricked somehow, but that didn't stop the quick sting of betrayal that worked itself into my heart. I figured Cherry was feeling the same shit in the moment, too.

"Something was wrong with me that night. I went to lie down in my office because I didn't trust myself to drive home. Couldn't drive anyway because I kept getting dizzy for no fucking good reason." Spinner turned to his wife, and his face crumpled into a miserable, pained shell of his normal visage. "Cherry had me convinced it was all just a weird dream and that I had fallen asleep at work that night because I was overworked and exhausted."

"I never suspected Chastity would pull a stunt like this because she was with you," her eyes turned to me to emphasize that point. "I thought she was finally happy." Cherry's voice pleaded with me to understand why she didn't think it was possible.

"You think you were drugged?" I asked my brother, while ignoring Cherry's assessment of her sister, since there wasn't a single thing about Chastity that had ever been happy or honest.

"It's possible. I thought I was coming down with something. I felt like shit the whole next day, too."

"When was this?"

"About two months before she took off," he confirmed.

"So, she found out she was pregnant, knew it was yours-" I started to recap, but was immediately interrupted by my brother.

"How would she have known it was mine?" he asked.

I shrugged my shoulders and glanced at Myra, remembering having this exact conversation with her not too long ago. "I guess I never trusted her because we never once had sex without a condom on." Myra flinched beside me and I pulled her close to me and held her tight. This wasn't exactly the best conversation to have with my current woman sitting beside me, especially since it wasn't the first time we'd discussed it. Having grown-up discussions about your past history was one thing, constantly having to face it being thrown at you, with details, that was something entirely different. Neither of the women in the room deserved to have to hear this bullshit.

"Do you have cameras at Rosy's?" Myra asked.

"We do," my brother answered. "Normally, we wipe old video files once they reach the six-month mark. Otherwise, it would be hell on storage."

"Too bad, or you could have proof that she was there," Myra mumbled out loud.

"Don't need it," Spinner told her as he held up the DNA test. "There's a baby out there that proves what she did." My brother groaned before dropping the papers back down as if they had burned him. "I was prepared to love that little girl as my niece, no matter what. I wasn't prepared to find out she was my daughter this whole time." What a goddamn mind fuck. If I could get my hands on Chastity, she wouldn't be long for this world. Two people on this fucking planet who didn't deserve this bullshit were my brother and sister-in-law. They were never involved in drama of their own, and sure the fuck would never step out on one another willingly.

Cherry was in tears beside Spinner as he acknowledged,

for the first time, that the baby had to be his. "She's done some horrible things over the years, dragged me into her troubles, but I never would have thought she'd stoop to this level," Cherry cried. Then she looked at my brother and lost it. "My identical twin sister raped you and now she's run off somewhere with your child. How can you even stand to look at me?"

I'd read the term 'ugly cry' in plenty of books since I picked up the habit of reading romance novels, but never had I seen it in action until now. Cherry was literally falling apart right in front of us.

"Come on," Myra whispered to me. "Let's give them some space to come to terms with what they just learned and to be able to work through it together."

Spinner turned his eyes on Myra. "Thank you," he mouthed to her while pulling his reluctant wife into his arms. I made eye contact with him and tried to convey the message, 'We'll find them'. He seemed to understand. My brother nodded at me and then really took hold of his wife, pulling her onto his lap and holding her so tightly, it almost looked as though it should hurt. The thing was, it couldn't hurt, because he was holding her together, and in the process, trying to do the same for himself. The last thing I saw before we left the room was my brother's shoulders shaking with the force of his own emotion.

"What a fucking mess!" Once the door was shut, I leaned against the wall while attempting to absorb everything we had just found out. I'd been envious of my brother before. He had Cherry and they had been perfect for one another from the start. Hell, it was the reason I tried so hard to make it work with Chastity. I wanted to recreate what they had.

"I feel like this is partially my fault for hoping it wasn't mine," I admitted.

"That bitch raped your brother. Nothing about that is your fault."

"I was still with her when that happened."

"Yep. You were with her, but what you need to remember is that she wasn't with you. She only pretended long enough to lay her trap and fuck things up for her sister again." Myra moved so that she was directly in front of me. Then, her hands slid up to frame my face and force me to look at her. "That bitch has been out to make sure her sister was just as miserable as her their whole lives. Do not take her bullshit on your shoulders. You were a pawn in her game. If you think that she didn't play her hand from the first time she turned you down, you're wrong."

We stood there for a long time, just like that, and I watched as the determination and firm belief in her words took hold in her eyes, and then transferred that belief to me. She was right. I'd made a bad choice, thinking I could tame the evil twin and have the cookie cutter relationship my brother and his woman had. That was where my fault lie. It didn't expand to include all the shit that Chastity pulled or her shit intentions through everything.

"Come on," Myra finally demanded after it was clear I had accepted what she had to say. "I think you require some Charlie time. Your BFF has new books she was telling me about. If you're a really good boy, maybe we'll try some of the steamy scenes out. At least, the ones that are comfy enough for me to do right now. We'll just bookmark the others until this bunny is born." She patted her belly, and it was the most beautiful moment of my life, because by calling her future son a bunny, she was acknowledging that while he might not be mine biologically, he was mine in all the other ways that counted. I'll admit to finding myself misty-eyed over the proclamation.

I also respected the fuck out of the fact that my woman acknowledged that I had a female best friend, and not only did she not have a problem with it, but she was encouraging it. Chastity always hated my friendships with Charlie, Liza, and Cherry. It just highlighted how right Myra was for me and how terribly wrong I'd been to try to force things with Chastity.

"I love you, gorgeous little momma." Her only response was to pull my face closer and kiss me stupid.

"I love you, too, my silly Rabbit." I smiled as she spoke the words into my lips. "Let's go check on progress, get some Charlie time, and give Spinner and Cherry their space."

"Do you want a big family, Myra?" I asked as we headed up the stairs. She turned to look at me so I could see the question in her eyes but she answered me anyway.

"I was an only child. I would have loved to have siblings so I guess three at the least."

"But maybe more?" I asked the question hopefully.

"If that's what I'm blessed with," she answered.

"That's good," I told her.

"Why? How many do you want?"

"My name is Rabbit, baby momma. I need to live up to it."

Myra's laughter was a balm to my soul as it carried us into the main room we used as our clubhouse bar. The mood was far too subdued for my woman's laughter, but I didn't care. Her genuine response fed my soul, and it was in serious need of sustenance.

29. MYRA

My brain was on overload and buzzing, and my heart wasn't helping the matter. Rabbit told me that he loved me, but more than just the words, I felt it in the way he held me and looked straight into my soul as he said it. Sure, it sounds silly and sappy, but coming from someone who thought she had been loved before, there was a world of difference.

I couldn't jump for joy or shout my love for him from the rooftops though because the clubhouse was a somber space. Spinner and Cherry were dealing with the devastating news that he fathered a child with her twin sister. It was the stuff of a bad soap opera, only it was really happening to people I cared about.

I left Rabbit with Charlie and begged off to the restroom to pee. I wasn't lying. I really had to go. I just didn't come back right away. Instead, I went to go find either Shameless or Rage.

I ended up finding both of them together.

"Myra?" Rage questioned.

"Something we can do for you, sweetheart?" Shameless tacked on, trying to sound a little nicer than his younger counterpart.

I shook my head. "There might be something I can do for you, though."

"What's that?" Shameless asked as he glanced to Rage. They seemed to be communicating something silently, but I didn't have time to figure out exactly what the message being passed between the two was.

"There are only so many places Chastity would go with a baby in tow," I explained. They both waited me out as I shifted my weight from foot to foot in a dance of nerves that was beyond my control. "She would either hide out locally or go home again."

"We figured as much already."

"Home is where my family is," I reminded them what I'm pretty sure they already knew.

"What are you suggesting?" Rage asked.

"If it will help find her, I will reach out to my family for you."

"Didn't you cut them out of your life for a reason?" Shameless asked in a gentle tone.

"I did, but finding that baby is more important than my issues with my family. They can't harm me anymore, especially now that my ex is dead. But Spinner and Cherry will drive themselves insane wondering and worrying the longer that baby remains out of sight. It hurts Rabbit and the rest of the club, too. My little bit of discomfort is worth it to alleviate that strain on all of you."

"You're one lucky son of a bitch," Spinner stated from

somewhere behind me. I turned on my heels to find both he and Rabbit had walked up and apparently heard what I had to say.

"Always spreading that beautiful heart of yours around, huh?" Rabbit asked me as he walked over and pulled me tight to his body. "I'd rather not use my old lady as she doesn't need the added stress while she's pregnant, but if Chastity isn't found in the next forty-eight hours, we'll revisit Myra's offer," he told all of them. "It'll take her at least that long to get back home anyway, unless she flew."

"We'd know if she took a flight," Shameless confirmed the answer to the question Rabbit hadn't actually asked.

"Sounds like a plan," Rage responded at the same time, before dipping his head to look at something on the monitor that was facing away from me.

"Find us if you need us," Rabbit called out before turning me around and walking me back to the main room.

"Are you angry with me?"

"I could never be mad at you for caring about our family and wanting to do whatever is necessary to make it better. I was a little concerned that you may have fallen in and clogged the toilet with your ass, and backwards drowned in there." I swatted him on the arm for the comment. "What? You were gone a long time and last thing you said was that you needed to pee. It sounded logical to me."

"Please," Charlie started as she massaged her own forehead. "Tell me he didn't actually tell you the 'she clogged the toilet' theory for why you were gone so long?"

"Oh, he absolutely did!" I informed her.

"That's it! You're banned from book club for a month, Rabbit!"

"What? Why?" He seemed truly panicked by the threat.

"You can't tell a pregnant woman her ass is so fat that it would clog a toilet. That breaks girl-code, even if it is true."

I turned to gape at Charlie as Tango and Liza snickered from nearby. Then I flipped them both off before slyly glancing at my own rear end, which they obviously caught because it only made them laugh harder.

"I'm growing a baby, things get wider!" My insistence just led to more laughter from the peanut gallery.

"Of course they do, honey," Charlie placated me as she patted my hand, like she hadn't just called my ass fat. She also threw a wink my way. I knew she was using me as a punchline to lighten the mood in the place. Suddenly, I was trying to think of 'your momma' jokes to help out, but I kept drawing a blank. Turns out, I'm not that funny, even in my own head. Maybe that was why I fell so hard for Rabbit. His antics were irresistible and I needed more laughter in my life. The next forty-eight hours were about to prove just how true that was.

30. RABBIT

IT HAD BEEN MORE THAN FORTY-EIGHT HOURS AND EVERY SINGLE one of my club brothers sat in church eyeballing me. "Does my hair have that fresh-fucked look or what?" I decided to break the tension with a little humor. I already knew what they wanted, and while I agreed it was time, I was loath to make things happen the way they needed to be done.

"We gave it all the time we could. She's had a good head start on us, but we need to worry what she'll do with that baby if she gets desperate," Iceman stated in his no-nonsense way. I was surprised to see him sober, but I guess a missing kid would make most good men snap out of their shit.

"I know. I'm going to ask that you let me try one more thing rather than involve Myra and her family."

"What thing?" Spinner asked.

"Do you give a shit what happens to Chastity?" I asked him.

"I could care less. It's my daughter I'm worried about."

"What about Cherry? Will she care?"

"After what her sister did? I'd like to say, 'no' but they are twins. I don't know how that will affect her."

"If we try this thing, chances are Chastity is dead."

"What the fuck is it that you want to try, Rabbit?" Rage asked, voice steady, but hands clenched like he was waiting for a fight.

I pulled Phoenix's number out and tossed it on the table.

"You want us to sic a psychopathic killer on her? What if he just kills the baby, too?"

"He's a tracker. Before shit went sideways with him and the Stoneridge Raiders, he never failed to track down a mark for them."

"He failed with your girl," Rage pointed out.

"On purpose. He came to see me once, before he showed up the last time he chased Chastity here."

"He has a thing for Myra, doesn't he?" My brother asked.

"I won't use her in this, in any way, if I can help it. We can pay for his services, though. I'm sure he could use all the money he can get his hands on since he's on the run now."

"Make it happen. I'll pay," Spinner agreed without hearing anyone else's arguments. "I don't want to use Myra either. She's a good girl. She shouldn't be played as a pawn because of Chastity's bullshit. There's been enough of that to go around already." Spinner's eyes met mine and I nodded. We were all that bitch's pawn at some point and like me, the others had all grown sick of it.

"If this doesn't pan out, she won't take no for an answer. Myra will reach out to her family, whether we ask it of her or not," I explained.

"Call him," Spinner demanded.

"I wondered when you might call," the voice on the other end of the line stated as soon as he picked up.

"How did you know?"

"I'm that good. Besides, I saw her with the baby."

"We need to find them, specifically the baby," I told him.

"So she is yours?" Phoenix asked, curiosity evident in his voice.

"No, but she's family," I admitted.

"She pulled a sister swap on your brother then, didn't she?" When I refused to answer, he tsked. "It's okay, you don't have to confirm. The baby will be brought to you in two days. I can't make it happen any sooner. The evil twin will suffer, though. That's our payment. We exact vengeance, the baby gets returned unharmed."

"You already have them, don't you?" I asked, causing my brother to stiffen. The whole atmosphere of the room changed as everyone in there was suddenly on high alert and paying close attention to the phone call.

"I've had eyes on her the whole time. We followed when she ran," he confirmed.

"Who is 'we'?"

"Not your concern. Two days," he offered once more and then hung up.

"What the fuck?" Spinner shouted. "He knew where she was all along? Why didn't we call him sooner?"

"I found the number in my pocket last night. It was the first time the idea to use him occurred to me."

"He better hope like hell that little girl is unharmed." Spinner spat out angrily. "What about Chastity?"

"Vengeance is his payment," I told my brother. Spinner nodded his acceptance and left church before it was dismissed. I turned a worried glance to Iceman. He waved me off though.

"His head is somewhere else and we can't blame him for that. Keep us up to date on any details or changes." Iceman glanced around at everyone. "That it?" He asked. When no one spoke up, he banged a gavel down one hard time. "Dismissed. We all still have a job to do. We aren't done until that baby is home. Don't care who is supposedly on it and bringing the kid back. Let's find out what we can, just in case."

Everyone else rushed out of the room to go do their parts, but I stayed behind, lost in thought. "What's eating you?" Iceman asked me.

"Could be me," I told him honestly. "That baby could have been mine. Hell, for all intents and purposes, it should have been mine. I was the one fucking her on the regular. Sometimes, I think I should have just lied and said it was. Would have saved Spin a whole world of hurt. Cherry, too."

"Yeah, but then they wouldn't have known what a devious, treacherous bitch that woman really is. Plus, Spinner would have hated you for keeping his kid as your own, no matter who her mother is, if it ever came out." He narrowed his gaze on me. "As long as that cunt was out there to tell the truth, you know it would have come out eventually. You did the right thing, even if it hurts them in the short term."

"Doing right doesn't feel so fucking good. What's this going to do to Cherry when they have that baby to raise?"

"We don't have all the answers, but something tells me

she'll be just fine. So will that baby. Despite her cunt of a sister having an evil penchant, Cherry is one of the good ones. Have a little faith, Rabbit."

"I fucking hope so."

"Come on, let's get out there. Where's your new woman right now?"

"Work. They called her in to fill someone else's shift."

"We have a man on her, just in case?"

"I sent one of the prospects, but I'm not sure how I feel about trusting that job to someone untested."

"Can't test 'em if they never pull important duty," Iceman reminded me.

"My woman is pregnant and a possible target of Phoenix because of the baby she's carrying and her association to the Stoneridge Raiders."

"You think Phoenix walking away before was bullshit until he could get to both women?"

"He kept saying, 'we' like he was working with someone else. That's the part I don't trust."

"Think it's her old man from the Raiders?"

"Nah. We verified that Phoenix killed Blaze and all of his blood relatives, supposedly. We have yet to find out why, though. The Raiders are keeping quiet, waiting for the heat to blow over from everything that went down." I knocked my knuckles to the table twice in a nervous gesture. "We might want to be prepared in case that club finds out where their princess ended up, or that their public enemy number one has been seen in these parts. There might be a reckoning coming our way."

"Fuck!" Iceman hissed. "I need to get my ass in gear.

Fucking president of the mother fuckin' chapter should know this shit and already be planning without his Road Captain telling him to."

"I honestly didn't think you would be this torn up over Carol," I admitted. Iceman had kicked his wife out and banned her from the club for her abhorrent behavior a few years back, but the bitch kept coming back for more and fucking with his head at every turn. Several of us were ready to see her on to the next life, but Shameless put a stop to our plans. He informed us that a man had to deal with his own ghosts.

"It's not even her, so much as it is everything I gave up for her."

"What do you mean?"

"She couldn't have any more kids after Steel. Too much scar tissue from how they butchered her when they took him out. I told her then that it didn't matter. I loved her, in the beginning. She let everything fester and rot inside, though. I gave up having kids for her. She wouldn't hear it when I tried to talk about adoption or hiring a surrogate. She still had working eggs and my shit worked just fine. We could have had a biological child, but she refused since she couldn't carry it herself. Easy enough for her to say since she already had Steel."

"You had Steel, too," I reminded him.

"Steel never looked to me as a father figure. He had Hopper for that, and I'd already been the man who stole his mom away from his dad, in his eyes, anyway. Didn't quite happen like that, but she never wanted him to know that I was with her first and she cheated on me with Hop."

"Why in the fuck would you take her back after that?"

Iceman's eyes came up to meet mine then. "Sheer fuckin' stupidity," were the words he chewed up like gravel before he spat them out. "When Chastity showed up again, I stopped the drinking because I was worried you'd make the same dumbass, blind decision I had all those years ago." He shook his head in disbelief. "First fuckin' time I even really noticed Myra was here with us. That shit snapped me back awake. So, I guess something good came from that Chastity cunt coming back and dropping her bombs on everyone."

"I don't drink often, if you need a reason to stay sober, or a person to do it with, I'm here," I offered.

"'Preciate ya, Rabbit," he turned to leave, but hesitated. "Go, relieve the prospect you have on your woman. You can keep us up to date via phone if need be." I stood, ready to burn rubber to the doc's office my woman worked for, but Iceman stopped me before I could get to the door. "Rabbit?"

"Yeah?"

"Take a burner, watch what you say to that Phoenix fuck. He claims vengeance is his payment, but we don't want whatever vengeance he's seeking to blow back on us."

"Understood."

31. MYRA

I WAS BOTH SHOCKED AND PLEASANTLY SURPRISED TO FIND RABBIT waiting for me when I got out of work. Although, the last time that happened, it was because the DNA test results were in. This time, I wondered if it meant something else.

"Hey bunny boy," I teased. A smile never appeared on his face, though. I glanced around and saw the truck sitting there. "You do know that I brought The Beast today, right?" Honestly, I was a little happy that the shitty weather in South Dakota would keep Rabbit off of his motorcycle for a while longer, because I wasn't ready to deal with the jealousy that came with not being able to ride along.

"I wanted to see you home safely," he finally told me as his eyes continued to dart around, as if he were waiting on a threat to jump out of the snowbanks or something. Fear crept into my bones instantly when I realized that was exactly what was going on.

"Did something happen?"

Rabbit stopped scanning long enough to look me in the eye then. "Let's talk about it when we get home, okay?"

"Okay," I answered back as we started moving toward my vehicle. Worry settled into my belly because Rabbit was never this serious, and while he was always watchful, normally it wasn't something you would notice about him. I wondered if they'd found Chastity? What happened to the baby? Was there another threat? All of those questions and more flitted through my head on the ride home. Never had a thirty-five minute drive felt quite so long before.

By the time we made it back to the house with Rabbit following behind in his truck, I was a ball of nerves. So much so that I just sat there, eyes darting around the driveway and the distant land all around us. The house that Rabbit had moved us into suddenly felt far too isolated. If someone was lying in wait, I didn't think there was a chance to get help to us in a timely enough manner. The dusky sky and the shadows the intermittent light threw across the space didn't help matters much. Everything felt far too eerie.

The door to the Suburban opened and Rabbit was there, turning off the engine for me, pocketing my keys, and helping me down from the vehicle. Then I was in his arms where all my worries melted away and I felt safe once again.

"I told you not to worry, don't do this to yourself. Let's get inside."

"It's been more than forty-eight hours," I mentioned, finally realizing that he probably needed me to contact my family. Rabbit didn't want me to have to get them involved because then I'd have to deal with the stress of my family knowing where I was and trying to get me back home.

"Shh," he hushed me again as we made it up to the gorgeous wrap-around porch that looked as though it belonged on an old antebellum house from the south-eastern US. The only difference was that the usual white pillars that went from ground to rooftop were actually trees on this house. The builders had felled trees, measured, and used them to form the behemoth pillars and give the anti-quated looking architecture a way to blend in with the forest around it. The deck was all natural woods too, leading right up to the stone and wood, two-story beauty of a house. It was like a country, mountain cottage, but on a much grander scale.

Once we got inside, Rabbit sat me down on the buttery soft, caramel-colored leather sofa as he made quick work of starting a fire in the beautiful stone-worked fireplace to chase away the chill in the room. The house had central heating, but it worked hard to keep up with the open space and high ceilings. We'd been lucky that the past two weeks hadn't seen anymore snowfall, although it was still cold enough that some of the snow that had been dumped on us previously still hung around.

"Myra?" Rabbit called me as if it wasn't his first time doing so.

"Yeah?" I answered blandly as he sat beside me.

"You don't have to contact your family." It took a few moments for what he was saying to sink in.

"You found her?"

He shook his head and the golden-brown hair that had fallen out of his usual man-bun skittered around his shoulders with the movement. "I called Phoenix."

"Phoenix? You mean *my* Phoenix? The one from my father's club?"

"Yep," he grunted the word out. "He's not *your* anything, though."

I waved the caveman bullshit off. "You know what I mean. Your club has a nomad named Phoenix, too. I heard the guys talking about him. I just wanted to be sure we were discussing the same person."

Rabbit nodded, understanding my logic a bit better. Then he sighed as his hand slid to my knee and began caressing up and down my thigh absently. "Phoenix has her already," he explained. Technically, I supposed he was telling me club business and I shouldn't have known this, but I was damn grateful he was trusting me with the knowledge. My heart melted a little more for him because it was something my own family and my ex would have never done for me. They'd never trusted me with anything, and now I knew why, because none of them were trustworthy.

"Why are you telling me? I asked without thinking.

"Because I don't want you freaking out and worried like you were today when I showed up to see you home."

"You said he has her. What does that mean?"

"He said he'd bring the baby to us in two days, but that Chastity was payment for doing so. He wanted to keep her for vengeance."

"Vengeance?" I questioned, as a shiver rolled through my body.

"Don't know what she ever did to him, besides witness Blaze's demise, but he sounded pretty serious about his price that needed to be paid."

"Is it horrible that I don't care what happens to her, so long as that baby is returned unharmed?"

"No. I think everyone feels that way."

"But you spent a long time being with her," I finally managed to choke out.

"I did, and the whole time I was with her, she was plotting and scheming. I think we both learned the hard way what unrequited, pretend love looks like. We saw what we wanted to see in our previous relationships, even though that wasn't the reality by a long shot. Being with you, even for a shorter time, has shown me the difference."

"Me too," I admitted. "What she did to Spinner was not okay. Doesn't he want his own justice?"

I think he'll just be happy knowing his daughter is safe and that she's young enough that she won't remember any of this."

"They're lucky," I commented absently.

"What do you mean?"

"Chastity and Cherry are identical twins. With Chastity out of the picture for good, Cherry can take over as the little girl's mom and no one will ever have to know the difference."

"We would have to be guaranteed that Chastity truly was never coming back if that were to ever work out."

"If Phoenix says he's enacting vengeance, then I guarantee she won't be coming back from that. I might have been sheltered from a lot of the club's underbelly before, but I still heard enough things about Phoenix. There's a reason he was their tracker and usually ended up handling the club's problems. He used to get angry because he did the enforcer's work more often than the enforcer did it, but he could never get an officer's position in the club."

Rabbit nodded but didn't otherwise respond. We sat there in the cozy living room, allowing the warmth from the fire to settle into our bones. The silence was comfortable and his nearness made me feel secure. Before I knew what was happening, I was in Rabbit's arms as he took me to the first floor guest bedroom.

"What are you doing?"

"Carrying you to bed, sleeping beauty."

"Well, beast, our room is upstairs!"

"Sweet, sweet baby momma, first of all, that's a different story. Second, you are carrying the weight of two people and I'm but one humble man."

"Did you just politely call me fat again?" I laughed, too sleepy to be indignant about it that time.

"No, love, I called you pregnant. We don't need me breaking my back on the stairs or accidentally dropping and hurting either one of you."

"Fine, but after the baby, you owe me at least one trip up those stairs in your arms."

"Your wish is my command," was his answer. "Until then, since you're wide awake again, how about I just make you feel like you're flying high enough to be up there anyway?"

"Oh yeah? How do you think you'll manage that feeling?"

Rabbit stuck his tongue out at me, wiggled the damn thing around suggestively, and then grinned. "Easy, baby, I can take you to heaven, it's up to you to grab a set of wings while you're there, though."

Rabbit did not even give me a chance to respond. Instead, he literally yanked my pants off of my body while I was mid-laugh, effectively shutting me the hell up. Okay, he might have been cheesy as hell, but he was my kind of cheesy, especially when he got all alpha possessive like that.

"Rabbit," I moaned as he kissed my thigh.

"Shhh, you're going to enjoy some me time," he told me while pointing to his mouth and continuing to grin like an idiot. "Then you're going to take a nap, and when you wake, dinner will be waiting for you."

"What about you?"

"I'm going to be a bad boy and eat my dessert before dinner, so don't worry about me."

Well, who was I to argue with that? My man settled my legs over his shoulders and kissed down each of my thighs until they had both received equal treatment. Then, he worked his way to my middle and started to feast on me. That was the only way to describe what he did because there was no mistaking that he enjoyed every second of what he was doing almost as much as I did.

Rabbit's mouth could win awards, and certainly, I'd be more than willing to give them to him after he brought me to two orgasms before climbing up behind me in the big spoon position and sliding inside. It was our first time going without protection, after both of us being tested, and if his groans were anything to go by, it was a feeling he would hate having to give up once I had the baby. He made slow, lazy love to me while gently massaging a breast and lightly strumming my clit.

"I want you to come one more time before I do, baby," he

whispered into my ear as I wiggled back and flexed my Kegel muscles for him. "Jesus, Myra, you keep doing that and I won't last."

I took it as a challenge and did it again, which forced Rabbit to smack my ass and attempt to hold my hips still, as if that could stop me from flexing internal muscles. I did it one more time and giggled as he groaned before he started to pound harder into my pussy.

"Okay woman, you asked for it!" Rabbit grabbed hold of my upper leg and held it up off the other one so that it was in the crook of his arm and gave him more room to move, then he used his fingers to deftly guide me into another orgasm as he hammered into me with such force that I had to throw my hands up above me on the headboard to keep from banging into it.

"Come for me, Myra," he grunted into my ear, his breath labored, as I tipped over the edge he already had me wobbling on. My contractions triggered his release, too. Rabbit bit down on my shoulder as he came, and then quickly dropped down and licked over the spot to soothe the ache he created. "Sorry," he whispered before kissing my shoulder once more.

"I don't know what you're sorry for, but you should definitely strive to be sorry more often," I teased him.

32. RABBIT

I WOKE TO FIND THE BED NEXT TO ME COLD AND EMPTY. MY HEART ticked up a few beats as initial panic set in at finding Myra already gone. I jumped up, threw on some clothes, and made my way out to the kitchen to find her sitting at the table with a calendar we usually hung by the refrigerator. She was erasing something as I slid in behind her, bent down, and nibbled just under her ear.

"What are you doing?" I asked against her tender flesh, causing her to both shiver and moan. Oh yea, my girl responded so well to my attention. It made me feel like the king of the fucking world. Chastity had always faked those reactions. Seeing it happen for real with someone made me wonder how I ever fell for the fake shit to begin with.

"Changing my appointment from tomorrow to next week."

"Why? Aren't you supposed to go more often now that you're so far along?"

Myra smiled up at me. "I love that you think of these things. And no, the every two week visits don't begin until my third trimester which will be toward the end of February. It is perfectly okay to reschedule this appointment. Your brother is going to need you by his side when the baby is brought back."

"Night and fuckin' day," I groaned.

"What does that mean?"

Shit! I did not mean to use my outside voice for that thought. "Earlier, I was thinking I should have known it wasn't real with Chastity. You keep proving to me the huge difference. I don't mean to keep bringing her up. It's not like I'm sitting around with that bitch on my mind in a good way," I added quickly so that she wouldn't get the wrong idea.

"Rabbit, I know what you mean. It's okay. I've had plenty of those moments of clarity about Blaze, too. It's worse for you, and I get that. She's in the center of all this on-going drama. If you weren't thinking about her, or making comparisons, I'd be worried. It's normal. It also shows that you appreciate what we have now and I can't be upset about that."

Her smile was radiant and genuine as she looked into my eyes. "Like I said, night and fuckin' day. You're the sunrise full of color and promises of sweeter things in my future. She was always midnight shadows and worry about what might be around each corner. I don't know how I found myself lost in that before."

"Fantasies aren't reality, but sometimes, we get swept up in them," Myra told me as she patted my hand before speaking again. "What day next week works best for you, in case they give me a choice?"

"Go with the first available, I'll work my schedule around it."

THE NEXT DAY, we all made our way to the clubhouse to await the arrival of my niece. Wherever Phoenix had been holding Chastity and the baby, it had to be completely off the grid. The club hadn't been able to find a single trace of Phoenix, Chastity, or the baby. Then again, we still didn't know who his partner in crime was either.

By noon, everyone's patience had worn thin. I'd called Phoenix three times only to be sent to a voicemail each time. "What if we trusted this bastard long enough to disappear with her?" Spinner finally asked. "He kept saying 'we'. What if she was working with him all along?"

"I highly doubt that," I told my brother, even as I had been wondering the same thing.

"Phoenix would never work with her. He likes genuine, honest people. If he finds you aren't those things, he cuts you loose immediately," Myra added.

"Incoming, Chevy Camaro headed in the lot," Rage yelled out as everyone got so quiet that you could hear a pin drop. "Woman with a baby," he called out again. Before long, there was a knock on the door. Shameless went to let the woman inside. As I positioned us close to the door, I was able to overhear what was being said.

"I have a package from Phoenix," the woman claimed. She had no discernible accent. Shameless opened the door to allow her entry.

"Who are you?"

"You may call me The Harbinger."

"The Harbinger?" Shameless repeated with a little disbelief in his tone.

"You have your road names, I have mine," she explained with a slight shrug of her shoulders.

"Come in," Shameless told her as he held the second set of security doors open for her. The woman, who was clad in head-to-toe black leather, and not much of it, took her time cataloguing each face she saw. When her eyes landed on Cherry and Spinner, she smiled grimly.

"I am so very sorry," she stated while heading toward them. "You should not be in a position to take this child. I need you to know that we were watching her, waiting to see what she would do. Phoenix said that she wasn't to be trusted around Myra." Her head swiveled until her eyes came in contact with my woman.

"You are the only woman I've ever felt jealous of. I think he would have loved you, if his brother hadn't sullied you first," she added as her eyes dropped to Myra's belly.

I moved to stand in front of my woman, because having some bitch tell my woman she's jealous of her and then talk about how she'd been sullied, didn't fucking sit well.

"No need for that. I don't harm the innocent. The guilty, now that's another story." Her eyes moved back to Spinner and Cherry. "She left this little one at a fire station. We retrieved her before any of them found the baby. It was too cold and the bitch didn't even knock, ring a bell, or so much as blow her horn to let anyone know she had been there."

Cherry gasped, shocked yet again by the cool indifference her twin was capable of. Personally, I was disgusted that I had ever chosen to be with a woman who could just dump her baby out in South Dakota, in the middle of fucking winter. The Harbinger moved forward and placed the baby in Cherry's arms. "In the diaper bag, you will find the original paperwork for the baby and also new documents. It is your choice which you use. The newer ones show that you are her birth mother and he is the father," she told Cherry as she pointed to Spinner. "Since you and the cunt were identical twins, your DNA will match the baby's, so no one can ever question it."

"How did you know?" Spinner asked.

"The bitch told us," The Harbinger admitted with a sparkle of something dark in her eyes. Cherry kissed the top of the baby's head, and held her tight. The Harbinger just watched for a moment before turning to Spinner, who was also watching his wife hold a baby that was his, but not technically hers. I could see the sorrow in his eyes for the hurt it must be causing his woman.

"Here," The Harbinger called out to get Spinner's attention before she attempted to hand him a piece of paper.

"What is this?" my brother asked as he glanced down at the paper.

"Latitude and Longitude of your closure," was all she said before she dropped the diaper bag and turned to leave. "Phoenix didn't want you to have that part, in case it ever came back on us, but I disagreed."

She glanced between Spinner and Cherry who pretended not to be paying attention. "It was better that we handled it. Your hands stayed clean. I thought you would always be looking over your shoulder if you couldn't confirm, though."

Spinner nodded, as if he agreed, but he did not speak those thoughts aloud.

"You have nothing to fear," The Harbinger told Myra as she walked by to get to the door. Once there, Shameless opened it for her. "You have such pretty toys," she told him after admiring the security system, and then she was gone.

"Okay everyone," Myra called out after clapping her hands together rather loudly a couple of times. "The Hastings have a new baby girl that they weren't prepared for." The entire room fell silent to hear what she had to say. "We need to get them prepared." She turned to Spinner and Cherry. "Why don't you two go to one of the rooms downstairs and get acquainted with your new daughter and the rest of us will work on getting everything you need for her." She moved closer to Cherry then and glanced down at the baby. "She's beautiful, do you have any idea what you want done for her room?"

My sister-in-law's eyes started leaking as she attempted to offer Myra a soft smile. "We don't know what kind of life she's had up to this point. So, she should have all the sweetness we can muster," was her answer.

"Sweetness," Myra agreed. "Got it." She leaned in and kissed the side of Cherry's head and whispered into her ear. Had I not been standing so close, I would have missed what she said completely. "I'm so sorry for your loss and the things she took from you, but you will be a wonderful mother. It already shows, and that little girl in your arms deserved you."

"All right guys," I called out. "You heard my woman! Let's go get Spinner and Cherry's house kitted out for their new baby girl."

33. MYRA

I<small>T WASN'T LONG AFTER THE BABY WAS DROPPED OFF BY THE WOMAN</small> who called herself The Harbinger, that Cherry convinced Spinner to take them home. I still felt like the rest of us had a job to do, but my part in doing that job got cut short by the club's president, Iceman.

"Prospect," Iceman called out as I plotted what we were going to need to grab from the store with Charlie and Liza. Two men stepped forward, both wearing ill-fitting kuttes that had the prospect rockers on them. "Take shifts, stand guard outside Spinner's place. Six hours on, six off until you're told otherwise by me. If you see anything out of the ordinary, hear something suspicious, you call for backup immediately. Every thirty minutes, I want an *'all clear'* text otherwise, got it?"

"Yes, sir," they both answered before taking off out of the clubhouse.

"Rabbit," Iceman bellowed. "I don't care what that freaky

bitch had to say, I want you and Myra close. Locked down on the premises for now, so we're not spread too thin."

"I have work," I interrupted.

Iceman glanced from my belly back up to my eyes. "Doc just put you on bedrest for the duration of your pregnancy," the infernal man told me without even missing a beat. I might have already known how motorcycle clubs worked, but that didn't mean that I was happy about being told I would no longer be able to go to the job I just got and desperately needed.

"Seriously?" I started to argue, but Rabbit pulled me back to his chest, a move that was meant to be a silent warning, while also being part protective instinct.

"Shh, everything will be fine," he whispered into my ear.

"Will it? I barely had that job and now they'll have no choice but to replace me."

"Doc will help you get another when the time is right," he assured me.

"I really don't think Phoenix will harm me." It was a weak argument, I knew. The man had already killed my ex, and God only knew who else from my family's club.

"I won't take the chance," he informed me.

"The club will put you on salary to help out around here when Doc can't," Iceman cut in. I also have a project I need your help with."

That didn't sound like it would be enjoyable. The Aces High Dakotas President hadn't been around much since I'd come here. Granted, he seemed to have pulled his head out of whatever hole he'd buried it in, but that didn't mean he was someone I liked or even knew well. I definitely hadn't built any trust for the man.

"My office," he demanded. "We'll talk there." The grumpy bastard didn't even wait around. He just took off, expecting we would follow. One good thing – for Rabbit – was he seemed just as shocked by his president's demand as I was.

"Let's just hear him out and then we'll make a decision," Rabbit mumbled as we trailed behind Iceman at a much slower pace.

"Have a seat," he demanded, once we were in the office with the door shut.

Like the good little boy and girl we were, the order was obeyed immediately.

"How badly do you want to remain off your family's radar?"

"Are you threatening to expose me?" I asked, completely taken aback by the prospect, even though I should have known better considering my own family sold me up the river in their own way. It was still settling into my bones that I never had a single person actually show me loyalty of any kind until I got here. I hated to think I had just deluded myself into thinking this place, and these people, were different. The roll of Iceman's eyes said that thought was preposterous, but I waited to hear the words too.

"I don't know what kind of outfit your family runs, but that's not how we do things here. We protect our own."

"Okay?" My one word reply was more question than answer and Iceman remained quiet, waiting. "I'd rather not have to deal with them at all. If I could fake my own death, without losing all of my schooling and hard work, I would."

"Because eventually, they will find you and your credentials are going to be an easy way for them to do that," he added.

"Have they contacted you?" I asked, suddenly nervous.

"No. I need to know, though, are they the type to hurt you, if you were found here?"

"I'd like to say no. Not physically, at least, but they did enough damage that I could never trust them again."

"Okay. We have several things happening right now and I'm going to need your help for some of them. First, we're diving into club business here. You understand what that means?"

"You'll be trusting me with information I wouldn't know if it wasn't important to what you need me to do." My answer was simple.

He nodded. "We have a deal that we help our southern brothers out with sometimes. There may come a time when we need medical assistance for our people as a result. Doc can't always be there to give it. That's where you would come in. You handle small, patchwork traumas until Doc can get to them."

Rabbit tensed behind me, indicating he wasn't exactly on board with this part of Iceman's plan.

"Second, I need help." He held his hand up and I could see the fine tremors rolling through it. "The shakes have been bad," he admitted. "Drying out is trickier than I thought it would be." It was my turn to nod in understanding.

"Just alcohol or drugs, too?" I asked. "And don't lie to me because it makes a difference."

"Just the sauce," he confirmed with a shy smile.

"We can work on that."

"Third," he continued like we hadn't been coming to an agreement already. "Doc does not want to be in charge of the BRATs' health any longer. We can't trust it to an outside source that might be easily compromised. Doc can train you so you can take over certifying health screenings, STI testing, drugs tests, and birth control for them."

"I'm only freshly graduated and licensed. I'm just a registered nurse at that. I'm not a doctor and suddenly you want me acting as a gynecologist, too?"

"Yes. Can you handle it?"

I watched the man then, taking in every nuance of him, his office, and the details of what he wanted from me. "You already wiped my credentials and work history, didn't you?"

Iceman grinned at me. "Not yet, but we do have a guy on standby. Quickshot will make sure you're a ghost, well and truly hidden from anyone who might want to find you."

I turned to Rabbit. "Are you okay with this?"

"Not exactly happy it was brought up to you without me getting a head's up," he complained while staring Iceman down. "But, I admit the plan has merit."

"One condition," I told Iceman as I turned back to him.

"Name it."

"The woman who Rabbit was with before, she will not come to me for anything."

"Then we'll let her go," Iceman told me.

"You don't have to go that far, I just won't be able to remain professional," I explained.

"Fuck!" Rabbit hissed from beside me, his hand clenched down on my thigh a little too roughly. I slapped at it, and he quickly let up. "I'm sorry," he whispered and I honestly wasn't sure if the apology was for squeezing my leg too hard or for having been with one of the club's BRATs.

"Sweetheart, I get it. I'm telling you, there's only one and she'll be dismissed if you can't handle treating her. I accept your condition."

"Okay. Then let's get started," I told him, shocking both men.

"Why don't you take the day," Iceman offered.

"Are your shakes going away without taking a drink today?" I asked defiantly. The man glowered at me but shook his head.

"Then let's get started," I repeated.

34. RABBIT

ICEMAN LEFT US ALONE FOR A MINUTE SO WE COULD DISCUSS everything before Myra jumped in and got started helping my President out with his problems.

"Are you sure about this?"

I watched as her shoulders slumped forward and then she dropped her head down into her own hands. "He's right," she mumbled through them before turning her head and glancing over at me. "Probably the only reason my family hasn't found me yet is because Phoenix caused so much havoc that they had to stop looking." She laughed then. "Or hell, for all I know, I don't even matter to them now that Blaze is dead. Anything is possible. Up is down and down is sideways. It's been crazy chaos since I found out about everything before I left Oregon. What I thought I once knew was never accurate and I think a huge part of me is still coming to terms with that."

"Maybe it would be easier to address your family, let them know you've moved on to a different life, and don't worry about anything else. It's not like they're going to come here and kidnap you."

Myra shrugged her shoulders and then leaned over so that she could rest her head on my arm. "I'm afraid to give them even a little piece of myself anymore. Even when they knew what was at stake, they couldn't help themselves. They still betrayed me to Blaze. It was like I didn't even matter. What I needed, it didn't matter. I can't live with the constant thought that I was never good enough to be their first priority."

"Hey! You are good enough. Those issues were their problems, not yours."

"I know that!" Her comeback was quick and a bit snappy. "Sorry, it's just that I don't doubt my own worth, I just don't want to diminish it by letting them back in either. So, the only choice I really have here is to live as quietly as possible. Iceman just offered me the opportunity to do that."

"I want to know that you're really okay with going ghost?"

"I'm okay with it as long as you don't have a problem being with a ghost?"

"What? Why the hell would I have a problem with it? If no one can see you, they'll never know you're secretly giving me ghost head at the table." She rolled her eyes at me, which was to be expected.

"I don't think that's how it works."

"Myra, you need to understand that you're mine. I'll take you any way I can get you. If you have to be a ghost to the rest of the world, you'll still be mine."

"What about if you want to get married? That leaves a

paper trail people can follow and if we do it under a fake name, then it isn't real."

"I'd never marry you under a fake name, but we can make it real and not have a paper trail all at the same time, little momma." I grinned at her then. "I accept!"

"You accept what?"

"Your proposal of marriage, my love," I teased her.

"Okay, well we'll have to make that happen at a later date. Right now, I have an appointment with your shaky, cranky president, and it's probably best not to keep him waiting."

"You didn't even flinch when I accepted your marriage proposal."

"That's because I'd marry you any day of the week, Rabbit. You're my person. If you think I'd ever give you up easily, you don't know me very well yet."

"Oh, I know you very well. Some might say, intimately."

"Some might say you should be lucky to know me intimately after how we met." I couldn't believe the woman. She said that with a straight face, too, and then she glanced down at my dick.

I gasped like a little, old, southern woman clutching her pearls after being scandalized in church on Sunday. "It. Was. Cold. Outside."

Myra cracked up right as Iceman came back into his office. "I'm not even going to ask what that was about. We getting started, or does Rabbit need more hand holding about his little problem?" Iceman winked at my woman.

"You too, huh? Where's the fucking loyalty around here?" I questioned them as I stood. Then I forgave my woman as I leaned in and stole a kiss from her laughing mouth, because that's all I wanted anyway – to make her smile again after her life just jumped another set of tracks she thought she was on. "Call me when you're done, I'll be right back here. I'm going to go grab some of our shit and bring it to the club-house while you're working."

"Okay, baby," she told me. When I was almost out the door she called out to me again. "Rabbit."

"Yeah, little momma?"

"I love you!"

"Love you, too." There was nothing else on this planet that felt as good as hearing those three words from someone who meant them wholeheartedly.

EPILOGUE - MYRA
SIX MONTHS LATER

CHARLIE WAS STARING AT ME, WHICH MOST LIKELY MEANT SHE HAD an inappropriate question brewing. "How does it feel to get a night off and out of the house?"

I glanced around and noticed that Rabbit was nowhere to be seen. He'd gone to the bathroom a few minutes ago. "Honestly? I'd almost rather be home. I miss him," I admitted.

"Aww!" Charlie squealed. "That's so sweet and wholesome," she managed to get out before the waterworks started. It was only then that I noticed she hadn't ordered an alcoholic beverage. I smiled knowingly as Rage made eye contact and grinned like the cat who got the canary. It was rare to see the normally angry-looking guy crack such a brilliant smile. What I wanted to do was jump up and hug him and Charlie, and congratulate them both on their news. Instead, I kept things chill with a slight tip of my head to acknowledge the fact that they weren't ready to make their announcement publicly yet. I turned to see that Cherry was watching Charlie's little crying fit with abject horror written on her face.

"I miss our sweet girl, too, but honestly, Charlie, it's not worth crying over," my sister-in-law insisted. Cherry had a baby to care for as well but she hadn't known the crazy hormone induced emotions that came along with pregnancy. I hoped, for her sake, that one day she might. I could tell that while she was happily raising their little girl, Cherry was still having a hard time with how the child had come into their lives. Spinner's eyes caught mine before lifting over my shoulder and grinning. I glanced around again, hoping to find Rabbit.

We had moved tables since we came in because there wasn't enough space for everyone once Charlie and Rage showed up. Liza and Tango had seats with us, too, but Liza had dragged her man off to go dance. The woman didn't give a rat's ass that there were strippers performing on the stage not far from the open floor area where she'd taken him. I loved her for it.

"I'm going to go check on Rabbit. He's been gone a while," Spinner stated before he got up and started to walk off. Whereas Cherry had problems with how their baby had come to them, Spinner was dealing with his own issues. The fact that he had been a victim of a sexual assault made him far more cautious and dare I say, jumpy when one of the guys suddenly disappeared from view for too long. He had also implemented the use of coasters inside the clubhouse and Renegade Rosy's that tested for the drugs commonly used to spike people's drinks. It wasn't a complete failsafe, but it was something that gave him power over what had been done to him.

"All right, we're taking a little break, the girls will be on the floor momentarily to entertain you guys!" The emcee for the night shouted through the speaker system. That was weird. They didn't often take breaks in a strip club. My brows furrowed, as did everyone else's at the table. The last time it had happened was when Rabbit had gotten up there and stripped for me when I passed my NCLEX. He had better not be stripping again, though. He was mine now and I wasn't willing to share his body with anyone, not even another person's eyeballs. My attention was immediately caught by Rabbit's voice as he spoke to his brother from just beside our new table.

"Have you ever taken a shit that just would not go down? There wasn't even anything particularly massive about it. The fucker just kept circling the Goddamn drain and getting stuck in such a way that it wouldn't hit the fucking hole and flush. You ever...?" Rabbit glanced up from fucking with his belt to look at Spinner only to realize that we had all moved to the large table closer to the bathrooms. Cherry, Charlie, Liza, Rage, Tango, and myself were all watching him. There was an uncomfortable few seconds before everyone burst out laughing and my poor love's face turned several shades of red.

"No, Brother, tell me more about how the massive shit you just took is a metaphor for how your life is circling the drain," Spinner deadpanned, much to the amusement of everyone else within hearing distance.

"Fuck!" Rabbit hissed. Then he turned accusing eyes

toward me. "You could have warned me that you guys moved to a closer table."

"Was I supposed to send you a text while you were wrestling your shit down the drain?" He came at me with hands extended in a choking gesture, as if he were going to throttle the very life out of me. It only made me laugh harder. "Put those things away, we all know where they've been, and I won't trust them until I see you wash for myself."

Even the men at the table were doubled over laughing at my man. "You certainly met your match with this one," Rage told him. "Couldn't have happened to a nicer guy!" He slapped Rabbit on the back as he took off toward the emcee's booth, presumably to find out why everyone was suddenly on a break. A few minutes later, Rage's voice carried over the speakers. "Mrs. Rabbit, you're needed in the back, please!"

"Mrs. Rabbit?" I questioned as everyone's eyes landed on me.

"That would be you," Rabbit told me as he slapped my ass and sent me on my way.

"What in the hell?" I muttered... When I got to the back, there was a woman, a dancer, lying on the ground while another held a bloodied towel to her torso.

"Please, help." The woman who had been injured called out to me. "I can't go to the hospital."

"Why not?"

"The man who did this works there, and they'll never believe me."

"Someone go get the emergency kit from the office," I yelled. This was my life now. I had been training with Doc for just such an occasion. For the longest time, I'd thought maybe the club was overpaying me.

"I need a name," Rage demanded.

"What are you going to do?" The woman, one of the newer dancers, asked him.

"We're going to take care of business. It'll be on tape," he told her as he pointed to the ceiling where the cameras were. "Now, either you can tell me who the dead fucker is or we can find out for ourselves and he'll still be a dead fuck."

She nodded and whispered a name just before passing out. "Don't worry, she won't be down long," I told him as I got to work checking her over, cleaning her wound, and sewing her back together. Luckily for her, the wounds were superficial, if a little deep. She'd live, but there would most likely be scars.

"Everything okay, baby?" Rabbit asked when he finally made it to the back to check on me.

"Rage is about to kill a fucker, this girl is getting a lot of stitches, and she's probably going to need a career change after this. Either that or a fantastic makeup artist."

"Damn," Sapphire grumbled. "She was one of our better dancers, too." I turned a glare up at her. "What? I'm just speaking the truth. We're all worried about her, but it will be a loss if she won't dance anymore."

"You need help?" I heard Rabbit ask someone. I turned my head far enough to catch Rage about to head out the back door.

"Nah, I'm taking a prospect with me. We'll give a call if we need backup for some reason."

While I didn't doubt Rabbit's skills at all, I was glad he wasn't heading out. I didn't need to be worrying about him in one place, our son in another, and my new patient, too. As if reading my mind, Rabbit pulled his cell phone out of his pocket and dialed a number. "Yeah, I need to know how he's doing. Then just say he's still sleeping. No need to be a dick about it. I might be needed later and Myra's patching someone up right now, so there's no telling when we'll get in."

I knew he was talking to Whiskey or Fox. They were on kid duty so that the rest of the grown ups could have a night out. My confidence in them as babysitters did not waiver, but I really just wanted to go home and snuggle my son, Noah. Still, I did my job first, and got the woman patched up. Then I gave explicit care instructions to Spinner who had come in to see what the problem was.

"We'll get her transported to one of the medical suites at the clubhouse for now. We'll call you in if we can't get a hold of Doc later, or if there are any problems," Spinner informed me before Rabbit took hold of my hand and started pulling me out the back door to where we had parked his motorcycle earlier in the night.

"We need to stop by the house and grab The Beast so we can go get our boy," I told Rabbit.

"No, we're not going to do that."

"What? Why not?"

"First, we're going for a quick night ride. It's August, we won't have too many more weeks of really good riding weather, especially for a night ride. Second, this is our first kid free night, Noah is with people we trust who assure me that he has been perfect for them so we're going to enjoy it. Third, our night might get cut short and I want to enjoy every second of the time we have alone together before that happens."

"Yes sir," I agreed, because all of his points made sense. Rabbit was still my person. The one I gravitated to more than anyone else on the Earth besides our Noah. He loved that boy just as fiercely as he loved me, and that only made me fall even harder for the guy. I found myself when I came to South Dakota, but more importantly, I found the real love of my life, too. There was no going back, only forward, no matter what drama might have just creeped into our lives. We'd handle it together.

THE END

THANKS FOR READING The Restart and the Remedy, book #3 in the Aces High MC - Dakotas Series

Please read/review the book, as this is how other readers find the books you love.

Don't forget to check out the other books in the Aces High MC - Dakotas Series.

- Dancing with Danger
- Whiskey Tango Foxtrot

Don't forget to sign up for my newsletter, so you never miss a new release!

https://christineandanne.myflodesk.com/newsletter

ACKNOWLEDGMENTS

As always, thanks to you – the reader! Without your support I wouldn't have the time to write all the words necessary for this giant motorcycle club world.

ALSO BY CHRISTINE MICHELLE

CHRISTINE MICHELLE

Kings of Anarchy MC: New Mexico

Property of Bigfoot

Aces High MC – Dakotas

Dancing with Danger · Whiskey Tango Foxtrot · The Restart and the Remedy

Aces High MC – Charleston

The Other Princess · A Love So Hard · The Princess and the Prospect · The Killing Ride · A Twist of Fate · Everlasting · A Year and a Day ·The Broken Beginning – Part One ·The Broken Beginning – Part Two

Aces High MC – Tallahassee

Crushed

Aces High MC – Sierra High

Walker · Trouble

Aces High MC – Cedar Falls

Redemption Weather · Proven · Smoke and the Flame · Redemption Duet Box Set

S.H.E. MC

Angel Girl · JoJo · Keys

Robeson Family Novels (standalones)

The Forgotten Wife · When the Last Petal Falls · A Different Husband

Standalone Novels

The Groupie Journal

Letters to Lily

His Bittersweet Regret

Bad at Love

TFO

The Fortunate Ones

T.I.E. Series

The Infinite Something · The Infinite Beat

Valhalla Rising

Revived

Dark Leopards MC (paranormal)

Ridden by Darkness · The B Team

Mirage Island Mates

Into the Grasslands · Beyond the Grasslands

Seasons Pack Series

Winter Wolves

The Ancients Series

Shadows of the Ancients · Falling into the White · Branches of the Willow · Bound by the Moon

Vukodlak Brew Series

Entwined · Enraged

The Awakening Series

Birthrights · Revelations · Incarnations

Death Viewers

Breathless

Upper YA Titles

The Voodoo Follies (PNR)

Catch a Falling Star (Dystopian Romance)

ANNE STORM

Savage Vipers MC

Wait For Me · Devastate Me · Surprise Me · Baby Me

Loved for the Holidays

Cupid Broke My Heart · Ghosted by Texas · Resolving Rumors

Cheating Hearts Series

The Homewrecker's Fate · The Regrettable Mistake

ABOUT THE AUTHOR

Christine Michelle runs on coffee and giggles as she writes her angst-fueled romance stories (motorcycle club, rockstar, paranormal, college, & other contemporary as well as women's fiction and marriage in trouble novels).
She is a mom to four humans (2 girls, 2 boys – all grown now).
When she's not writing books, she enjoys reading, drawing, hiking, or feeding her soul with live music at concerts.
Christine is a traveler and has lived all over the USA (and

other parts of the world). She currently lives in San Antonio, Texas with her two fur babies.

Universal links to everything
(website, social media, book links, and more)
https://linktr.ee/christinemichelle

facebook.com/M00nlitDreams

instagram.com/christinemichelle_annestorm

tiktok.com/@christine.michelle.books

com/pod-product-compliance